KUMARI
GODDESS
OF GOTHAM

Amanda Lees was born in Hong Kong of British parents and survived both a convent boarding school and subsequent incarceration at a Jesuit boys' school.

A onetime stand-up comedian, she teaches presentation skills to authors and conducts workshops on story and dramatic form for children and is also now a successful author, actress and broadcaster.

She has lived all over the world and now resides in London.

KUMARI

GODDESS OF GOTHAM

AMANDA LEES

Piccadilly Press • London

Thanks first and foremost to Peter Cox, a good friend as well as a great agent. Also to the fantastic team at Piccadilly, especially Brenda Gardner, Mary Byrne, Melissa Patey and Anne Clark, my stalwart editor. Special appreciation to the sales team who are out there on the frontline, led by the lovely Finette. And of course a big thank you to my family and friends who are always there for me. Most of all, I would like to acknowledge my mum for giving me so much of what ultimately led to this book. I hope that its humour and sense of adventure are a true reflection of her spirit.

First published in Great Britain in 2007
by Piccadilly Press Ltd,
5 Castle Road, London NW1 8PR
This edition published 2008

Text copyright © Amanda Lees 2007

A catalogue record for this book is available from
the British Library

ISBN-13: 978 1 85340 956 1 (trade paperback)
1 3 5 7 9 10 8 6 4 2

Printed and bound in Great Britain by CPI Bookmarque, Croydon
Cover design by Simon Davis
Cover illustration by Anna Gould
Set in Stempel Garamond and Trajan

In memory of my mum

CHAPTER 1

An orange moon hung low over the hidden kingdom, tingeing the snow-capped peaks that surrounded it, protecting it from the prying eyes of the world beyond.

Unmarked on any map, it was as if the kingdom did not exist. Spy satellites swept over it, registering nothing. Nestled deep within a distant mountain range, the kingdom lay untouched, as it had done for eons.

Which was all very well for those who liked things the way they had always been.

But not so great for a goddess-in-training who longed for a bit of life.

Tucked up in her bed, Kumari tossed to and fro. Her silk sheets twisted beneath her as she thrashed around in her sleep. The nightmare was back again, this time worse than before.

'Mamma,' she murmured. The sweat trickled down her face.

She could see her Mamma so clearly in her dream, walking ahead of her, but as fast as Kumari ran she could not catch up.

'Mamma!' she shouted, but the words stuck in the back of her throat. However hard she tried to scream, she could not make a sound. And all the time her Mamma carried on walking, blissfully unaware of the danger that lay ahead . . .

Kumari could see it – knew just what was about to happen. But there was no way she could stop her, as hard as she tried. It was like running in quicksand, yelling into the wind. A great gulf yawned in front of Mamma, ready to swallow her up. And then – her Mamma was gone, falling into the darkness . . . disappearing into a void from which she would never return.

Kumari woke with a start. She was sitting bolt upright, arms outstretched, empty. *I couldn't reach her*, she thought miserably. *I failed Mamma. Again.*

A tear rolled down her cheek and slid, salty, inside her lips. Her chest ached with emptiness; her heart felt hollow inside. And then she remembered. This was the night of her grand plan. The night she might – just perhaps – kill off the nightmares at last.

The moonlight shone through the arched windows, casting shadows along the floor. It was well after midnight; soon bird-

2

song would herald the dawn. Flinging back her rumpled sheets, Kumari threw herself out of bed. Badmash, her baby vulture, sighed and rolled over into the indent she had left. His feet were twitching, a sure sign he was dreaming. And whatever those dreams consisted of, it was a safe bet they involved food. Kumari leaned over and tickled his fat little belly.

'Badmash, wake up,' she hissed. 'Tonight's the night!'

Badmash opened his beak and let out a squawk of protest. Instantly, Kumari clamped it shut again. The last thing she needed was to get caught. She *had* to talk to Mamma – speak to her just one last time. And the only way to do that was through the Great Summoning Ceremony itself.

The Great Summoning Ceremony: the most difficult of rituals. In attempting to bring her mother back into this world she might well destroy them both. Mamma was caught between two states, unable to make the final transition from queen to total goddess. Owing to her untimely death, she was in the most dangerous place of all. One slip of the tongue and it could so easily go wrong. Her Mamma might end up in limbo forever if Kumari made a mistake.

The gods were not to be trifled with, even if you were a trainee one yourself. Incur the wrath of the heavens and the repercussions could be dreadful. Kumari did not relish the prospect but, still, she had no choice. Already she scented danger on the wind, could feel it stalking the palace corridors. And so tonight she would perform the ceremony. Get the answers she craved.

There was just one tiny problem: she had never *actually*

managed it. Never summoned up a god before, despite the Ancient Abbot's best efforts. She could imagine her teacher now, his hands sketching shapes in the air.

'This is how you do it, Kumari. See – sweep down and towards you!'

Looked so simple when he did it.

'It's not working,' she sighed.

'Why not try it this way? Come, child, focus your energy. Magic is all in the mind, Kumari. In the mind and in the heart.'

As teachers went, the Ancient Abbot was rather dull. But he knew more about rituals than any man alive. And it was not his fault he was so old. Sometimes he forgot entire incantations, stopping dead in mid-sentence. Other times he muddled them up, with spectacular results.

Age was honoured in the kingdom, a fact that occasionally drove her nuts. It was tough to be thirteen in a place where one hundred was considered young! Even harder to be a girl-goddess, with all that it entailed. How she envied the ordinary citizens, hearts carefree, minds untroubled. Of course, it was all down to Papa and Maximum National Happiness.

It was Papa's job to generate National Happiness, but lately he seemed lost. As far back as she could remember, Papa had worked away at the holy fires, stoking them up with love and care, sending the smoke of Happiness to his people. Its haze drifted across the valley kingdom, infusing it with well-being. Except the haze was all but gone, the skies dishearteningly empty. National Happiness had not been at maximum for a long time, not since Mamma's death eight moons before.

4

Was it really eight moons? It felt like a heartbeat. A heartbeat that ached with unanswered questions both for herself and Papa.

Kumari could see Papa now, sitting alone by the holy fires, unable to conjure up more than the odd wisp instead of the great clouds that had once billowed forth. Papa's Powers had deserted him along with the ability to maintain Happiness. It was as if something was sucking the very life force out of him, rendering him impotent and withdrawn. As the holy fires dwindled, so did Papa's spirits. The further the king sank into deep depression, so the kingdom followed suit. OK, so Happiness was not everything, or so the Ancient Abbot said. But then what would *he* know – he was a monk, for heaven's sake.

There was only one thing to do and that was to speak to Mamma. She had to find out what had happened, how she had really died. Only one person would tell her the truth and that person was Mamma. And how Kumari longed to hear her voice, to be soothed by its familiar sound. Since before she could remember, Mamma had sung her to sleep, had told her stories of fairies and dragons, had murmured her name. Later, she had been her source of wisdom, teaching Kumari of the ways of the world, talking about its biggest mysteries: magic, the meaning of life. Boys. Already, though, the sound of Mamma's voice in her head was fading. It was as if someone was wiping all the good memories from her mind, leaving nothing but hurt.

Tonight was the perfect night, the night of the Murmuring Moon. All over the kingdom, hundreds of people were gazing up at it, whispering their wishes in the knowledge that the gods would grant just one. Each year the lucky winner would give thanks at the temple while the losers smiled nicely and muttered snide asides. Well, as far as Kumari was concerned this was one lottery she was about to fix. She had a hotline to the gods and she intended to burn it up.

Time to get moving. This mission called for mountain gear. Hardly a fashion statement but then no one would see her anyway. Her winter robes were what her Ayah called 'sensible', hanging like a red tent to her ankles. Beside the ladies of the court, she looked like a scarlet blob. A blob with a scowling face poking out of the top, pale and unadorned. Not that she particularly wanted to paint her lips or totter round in tight skirts. It would be nice to have the option, though, instead of always being treated like a kid.

Next, her ceremonial bag, stashed in its secret hiding place. OK, so it was the back of her wardrobe. But it did the job. The strand of hair was still there, exactly as she had left it, laid just across the door handles so that she would know if anything had been touched. You couldn't be too careful, as Mamma's death had proved. If they were able to get to Mamma then Kumari could well be next in line. As for Papa's malaise, Kumari was sure it was something more than grief. If even the god-king could succumb to outside forces, what hope was there for Kumari? Gain access to her magic tools and they were halfway there. Of course, she had no idea who *they* were, it was just her suspicions. It made it all the more important to guard her things. Through them they could harm her.

Until the day they ascended the Holy Mountain, a living god or goddess was vulnerable. Like her Mamma and Papa, one per cent of Kumari remained mortal. Find that weak spot and you could kill off the human part, consigning the living god or goddess to the endless night of a limbo state. Someone had done that to her Mamma and it would take an awful lot to set her free. Now not even Papa was strong enough to rescue Mamma and the gods could not intervene. Only one of her own blood could save Mamma. If she found out how Mamma had been murdered, Kumari could help her heal and send her on, up the Holy Mountain to join her fellow deities instead of languishing in its foothills, unable to go forward or come back.

Whoever it was had known where to strike, and that knowledge was kept from all but a very few which meant it had to be someone close to the royal family, perhaps even in the palace itself. Then there was the mystery of her death, the complete lack of evidence. There were only three ways to kill a living goddess: one being with the sacred sword. But that was kept under lock and key in the temple, guarded by the monks day and night. For the sacred sword was also vital to the first and most important Power of them all: Power No 1, the Power to be Invincible. Of the Eight Great Powers to be gained by a trainee god or goddess, this was the hardest to attain.

The second way to kill a goddess was to turn her own magic against her but that, surely, would leave its mark. There had been no marks on Mamma. It was all very strange. Whatever the circumstances, it was clear Mamma's death was no accident. Someone else had had a hand in it, and that some-one was very powerful. Only a person with great influence could have murdered a living goddess like Mamma.

Aha, here it was. Her ceremonial bag and it looked intact. Better check the contents one more time. This was too important to mess up.

Summoning Cup
Cowrie Shell
Incense
Charcoal
Incantations Part One (in hardback)
Journal
Firesticks

It was all there, present and correct. Kumari slung the bag over her shoulder. It rucked up her sleeve, exposing her amulet. The silver bracelet round her wrist was Kumari's most precious possession, a gift from her Mamma that was intended to keep her safe. And so it would, if only Kumari could remember the mantra that activated it. Mantras were not her strong point. They all sounded the same. Still, she loved her amulet. It made her feel closer to Mamma. As if Mamma were protecting her through the slender band of silver that she always wore.

Catching sight of it, she felt a rush of courage. All she had to do now was get past the guards to the western door. Once free of the palace, she would climb the hills opposite the Holy Mountain to perform her ritual with the dawn. The Great Summoning Ceremony had to be conducted in direct sight of the mountain. In its foothills Mamma languished, and it was from there Kumari hoped to summon her. The ascent was steep and dangerous; she needed to move swiftly. Too much haste, however, and she could make a fatal mistake.

Carefully, she replaced the raven strand of hair and tiptoed towards the door. Scooping Badmash from her bed, she tucked him under one arm. Badmash glared up at her beadily but refrained from opening his beak. On the threshold, Kumari paused, listening for telltale creaks. Night watchmen patrolled the corridors. Bump into one of them and all was lost. They had strict orders to protect her, and that included from herself. No one left the palace alone at night, especially not the girl-goddess.

Her heart was thumping so hard she could swear someone would hear it. It was now or never. She lifted the latch . . .

The corridor was still, the butter lamps burning low. She glanced towards her Ayah's door, half-expecting to hear her snore. Generally, her Ayah snored so loudly it reverberated right through the floorboards. Tonight, however, all was silent.

Her Ayah slept in the next room, as she had ever since Kumari was born. Protocol demanded that the girl-goddess had a nanny, even though her mother had not been keen. Happily, the Ayah was a distant cousin and so kind it was impossible not to love her. It had been the Ayah who had held her tight the day they bore Mamma away.

As they carried Mamma, cold and still, to the foothills of the Holy Mountain, Kumari had followed, holding on to her Ayah. They had placed Mamma's pallet by the river that

9

separated the Holy Mountain from the kingdom. Wide and very deep, its waters ran icy cold from the snowy peak. The mists had descended, rolling towards Mamma. Then the waters rose and took her pallet, sweeping it towards the distant shore. There she would awake to the living death of limbo, blessed with all her attributes of youth and beauty, cursed to remain stuck. The first step was to avenge Mamma's death, to break the murderer's curse. Then she would be free to ascend the mountain and take her rightful place among the gods.

'I'll find them, Mamma,' whispered Kumari as she gazed at the waters with streaming eyes, clutching her Ayah's arm with whitened fingers until the pallet disappeared from sight.

'I will look after you,' said the Ayah. 'I will take care of you.'

And so she had, although it was never the same.

Kumari could still feel her Mamma's slender fingers stroking her face gently. Occasionally an unseen hand would brush her cheek and she knew it was her mother. Some people would say she was crazy and so she kept those thoughts to herself. But Kumari *knew* she was there, so close and yet so far. It was why she had to do this, for herself and for Mamma.

Here was the Ayah's door. Best to go s-l-o-w-l-y. Somewhere around here a floorboard squeaked. This might be the one . . . Toes down first . . . Nothing. On to the next one. Aha – a creak. Step over it very carefully. Excellent! Home and dry. Past the first butter lamp, then the second. Stick to the shadows at all costs. Weird that her Ayah wasn't snoring. No time to ponder. Keep going.

One down, two to go. There was Papa's room at the end. Before him, the RHM. Ah yes, the Right Hand Man. Her least favourite person in the palace. In the universe, in fact. OK, so her universe ended at the borderlands, gateway to the World Beyond. And what little she knew about the World Beyond she had heard from the RHM. Frankly, having listened to all his tales, she rather wished he would move there. He would fit in really well, wrinkling up with the rest of them.

They lived short but terrible lives in the World Beyond before their bodies crumbled to dust. Or at least, that was what the RHM said in their Social History sessions. Personally, she thought it sounded rather interesting, all this stuff about ageing. How weird would it be, seeing your face shrivelled up like a walnut?

OK, so it was unlikely. Impossible, in fact. Amongst the many gifts bestowed on a girl-goddess, Kumari had been granted eternal youth. Even the ordinary citizens of the kingdom aged at a rate that was barely perceptible. Most lived to be well over three hundred, their skins still unlined, their hair black and thick. Maybe she could just slip over to the World Beyond, take a peek at these people. She'd be so close to the borderlands tonight. It would only take a minute. Even as the thought popped into her head, so did the RHM's voice.

'Time moves faster in the World Beyond. You would have but a year and a day as they measure it. A year and a day, Kumari. And then you would die!'

11

Ah yes, the one other way to kill a goddess. Consign her to the World Beyond where she would be subjected to their physical laws. There, far away from the Holy Mountain, she would be unprotected from Time's ravages, helpless against the World Beyond's greatest disease. A year and a day before Time claimed her for its own, treating her worse even than a mere mortal, as it once would have treated the RHM.

Oh, he was safe now, all right, secure in the kingdom. He would live as long as all the other citizens, privy as he was to their secrets, breathing in the haze of Happiness, although it had not always been that way. The RHM himself was from the World Beyond. Found abandoned as a young boy in the borderlands, it was Papa who had rescued him, brought him to the palace, treated him as his own. Educated him, cared for him and finally inflicted him on his daughter. For that, she all but cursed Papa every time the RHM spoke.

After all, she was the one who had to listen to him droning on day after day. He had a voice that drummed right through your skull and scratched at your brain. In fact, she could hear it right now.

Really hear it, out loud!

She was hovering outside his door. There were voices coming from inside. A muffled shout then a gasp. A sudden thud. Then a murmur. That had to be the RHM. He always spoke softly. Somehow it made what he said more important. More sinister, even. The second voice again, rising in anger.

'Pay up or I'll . . .'

Thud, thud. Then silence.

Hmmm, *very* interesting. And in the middle of the night.

Who was the man in the RHM's room? And what had he been talking about? Some business transaction, it seemed, but at a very strange hour. On all her other expeditions around the palace in the small hours, she had never known the RHM to stay up this late. It was a puzzle she picked over all the way to the western door.

As it clicked shut behind her, she forgot all about the RHM. Cold night air filled her lungs; the adventure was just beginning. She could make out the shapes of yaks dozing in the meadow alongside the palace as she stole past. *Smelly beasts,* thought Kumari, as one let out a prolonged fart. The meadow was fringed on the far side by forest, the intermittent moonlight picking out the twisted trunks of oaks and rhododendrons, casting them into monstrous curlicues that appeared to be alive.

On the edge of the forest, she hesitated. It looked different in the moonlight. At night, strange sounds emitted from every leaf and branch, odd rustles and creaks. *Don't be so ridiculous,* thought Kumari. They were only trees, after all. Still, she strode through it as fast as she dared, given that the branches hung so low. As the forest grew denser, she began to feel claustrophobic. For once, she was glad to be both small and slight. A larger person would have found themselves impaled on a thousand twigs.

Suddenly, her head was jerked backwards. She froze, stifling a scream. Very slowly, she turned around. Her hair was caught up on an aged oak, its gnarled branches grabbing like grasping fingers. Kumari blinked at them once, twice. She could have sworn they moved.

13

Don't panic, she thought. *Just untwist your hair verrrrry carefully*. She began to unwind the long, black strands. The branch swayed, reaching for her face. Her hair was stuck fast, however much she yanked at it. The twigs were scratching, stabbing at her eyes. She tried to twist to one side. And then, suddenly, she felt it, a gentle caress on her cheek. An unseen hand released her hair. She was running, free. Crashing through the forest, not caring who heard her, stopping only when she had reached the slopes beyond, sending a silent thank you to Mamma.

Safe above the tree line, she stood gasping for breath. A feeble squawk penetrated the sound of blood pounding in her ears. She pulled a seasick Badmash from her pocket.

'You poor thing,' she murmured, cradling him in her hands.

Badmash tottered theatrically and collapsed against her chest.

'OK, OK,' she said. 'Enough now, Badmash.' Badmash was a great pet – but he did like to be a drama queen.

Kumari clambered up the mountainside as it grew steadily steeper, Badmash perched on her shoulder, stubbornly refusing to fly. She had done her best to teach him, trying every trick in the book. After all, it was something she herself had to learn, one of the Eight Great Powers: the Power to Levitate or Fly Through the Sky. Power No 6.

So far, she had acquired precisely none. It was not a brilliant record. Before she could become a fully-trained living goddess, she had to pass all eight tests. By now she should have passed at least one, two if she was really going some. It was not like she didn't want to learn, just that somehow it

14

seemed such an effort. Some Powers were more fun than others. Take the Power of Extraordinary Sight, for example. Among other things, it meant she would be able to see demons and spirits as well as discern the truth. Then there was the Power to be Invincible whenever she wielded the sacred sword. As for the Power to Move through Mountains – how cool was that?

OK, so she had failed to gain even one Power. It made success tonight all the harder. And this was no ordinary ritual. This was the Great Summoning Ceremony itself. The means by which a god or goddess could be brought into another realm to offer help or, in this case, provide answers. Summoning would not free Mamma, however. She would return to the limbo from whence she came. The very act of Summoning was dangerous which was why, for once, Kumari had applied herself. Time and time again she had practised in the privacy of her bedroom. Somehow, she always got the words wrong. There were too many other things to think about.

A lot of the time, for instance, Kumari wondered what it would be like to be normal. To roam the streets of the kingdom unobserved, to have a friend. She had no proper friends, apart from Badmash. And he did not really count, being a small, bolshy baby bird. What was so wrong with normal after all? Normal was better. If she were normal, she could giggle with the other girls. She could dress in something other than red robes that covered her like a sack. She might even get to cut her hair into something resembling a style. If she looked more normal, then boys might actually glance her way instead of casting their eyes to the ground on the rare occasions she passed by.

15

Oh, she knew why they did it. It was out of respect for her status. No one could gaze upon the girl-goddess except the courtiers and the king himself. Which kind of put paid to any chance of her ever getting a kiss. Not that she really wanted a kiss. Well, not just from anyone. Kisses sounded, well, *slobbery*.

Although one from Tenzin might be nice.

Kissing. Another mystery. In fact, she had no idea how to do it. It was one of those questions she could not ask anyone, not even her Ayah. Mamma would have known what to say, would have taken her seriously. She would have understood how much Tenzin meant. Would have told her what to do.

The thought of Tenzin sent butterflies flapping wildly about her stomach. Which annoyed Kumari because she liked to be in control. Or at least that was the theory. In practice, it was really hard. In which case, it was better not to think about him. Which was also pretty tough.

So caught up was she in her thoughts, that Kumari did not realise quite how far she'd climbed. It was only when she stumbled and had to right herself that she paused to look down.

Far below in the valley she could see the lights of the palace. A beacon always burned at each corner to let the people know they were safe. Although frankly, what with the Happiness deficit, the people were growing restless. Kumari's gaze shifted to the royal wing. She squinted, trying to make out poor Papa's window.

There it was on the corner, beneath one of the seven gilded pagodas that adorned the palace roof. A dim glow was visible within; Papa could no longer sleep with the lights off. Next to his room, the RHM's was in darkness. She remembered the voice raised in anger, the RHM's soothing tone, then the thuds. He had been trying to shut someone up, that much was obvious. But what about and why? And in the middle of the night? As the god-king's closest aide, the RHM was extremely powerful. He could easily deal with someone by daylight through the usual channels. Unless he did not wish to be discovered.

It occurred to Kumari then that the RHM could be her suspect. He had the opportunity, the influence. But what about the motive? The RHM had appeared to love her Mamma, certainly to respect her deeply. No, it could not have been the RHM. He had no reason to kill Mamma.

Bored now of staring at the palace, Kumari's perspective widened. She swept her gaze over the valley, settling on a house in the Court Officials' District. Tenzin was the son of the Royal Treasurer. It was how she had first come to lay eyes on him, accompanying his father to court. Unlike all the other boys, he had dared to look her in the eyes, glancing at her sideways with an amused glint.

How dare he, had been her first thought, followed by a rush of admiration. The boy had guts, not to mention a cute smile. Of course she had turned away, lifting her chin a touch haughtily. And then ruined the entire effect by glancing back when she thought he wasn't looking. Naturally he was and naturally he had grinned triumphantly. Kumari could not help but grin back.

Right now he was asleep, as far as she could tell from his

darkened house. Or maybe lying there in his bed, thinking of her . . .

Don't be ridiculous, she told herself. Tenzin had far better things to do. Like hang around with the other kids with whom he attended school. Kumari had never been to school. Instead, she had the RHM and the Ancient Abbot.

It made it much harder to get away with anything, being the only kid in class. But Kumari had her methods. Take tonight, for instance. It made it all the more exciting, knowing how furious they would be if they found out. Except, they were not going to find out. She would be back in her bed just after dawn.

Huddled against a boulder, knees drawn up, Kumari stared at the changing sky. Indigo was giving way to grey; soon the sun would splash it with golden streaks. Across the valley, she could barely make out the contours of the Holy Mountain, its foothills shrouded in mists, its peak crowned with cloud. She stared at the foothills, wishing that, just for once, the veil of the mists would be ripped apart. Hidden by it, her mother lingered, gazing back at the land she still loved.

The Holy Mountain was blessed, its tip the most sacred spot of all. The summit cloud acted as a screen, shielding the gods from mortal gaze. The only way to ever see a god was to summon one from the mountain and the ability to do so was only handed to a few. The Ancient Abbot had taught her the words, the formula written in her ritual book. But words were nothing without magic. And magic involved risk.

Summoning was not entirely safe for either side. You never quite knew what might appear. In Mamma's case it was doubly

18

dangerous, alone as she was, unprotected by the other gods.

'Summoning,' the Ancient Abbot said, *'is only to be used in extreme circumstances.'*

Well, these circumstances *were* extreme. How else could she communicate with her Mamma? And Mamma would understand; she had always urged Kumari on.

'Be strong,' she would say. 'Fight for what you believe in, Kumari.'

Well, she believed in her mission. She believed it was the only way. Kumari stared harder at the mountain and murmured, 'Mamma.'

A tear trickled down her cheek. She brushed it aside, furious. 'No tears,' Mamma always said.

'No tears,' whispered Kumari.

Nestled in her robes, warm against her belly, Badmash glanced up and let out a squawk. Kumari looked down and smiled. She had almost forgotten his presence.

'Soon, now,' she soothed. 'You hang on in there.'

Badmash was growing restless, his belly growling for food. Any normal bird would have gone foraging for a few worms. But Badmash was no normal bird. In fact, he hardly considered himself a bird at all. It was why he refused to fly, or so Kumari theorised. In any case, it gave him a human-sized appetite along with a lot of attitude.

Very soon, though, the sun would rise, a sudden slash through the grey cloud. The cold mists would be ripped by light, night turning swiftly to day. It was alchemy itself and Kumari loved it, the bleak mountains bathed in sudden gold, the frosty sky on fire. Each jagged peak would salute the sun

19

as the valley awakened. Demons would scuttle back inside their caves. Eagles would swoop in delight.

With the dawn, she would perform her ceremony, then slip back to the palace. They could be there by breakfast time, with her Ayah none the wiser. The Ayah brought breakfast each morning, laid out on a silver tray. Yak yogurt and honey for Kumari, a whole mouse for Badmash. At first the palace cook had protested so now the Ayah simply slipped one on the tray in transit. It was pretty impressive, come to think of it, having an Ayah who could handle a dead mouse.

A sound cracked through the air, the snap of a twig breaking. Whirling round she saw nothing save a ragged shrub swaying in the wind. Little grew above the tree line; the climate was too harsh. The wind was bitter, unrelenting, unlike the balmy valley below. Kumari dropped her head to her knees and pulled her robes tighter. Alone on the hillside, it felt as if the dawn would never come.

Thoughts began to taunt her. Just who was she kidding? Imagining she could summon up her Mamma. She was nothing but a joke. She had not passed a single one of her Powers, for heaven's sake. And at this rate she never would. Call herself a trainee goddess? Trainee *dingbat* more like.

And then she felt it, a flash of warmth on her back. She whipped her head up to see the mountain. Above it, the sky blazed, aflame.

Hastily, she pulled out her book.

'Place incense on charcoal,' she muttered, reading out the instructions. She had done this a hundred times before but this time she had to get it right.

The firestick stubbornly refused to light, no matter how hard she flicked it.

'Stupid thing,' cursed Kumari. The sky was getting lighter. Then, with a whoosh the firestick ignited. With trembling hands, she applied it to the incense. A wisp of fragrant smoke curled into the sky, scenting the air all around. Rising to her feet, book in hand, Kumari read over the next bit. From his perch on her shoulder, Badmash cooed. He did so love a good ritual.

'OM TARE TUTTARE TURE SOHA
OM TARE TUTTARE TURE SOHA
OM TARE TUTTARE TURE SOHA . . .'

Kumari chanted, feeling a little silly. That was part of the problem. The words just felt all wrong. *This is your one shot*, she thought. *Come on girl, give it all you've got.* Breathing in until her ribs felt like they might crack, she threw back her head and howled:

'OM TARE TUTTARE TURE SOHA
OM TARE TUTTARE TURE SOHA . . .'

Swaying backwards and forwards, Kumari did her best impression of the Ancient Abbot. He might be an old guy but he could chant with the best, voice rising higher and higher, making the whole temple echo. One day she fully expected him to take off and hit the temple roof. Now and then it gave her the giggles, which she had to stifle in her sleeve. Today, however, was no laughing matter. It felt as if her whole life rested on this moment. To see her mother one more time, she would happily die for that.

On and on Kumari chanted, working through all the

verses. For once they came easily, without her having to glance at the book.

'HOWL WIND, ROAR THUNDER . . . '

She blew into her cowrie shell.

'RIP HEAVEN'S VEIL ASUNDER . . . '

She waved her firestick aloft.

'THROUGH FLAME, THROUGH FIRE,
THROUGH HELL ITSELF COME FORTH!'

On and on she chanted, beating the ground beneath her feet, summoning up the spirits from the earth and sky, from the heavens and the depths. Around her the wind howled, shrieking with a thousand demonic voices. The mountain trembled as the spirits woke and shook it in a rage. A sheet of fire shot from the distant peak. Thunder rumbled in anger. The gods did not give up their own without a fight, even when they were stuck in some nether world.

At last, Kumari slumped to her knees, spent, her head bowed, her heart broken.

She had done her best, given it her all. And *still* there was nothing. She would never see or hear Mamma again. Never get to the truth. Never find out who had killed her. Never be able to sleep in peace.

Then she felt the sun burst across her face, the first shaft of daylight. Snapping open her eyes, she was all but blinded.

And there – before her – stood a shape, silhouetted against the fiery skies.

The sunlight picked out the edge of scarlet robes, casting a halo round a hooded head. A hand reached for Kumari, its touch the one she craved. She could smell Mamma's familiar

22

perfume, see the royal ring on her finger. Although her face was deep in shadow, she knew this, at last, was her mother.

'Mamma?' She took a step forward, face lifted in longing.

Cold fingers closed around her own.

Then everything went black.

CHAPTER 2

A great roaring filled her ears, a sound unlike any she had ever heard. Strange smells filled her nostrils: leather, sweat and *something else*. Her head was being flung around, her body jerked side to side. She tried to roll with the motion, as if she were on a boat. The roaring changed in tempo, increasing and decreasing. There was an earsplitting squeal and the motion abruptly ceased.

'What is it? What's happening?'

The man's voice came from beside her, speaking roughly in a tribal tongue that she recognised. It was the dialect used by the warlords who plagued the western borderlands of the kingdom. Dimly Kumari recalled feeling a sharp pain in her arm and then an endless sleep punctuated by movement and sounds: yet more voices, being shoved around, manhandled as if she were a potato sack.

'It's the Macy's Parade,' came another voice from her other side. 'Dumb cab driver's taken the wrong cross street.'

A sensation welled up inside Kumari. Desperately, she tried to speak. Her tongue felt swollen, her throat dry as dust. Finally, she managed to croak.

'I'm going to be sick!' she rasped.

Instantly, there was pandemonium.

'She said *what*?'

'She's going to be sick!'

'Open the darn window!'

'No – open the door.'

'Keep a hold of her, you idiot!'

One of them grabbed Kumari's shoulders and propelled her forward. She was stepping down from some kind of coach, although she could see no horses. The vehicle was bright yellow, the hard ground beneath her feet a dull grey. She glanced up at the sky. Instantly, the world tilted sideways. Stretching up, touching the heavens, immense towers surrounded her. Towers ten times higher than the palace walls, thirty times higher even. So tall were these towers that they blocked out the sun's rays from the earth. Diamond shards of light shot from the summits, citadels of the gods, surely. Kumari stared, awestruck. Suddenly, her guts lurched again.

'Hurry!' shouted a voice. 'We have to get the kid out of here.'

25

'Pipe down,' said another, closer to her. 'Can't you see she's not well?'

As Kumari retched over and over, her mind began to steady. The hands that held her head were strong, their grip unrelenting.

'Where am I?' she muttered. 'Who are you people?'

No answer from alongside. She retched again, deliberately. These men meant her harm. She had no idea who they were. What was she doing here, in this place of towering pinnacles?

Last thing she knew, her spell had worked. She had summoned up Mamma. Somehow, though, Mamma had gone. Again. And she was *here*, with these people. Had her magic gone wrong once more? Was this some sort of demonic mirage? No, this felt all too real. Fear trickled down Kumari's spine, landing at its base with a jolt. She must be in the World Beyond. At the mercy of Time! The mortal enemy, its sands unstoppable . . .

More sensations began to filter through; the sounds of people talking and walking. In the background, that roaring sound. Other noises, strange and startling. A hooting and a honking; a distant, whooping wail. Her eyes focused on scraps of paper carelessly tossed in the gutter. She glanced at her wrist; her amulet was gone. Her cherished silver bracelet, a gift from Mamma. Without it, she felt naked, more defenceless than ever.

'You done, princess?'

She had almost forgotten the man still holding her. An idea popped into her head. She let her body go slack.

'What the . . . She's fainted!' shouted the man.

26

'Get her back in here,' yelled the others.

At that very moment, Kumari kicked out with all her might. She heard a sharp crack as she contacted with the man's knee. 1–0 to her! An angry bellow of pain. And then she was running. Racing down a dull grey path, along the gulley between the towers, heels pounding, arms pumping, dodging people, in and out. They passed by in a blur. Faces streaking, featureless. Noises fading into nothing. *Run! Hide! Get away!* Chest exploding with the effort. Squeezing through the mob. Too many people, getting tighter and tighter.

Behind her, she heard a shout. The men were gaining on her. She began to push through the crowd, her slight figure disappearing amidst the throng.

'Excuse me! Excuse me!' she screeched but no one appeared to understand. 'I've been kidnapped!' she shouted but nobody seemed to listen.

The mass grew solid, an impenetrable human wall. She had reached a dead end. A quick glance over her shoulder. The kidnappers were right behind her, shoving their way through the crowd. There was no escape. The only way out was forward. Any moment now they would spot her and then she was finished. There was nothing else for it. She had to climb over these people. Scramble up on to shoulders, use backs as stepping stones. Never mind the shouts of protest. This was life or death – hers!

Eyes swivelled round, people glaring and grumbling. One or two let out an encouraging cheer. Someone offered her a hand. And then she was at the front, staring down into a wide avenue. Closing her eyes, she dived, twisting and turning as she fell. She landed with a thump, rolling over and over. Shouts rang out from the crowd, shouts that contained a warning note.

She heaved herself up. There were guards marching straight towards her. At least, they looked like the palace guards, their insignia glinting in the winter sunlight. Those in front were banging drums, grim-faced in concentration. The guards were only feet away when Kumari flung herself to the side. Her efforts were not quite enough; the guards had to break ranks to avoid her.

'*There she is!*'

Another cry from the crowd, one in a language that she understood. The kidnappers were yelling to one another, pointing at their prey. Scrambling to her feet, Kumari tried once more to run. Weaving in and out of the musicians, dodging trumpets and whirling sticks, panic-stricken as on and on they came, knees lifted in unison. Fluffy pom-poms caught her on the cheeks. A flag bearer bore down. Breaking through the rear of their ranks, she could see more marchers approaching.

Above them, something strange and wonderful: a giant dog flying in the sky. For a moment, Kumari gaped. The World Beyond was bizarre! Another yell and she tore her eyes away. A man was heading towards her. She glanced at the crowd lining the avenue – an unbreakable phalanx. Turning, she ran the other way, straight through the procession. Racing for the giant dog, towards the people beneath it. Their eyes were wide with surprise, their mouths open, calling. Ignoring them, she kept going, head down in determination.

28

Once again, a roar filled her ears but this was the roar of a hundred thousand voices.

And then a more familiar sound, the clip clop of horses' hooves. Rows and rows of splendid beasts, ridden by men in uniforms. The horses were drawing to a halt, standing in formation. Beyond them, a magnificent coach on which an old man sat in state. This had to be the king; his robes were red, trimmed with white fur, his throne ornate. Piled around his feet were brightly wrapped packages, offerings perhaps from his subjects. A splendid beard sprung luxuriantly from his smiling face, crowned as it was with a scarlet cap.

Brushing through the horses' flanks, Kumari ran towards the king, arms outstretched in supplication.

'Oh, please,' she gasped. 'Please. You have to help me. I, too, am of royal blood! I have to get home! I have to get back to my father's kingdom!'

The old man peered at her from his throne. Alongside, his handmaidens twittered.

Kumari tried once again. 'Your majesty, I have been snatched from my homeland!'

From beneath his white whiskers the old man spoke. His words were unfamiliar. From his reaction to her desperate pleas, it seemed he found her equally incomprehensible. She felt the anger rise up. This was ridiculous. How hard could it be? *Anyone* could see she was a goddess.

'Look, your majesty, I realise I'm interrupting here. But really, you have to help me out! You know, one royal person to another!'

Hands on hips she stood, chin jutting in determination. And

still the old guy gawped at her. To Kumari's astonishment, he was beginning to look nervous. The handmaidens started to back away, the bells on their hats jangling nervously. Exasperated, Kumari stared them out. What was with the weird outfits?

Tears of frustration began to well. Any minute now her captors would be upon her. She threw her head back and howled in despair. Suddenly, a strong arm grabbed her. She felt herself being hoisted up, lifted from the ground. Kicking and screaming she tried to break free. The arm held her firm as it flung her down across a saddle in front of him. As hard as Kumari struggled, there was no fighting this new assailant.

Twisting round on the saddle, Kumari stared at her attacker. She caught a glimpse of a shield-shaped badge gleaming against a thick, blue jacket. Across one shoulder, a leather strap; on one hip, a holster. As the man kicked his horse into a trot, she felt the cold clutch of fear. The guy had a gun. Kumari hated guns, had only ever seen the ornate replicas kept in the museum. They were banned from the kingdom, although the occasional shot rang out from the borderlands. Hunters and warlords liked to perpetrate the evil of these weapons. And now she was inches from one, being carried off she knew not where.

'Let me go,' she snarled. 'My father will have you for this!'

The man stared ahead.

'How dare you!' she snapped. 'I am a *goddess!*'

No reaction. Not a blink. Clearly he had no respect for anyone, let alone an immortal.

30

'Very well,' she announced in the haughtiest voice she could muster. 'I shall now banish you to the fires of hell!'

Easier said than done, especially when it was yet another feat she had never managed. She tried first one incantation then another, finally combining a bit of both:

'BY THE CRIMSON ROBES I WEAR
BY BASILISK AND BLOODSTONE
BY THE GARLIC IN THE FIELDS
BY THE POPPIES AND WHAT THEY YIELD
I BANISH THEE FOREVER!'

Pausing for breath, Kumari glanced at the man. Not so much as a twitch from him. Really, he must be made of stone. That or her magic was way off . . .

Eventually, she gave in, slumping across the saddle in exhaustion. When at last the horse drew to a halt, she scarcely bothered to lift her head. Helping her down, the man kept his grasp tight. Kumari, however, was beyond running, beyond anything except black despair. She was taken through a doorway into a dim lobby. Before her stood a large wooden desk and behind that another man. This one, too, wore a uniform, similar if less pristine. He peered at her from over the desk and tapped his pen against his teeth.

'So this is the kid who accosted Santa Claus?'

Then she was being handed over and led away down a corridor. She did not bother to look back; one captor was becoming much like another. They placed her in some kind of cell, barren, bleak and cold. Sinking down on to the solitary bench, Kumari cradled her head in her hands. People came and went; occasionally they spoke to her.

31

Their words were beginning to make a bit more sense, which meant she was starting to tune in. She hated to admit it but the RHM had a point. If she'd applied herself to the Gift of Tongues, none of this would be so hard. She'd have had instant communication instead of this fuzzy noise in her ears. Been able to speak their tongue instead of struggling to be heard.

What kind of place was this, anyway, where they incarcerated a kid? OK, so they left her door ajar. It was not exactly a great welcome. She could try and make a run for it but the odds were pretty lousy. Outside she could see them sitting at their desks. It would be impossible to get past so many. Besides, they all had guns, parading them proudly. Given that her strike rate on magic was not so hot, it seemed she was pretty much stuck.

Eventually, two female guards brought some food, or at least that was what she assumed. Kumari stared as they mimed eating. These people were insane.

'Cheeze-birrgirr,' said one.

'Frahze,' said the other.

Kumari glared at the package they handed her. This had to be a joke. Food served in a bag? Not even peasants ate out of paper! She could forgive the lack of deference. Obviously they had no idea who she was. But making her eat like this was tantamount to torture.

She glanced up at the women. They motioned towards their mouths again. Kumari rummaged inside the bag and pulled out a box. Opening it up, she saw an object. It was the only way to describe it. A circular *object*. They expected her to *eat* this? Gingerly she poked at it. Her finger sank into a bread-like disc. Ever so carefully, she raised it. *Eugh!* Her nose wrinkled in disgust.

A yellow ooze spilled from underneath. She scraped at it experimentally. Beneath it lay something else. Kumari bent close. She could not believe her eyes. They wanted her to eat this shrivelled, grey-brown *thing*. Pushing it away, she shook her head. The guards looked at one another. Shrugging, they left the cell.

'She don't like cheeze-birrgirr?!' said one, clearly mystified.

Kumari's stomach let out a rumble. Despite herself, she was hungry. *Should I risk it?*, she wondered, bending forward again to take a cautious sniff. Digging in the paper bag she found another sack. Inside that, pale strips, possibly some sort of vegetable. Alongside the strips, a tiny pot, its contents red and sticky. Emboldened, she stuck her finger in and, extracting it, licked. A smile creased her face. *The stuff was exquisite!*

Picking up a yellow strip, she inspected it. It looked pretty harmless. Shoving the strip inside her mouth, she crunched. The thing was tangy with salt. *Stupendous.* Throwing caution to the wind, Kumari dipped the strips in the red sauce. A few moments later, she was sucking her fingers, delirious. Whatever these things were, she needed more. At once.

Dubiously, she eyed the bun thing again. It looked positively dangerous. Her stomach let out another growl. *What the heck*, thought Kumari. Holding her nose, she took an enormous bite. The 'cheeze-birrgirr' was not so bad, a little bland but edible. Determinedly, Kumari chewed. She would need all her strength to escape.

Outside, at his desk, Sergeant Rooney was in a quandary. The kid was obviously not from the United States but from quite where was another matter. There were so many tourists in town for the parade that she could be from any place in the world. In all his time working the 14th precinct, Sergeant Rooney had not seen anything like it. Sure, he had come across all types. But this kid was pretty different. There was something about her, something strange aside from her garments. A certain look behind those eyes, an imperiousness about her bearing.

'I tell you, that kid is *someone*,' he said to his buddy.

'Yeah, they're all someone,' scoffed his buddy.

'No, I mean *really* someone. Like, you know, important.'

The other officer scratched his head. 'Yeah, OK, whatever.'

Soon Child Services would be here. Then she was no longer their problem. What with the parade and all, it had taken time to find someone. Imagine the kid running through the marching bands, accosting Santa Claus. It was a miracle there had been no accident. Sergeant Rooney sighed aloud.

'I'm Lisa Anderson.'

A young woman stood before them, straight blond hair hanging smooth to her shoulders. Her blue eyes were steady, her handshake firm, her face sprinkled with a few freckles.

'From Children and Family Services,' she added.

The other officer glanced at his watch. 'You're the babysitter, right?' he said, gruffly. 'You sure took your time.' These welfare types always sounded so superior.

'You try getting across town today,' Lisa Anderson snapped back. She might look fragile but there was no messing with her.

'She's through here,' interjected Sergeant Rooney, throwing a look at his colleague. Sometimes he could be such a jerk.

The welfare woman smiled slightly.

Sergeant Rooney had a soft spot for kids: so far, he had thirteen grandchildren. His heart went out to the little girl. What kind of parents would let her get lost like that? Surreptitiously, he wiped a tear from his eye, then addressed himself to the holiday roster. He marked himself as on vacation for Christmas and New Year's with a small grimace of satisfaction.

Lisa Anderson bustled down the corridor, following the officer's broad back. Cops, they were all the same. Made her job twice as difficult. Under one arm, her briefcase bulged, paperwork spilling from its split seams. There would be more forms to fill in with this one, an endless barrage of documents. At the door to the holding cell, the officer gestured.

'The kid's in there,' he indicated with his thumb, then turned on his heel.

Slipping inside the cell, Lisa's eyes fell on a red bundle. One tiny foot dangled over the bench, encased in a flimsy sandal. Sandals in November – now Lisa really had seen it all.

Bending forward, she brushed the little foot with her finger-tips. The copper skin felt icy.

'You poor thing,' Lisa murmured. Amazing how this job could still get to you. At the sound of her voice, the bundle stirred. A sleepy head raised itself from within. Lisa found herself staring into the most remarkable eyes, at once inno-cent and knowing. A curtain of raven hair fell straight around a perfect face. Despite her dishevelment, the child was breathtaking.

'Hi, I'm Lisa,' she offered, holding out her hand.

The girl stared in bewilderment.

'I've come to take you to a foster home,' she continued.

Still, the girl gazed at her, dumbfounded.

With a sigh, Lisa helped the girl up from the bench. They would need to find an interpreter. Although goodness knows what language this girl spoke – some kind of Asian dialect, she would guess. Brightly, Lisa chivvied the girl along, sign-ing the appropriate paperwork. The kid's head remained bowed until a sudden commotion in the corridor brought it snapping up.

A couple of officers were herding in four foreign men. The men were jabbering excitedly in their own language, clearly trying to protest. At the sight of them, the kid cowered, grab-bing at Lisa's arm for support.

'It's OK, honey,' soothed Lisa. 'Those guys aren't coming this way.'

Sure enough, the officers led them off to be processed although the kid trembled until they were out of sight.

'Come on, sweetie,' said Lisa. 'Don't worry, they didn't see you. Time to get you out of here. My car's parked out back.'

Outside, Lisa settled her into the car, showing her how to do up the seatbelt. All the way uptown to the Bronx, her conscience nagged at her. As gleaming skyscrapers subsided into the low-rise sprawl, her heart, too, began to sink. It was hardly the greatest environment in which to place a girl like this. But there was nothing else Lisa could do; nowhere else to put her. Besides, it beat staying in some institution. Mrs Hernandez might be a little kooky but she had a good heart. Finally, they arrived outside a shabby apartment block.

'We're here,' said Lisa.

As she helped the girl from the car, she consoled herself that this was temporary. Probably even now her parents were frantically trying to find her. They must have got split up in the crowd. At least it seemed the kid was not a trafficking case. Those were the ones Lisa found the hardest. Children smuggled in and out of countries, their fate too awful to contemplate. This girl was one of the lucky ones. At least now she was relatively safe.

The apartment door swung back. Kumari blinked in astonishment. The woman who filled the doorway was as wide as she was tall. *Oh my goodness,* she thought. *This woman is a giant plum.* A shiny purple top strained to cover an ample chest while her bottom bulged over burgundy leggings that cut in halfway up her calves. Her skin was bronzed, a shade darker than Kumari's, her hair a dazzling confection of twisted curls topped off with mauve tips.

Unsmiling, she led them through. The noise was deafening.

In the corner of the shabby room, a box blared out at full volume. Kumari was mesmerised; across a glass screen pictures moved. There were people inside that box – how did they shrink them like that? This was powerful magic indeed. A face filled the screen, a man with bouffant hair and orange skin. Even as she watched, the man disappeared to be replaced by a chicken dancing.

'Honey.'

'Hey, sweetie.'

White noise buzzed through Kumari's brain, as it did each time these people spoke to her. The sound seemed to grow louder and louder. Frantically, she scanned the room. She had to get away from this place, this terrifying purple woman. They were between her and the door. She could only think of one way to go. Maybe those people in the box would help her . . .

Taking a deep breath, Kumari leapt headfirst for the screen. A sharp crack and she fell to the ground, clutching her skull in agony. Stars danced before her eyes. The room whizzed round and round. She could feel herself falling down, down, giving in to darkness once more . . .

CHAPTER 3

Her headache was beginning to subside as claustrophobia set in. She had awoken in a room so small that she could touch both walls at the same time. Which is exactly what she did.

It beat staring out the window right next to the bed or counting the cracks in the wooden floor.

Beside her lay a pile of clothing that the plum-clad woman had left. She unfolded the first item: a thick, grey hooded top. Next, a pair of rough, blue trousers such as a peasant farmer might wear. With a grunt of disgust, Kumari flung them to one side. OK, so she was not exactly hip, but even she had her limits. She would wear her red robes for the moment, dirty and stained though they were. And then she remembered. She still had her ceremonial bag, concealed in the folds of her robes. Excitedly, she rummaged through it. Her journal was there. Everything else had been left on the hillside, but this, the most important item, was safe in her hands.

All her notes on secret ceremonies, all her innermost thoughts, hopes and wishes. The stuff she would hate anyone else to read, especially the bits about Tenzin. Most precious of all, the miniature portrait of Mamma, tucked carefully between the pages. Extracting it, Kumari placed it on the pillow before leafing through her book. Was it really only one moon since she had written these words?

Imperial Blessing Day. Boring. Was yawning so much into my sleeve, I forgot to keep an eye on Badmash. Next thing I know, he'd eaten the Holy Honey Cake meant for Papa. By the time I realised, all that was left was a pile of crumbs. Papa was unimpressed to say the least - I had to banish Badmash to my bedroom. Saw Tenzin in the front row but pretended not to. Ha! Should have seen his face!

Or this entry, dated a few moons earlier:

Today there was a procession with Mamma's portrait. All the school kids threw flower petals. I wish I'd been with them instead of all alone on my palanquin. I kept my head down – my eyes are so puffy and red. I don't want anyone to see them, especially not the person who might have murdered Mamma. I don't want them to think I'm suffering. It's much better to appear strong.

And then there was one even earlier, the ink blurred by

teardrops. Kumari stared at it hard, her eyes pricking once more.

They took Mamma away today. I miss her . . .

'I miss her,' whispered Kumari.

Now it seemed she would never get her back. She missed Papa too, in a different sort of way. Much as she loved her Papa, at times she felt as if she hardly knew him anymore. Right now, for instance, she had no idea what he would be thinking. He might not even have noticed that she'd gone until someone else pointed it out. Even when he was well, Papa was somewhat distracted. It was not that he didn't care, more that he had so much on his mind. It must be hard being a god-king, with all that responsibility to bear. Or so Mamma had always told her. Poor Papa. Since he had started to get sick, he had become more remote than ever.

Closing her journal with a sigh, Kumari tried to work out what to do. Although this room had no bars, it was as much a prison as the last. She had no knowledge of the World Beyond apart from the RHM's tales. No means of communication. No way of getting home. If she tried to escape, she would be lost in an instant. She was stuck in this foreign place without her only friend. Her heart twisted at the thought. She could not bear to think of Badmash, to wonder what they had done to him, even to hope he was safe. She only knew that he was no longer there, her constant companion. They must have abandoned him, or worse. Now she was truly alone.

The realisation bit deep. Kumari doubled over with the pain of it, rocking backwards and forwards, resting her head on her knees. She wanted to howl aloud, to scream out her helplessness. Instead, she tried to think. There had to be a way out. Cocooned in despair, she became aware of a ticking noise. Glancing at the door, she saw an instrument above it, circular in shape, numerals arrayed around its edge. As she watched, a thin arm swept round the circle while two others pointed in turn directly up and down. Fascinated, she stared as each arm shifted position, the two fractionally thicker ones moving slowly, the thinner one keeping up its continuous sweep.

This instrument measured something, that much was obvious. And then it dawned on her. This thing was apportioning Time!

Its markings were gradations, signposts on its remorseless sweep. Kumari shrank in horror. *This was a clock*, mechanically counting down the days. For the people in the World Beyond, there was no escaping Time. It hung over them like a sentence, the clock taunting them with the evidence. Look at me, it mocked, see how swiftly your life is passing. Listen to me ticking it off. Work out how much you have left.

Kumari shut her eyes. She could feel the weight of it. Now *she* was trapped, too. And she had but a year and a day. A year and a day in the World Beyond and then she would succumb to it. Time would claim her for its own, as it did everyone here. No longer protected by the Holy Mountain, she would die many miles from home. The breath stalled in her chest. A gulp choked up her throat.

'Help me,' she sobbed.

The ticking intensified, matching the throb in her temples.

42

It grew so loud that it filled her mind, blocking out all other sound. *Tick, tick, tick. Tap, tap, tap.*

Once again, Kumari lifted her head. She waited, listening, and heard it again. Not a tick – but a tap. Her eyes flicked to the window. The tap had a hollow sound. Like fingernails on glass. Or perhaps even the beak of a baby bird . . . She could make out a shape through the grimy pane, a shape at once blurred but familiar. Pressing her nose to the glass she took a good look.

'Badmash!' she cried.

Kumari wrenched at the window, trying to open it. At last she succeeded and Badmash crawled through the gap. Bedraggled, emaciated, he fell into her open arms. His half-closed eyes showed delight, despite the exhaustion of his journey across the world.

'Oh, Badmash,' Kumari crooned. 'How on earth did you find me?'

His feet were gnarled, his claws broken as if he had clung on to something for dear life.

Gently, she stroked his feathers. Under her fingertips, she could feel his ribs poking through. And then something else; a hard ring around his neck. Parting his feathers, Kumari exposed a band of silver.

'My amulet!' she cried. 'Badmash, you clever thing!'

He must have found it on the hillside and wriggled his head through it. Dropping a kiss on his beak, Kumari slipped the amulet on to her wrist. It gleamed against her skin and instantly things seemed better. If only she could remember how to activate it. Then she would feel truly safe.

Just at that moment, there was a knock on the door. Hastily, Kumari shoved Badmash under the covers. A few seconds later, the purple woman squeezed into the room.

'Hi,' she said brightly, exposing her teeth again.

'Hi,' mimicked Kumari. This must be their form of greeting. The buzzing was back in her ears but she did her best to ignore it. Instead, she parroted. It seemed like the best idea.

'Meeeee Maaaaa,' said the woman, pointing a finger at her ample chest.

Kumari gawped at the finger. It was adorned with the biggest ring she'd ever seen. Come to that, so were all the others. It was amazing she could even lift her hand.

'Meeee Maaaaa,' Ma repeated, raising her voice and speaking slower. 'Me Ma *Hernandez!*'

Ma pointed to the clock and then held up seven and a half fingers, a manoeuvre that involved much complicated knuckle bending.

'Gotta go get food. Be back soon.'

Kumari nodded and smiled. She had no idea what Ma meant. It was best to keep her sweet, though, until she could work out some escape plan. She leaned back on the pillow, as if to indicate she would rest now; lull the woman into a false sense of security while she worked out what to do. Unfortunately, however, she had miscalculated. As Kumari settled back, an angry squawk rang out. Hastily, Kumari coughed. Ma's eyebrows shot up. Kumari coughed again then yawned, indicating Ma should leave. *Just go*, she thought fiercely. Mercifully Ma did. When the door clicked to,

Kumari let out a long breath.

'That was close,' she scolded Badmash, hauling him out from his hiding place.

Badmash nibbled her cheek. She could never stay cross with him for long.

Kumari waited a moment, listening, after the front door finally banged shut. Silence reigned in the apartment. Even the talking box held its tongue. Cautiously she crept from her room, cradling Badmash in her arms. She tried the front door. Locked. These people were not stupid. Other doors led off the hallway. The first one she tried was also locked. The second opened on to a cupboard stuffed with sheets and towels. The third hung off its hinges, revealing a narrow room lined with more cupboards. Cautiously, she opened the nearest. It contained nothing but cracked plates. Another cupboard, larger and shinier, enticed her further along. She grasped the handle on the front and hauled its door open to reveal shelves. A blast of cold air hit her in the face. Light shone into her eyes.

Startled, Kumari leapt back, banging her elbow on the sink behind. This was some kind of magic cupboard, she could tell by the fine mist that wafted out. On its shelves were packages. She picked up a box at random. The finger-shaped cake she pulled from it looked nothing like its picture. Exploding creamily in her mouth, it was like eating sweetened cloud. She offered some to Badmash. Big mistake. He stuck in his beak and sucked the cake dry of cream, gobbling the remnants with fierce concentration before looking up for more. Kumari fed him the rest of the box but still he looked hungry. She reached into the cupboard again and pulled out a canister. There were red symbols emblazoned across it that read E-A-S-Y C-H-E-E-S-E.

No idea what that means, thought Kumari, pressing the button on the top. A yellow stream shot forth, entangling Badmash in a sticky web. Kumari began to giggle, offending him deeply. He might be a baby vulture but Badmash had his pride. Squawking with outrage, he began to jump up and down on the button. His first two attempts missed. The third hit her wetly in the ear.

'OK, OK, truce!' she cried, wiping his efforts from her earlobe. Thirsty now, she grabbed a bottle from the magic cupboard and held it up to the light. The contents appeared dark, a gaseous, murky brew. Steeling herself, she took a slug.

'Urk!'

Instantly, she spat it out. Her tongue was tingling, her taste buds dancing. Actually, this stuff was not so bad. She took another swig.

Piling a plate with all the food she could find, Kumari decided to explore some more. She tucked the bottle of brown liquid under her arm. It made her feel curiously alert. The next room along turned out to be Ma's bedroom. She could tell by the outsize clothing draped over every surface. Ma certainly had unusual taste, as well as a penchant for fancy footwear. Kumari slipped her foot into a silver shoe, its sole stacked and squishy. She hopped up and down a couple of times, admiring the fluorescent flash on one side.

Spying a pink, sparkly cap she jammed it down on her head. Rummaging through the piles for more, she unearthed a long scarf made of feathers. Adding a frilly jacket, she gazed at herself in the wardrobe mirror. The sleeves hung a foot from her hands; the cap obscured half her face. Pleased with the effect Kumari began to twirl, faster and faster. Slithering down, the feather scarf tripped her up and she fell backwards on to the bed. She seemed to sink forever into its soft embrace, its aged springs sighing soggily. Compared to the unyielding wooden beds in the kingdom this was a positive invitation to play. Scrambling to her knees, Kumari began to bounce, higher and higher. Whooping with delight she flung herself around, Badmash flapping beside her.

All of a sudden, she noticed that Badmash was no longer there.

'Badmash? Where are you?'

She found him trembling in a corner.

He was staring at a table half-hidden by a screen. Upon it sat a candle, carved into the shape of a skull. Adorning it, a crown of leaves. Before it, a dish of incense. Kumari wrinkled her nose. It smelt resinous, familiar. The whole arrangement sat on a golden cloth draped across the table.

'It's OK, Badmash,' she cooed. 'It's only an altar.'

So they had altars in the World Beyond. Which meant ceremonial magic. Maybe it was not so different to the kingdom after all. Only Time would tell.

The sound of the front door opening sent Kumari scuttling back to her room, shedding Ma's clothes. Not two seconds after she had shut her door, it opened again.

'Hi,' said a friendly voice. Two voices in fact. Two smiling faces stared at her, almost identical in every respect.

'I'm LeeLee,' said one.

'And I'm CeeCee,' said the other.

Kumari gawped at them. She had never seen two girls look so alike. They didn't look to be much older than her which made them Ma's daughters, she would guess. There was a resemblance to Ma in their eyes and in their mouths although their hairstyles were more sober, tied back neatly behind their heads.

'Oooooh, cuuuute,' said CeeCee, suddenly spotting Badmash. Too late, Kumari realised he was still perched upon the bed. Sweeping him up in her arms, CeeCee cuddled him as LeeLee petted him. Or maybe it was the other way round. Kumari felt thoroughly confused. Still, they appeared to like Badmash, which was a great relief. She had been so afraid they would refuse to let him stay. Not everyone liked small, scruffy birds.

While CeeCee carried Badmash, LeeLee took Kumari by the hand. Together, they lead her through into the room dominated by the talking box. At the sight of its screen, Kumari's head began to ache. Patting the long, squashy seat in front of it, the girls gestured to her to sit down.

'You hungry?' asked LeeLee, opening her mouth and pointing inside.

Kumari shook her head. Goodness knows what they would produce.

'OK,' said LeeLee and sat down beside her. CeeCee sat on the other side, stroking an almost comatose with pleasure Badmash.

One of the girls pressed a button and instantly the talking

box sprang to life. Within seconds, Kumari was once again mesmerised, lost to all but its magic. The World Beyond certainly was a curious place. Whatever next?

Sonny Hernandez skulked by the kitchen door. His mom refused to give him any cash.

'Not until you mend that door,' she scolded.

'Yes, Ma,' he sighed.

'And another thing, Sonny. I don't want you bringing those boys here no more.'

'What boys?'

'You think I don't know? I got eyes everywhere, son.'

Sonny gave the door a surreptitious kick. It was not fair, the way she treated him. Always on his case about something. She didn't treat his sisters that way. Just because they were twins, it didn't make them special. They were in there now, cooing over the weird kid with the ugly bird. Kid didn't even speak English. Just sat there in her funny clothes.

'Where's that kid from, anyway?' he muttered.

'You leave her alone,' said his mother. 'That child's been through enough. Running through the parade like that. Girl could have been killed. No one's any idea where she's from or if she has any folks. Makes you wonder how she got here, her and that darn bird.'

'They don't know where she's from?'

'Nope. She just appeared, all on her own.'

'What, like from nowhere?'

An idea was forming in Sonny's mind.

'Something like that,' said Ma. 'It's a mystery, that's what

49

it is. You know, like on that TV show. That guy who suddenly appears. Can't remember nothing, not even his own name. What's that thing he's got called? Amn . . . something. I forget.'

Sonny hung back as his mother waddled through into the lounge, in her arms boxes of pizza which she proceeded to hand round.

'Sonny, come get your pizza.'

'Just washing my hands, Ma.'

Had Ma paused for thought, she would have considered this odd. She was far too busy, however, sinking her teeth into a Hot One. Seizing his chance, Sonny snuck to the phone.

'Uh, yeah, *Daily News*? Got a story for you guys. You get the details for dough, man. You know what I'm saying?'

Sonny Hernandez was not known as Ratboy for nothing. He combined a rodent's low cunning with its fondness for a free lunch. His latest scam was selling stories, a nice little sideline. So far, he had ratted on an ex-soccer star now peddling dope, and the sleazebag trainer of the local swimming squad. As he waited to be transferred to the news desk, a smile stole across Sonny's face. This story was definitely worth a few bucks, he could feel it in his bones. Sell out that kid and he could pay off what he owed. Sonny began to hum under his breath.

Suddenly, life was looking good.

KUMARI'S JOURNAL
(TOP SECRET. FOR MY EYES ONLY.
EVERYONE ELSE KEEP OUT!
THIS MEANS YOU!)

The World Beyond
First Night

It's so noisy here I cannot sleep. Those things with wheels rush up and down all night. I can hear people shouting in the street and other sounds. I have no idea what they are. The light shines in through the window so brightly I can see to write – far brighter than moonlight. Weird thing is, I can't even see the moon or stars. I need to find the moon to work how long I've been here.

If I can work out how long I've been here already, I'll know how much of my year and a day I have left. But there doesn't appear to be a moon. Instead, the sky is a kind of orange. At least Badmash is asleep. He looks so tired it makes me think he must have travelled far which means I must also have come a very long way from home. The scariest thing is not knowing where I am.

These people seem to be friendly enough although I don't like the way that boy stares at me. I think he must be Ma's son, the brother of those girls who look the same. Except for the boy, they are all very kind, although I suppose it could be a plot. They could be working with those men who snatched me. At least those guards with guns have got them now so they can't take me again.

I don't think the people here are working with those men, though. I trust Ma – she's a good person. She has gentle eyes and a kind face. She reminds me of the Ayah a little bit, like a big, soft cushion (in a nice way). I like her hair – it's mad. And her clothes are something else. But I wish I could understand what she says. The words just don't make sense. The RHM would feel so smug – 'You should have listened,' that's what he'd say. Yeah, right. 'Accessing the Gift of Tongues.' I mean, it didn't seem exactly relevant before all this.

I wish I was back home. Everything here is really strange. Even the food they eat is bizarre. Instead of plates, they seem to use boxes to eat from and all the food appears to come from packages. I'd give anything for a bowl of spiced lentils and rice. Or maybe the Ayah's special momos. Tonight we all sat looking at the talking box and ate some kind of bread and cheese thing they called 'peetza'. Do people watch the box every night? Or do they read or talk or practise rituals? The talking box is pretty cool, although I still can't work out how they get the people in it.

There certainly seems to be some powerful magic in the World Beyond – I don't know yet just how strong. They might even be using some now to keep me here, although I'm sure I would feel it. Plus I have my amulet back – that must be doing something to protect me. Or it would do if I could only remember how to activate it.

It's not like I can test it by trying to escape, seeing as I don't even know where I am, right now. What's the point of running away if you don't know where you're heading? I don't know a single person in the World Beyond so it's not like *there's anyone to help me, anyway. I did try with that king guy but it was pretty clear he didn't recognise a fellow royal. The best thing to do is sit tight and think. At least, that's what Mamma would say. I can see her picture now on the pillow beside me. I miss her more than ever.*

CHAPTER 4

Kumari tiptoed into Ma's bedroom, casting a last, nervous glance through the living room door. Blue light flickered from the talking box. Poking above the couch in front of it, she could see the backs of three heads. Ma and the two girls were watching a small, yellow boy called Bart scrawl in chalk across a blackboard. The angry young man had left some time before. Now she had her chance.

Tucked in her pocket, Badmash snoozed, exhausted from his endeavours. Kumari refused to be parted from him, not even to take a bath. It was where she was supposed to be right now, immersed in the tub Ma had filled for her. Instead, she was here, in Ma's room, standing before the altar. Holding her breath, she stood before it, feeling her throat tighten and fill. If she could only call upon the gods to help, they would get her out of here. But she had tried so many times and each time she had failed.

'OM TARE TUTTARE TURE SOHA
OM TARE TUTTARE TURE SOHA
OM TARE TUTTARE TURE SOHA . . . '

Once again she was chanting, eyes closed, body swaying. Had it worked on the mountainside or not? She couldn't tell. She had smelt Mamma's perfume, seen the royal ring on her finger. And yet Mamma's touch had felt *different*, somehow. Colder. Less tender. Of course it would feel different. Mamma was different, for heaven's sake. Caught halfway between two states. No longer the Mamma she once was.

Kumari opened her eyes again. The room remained unchanged. No divine presence cast its light upon the heaps of clothes. No holy wind stirred up the dusty air. She was quite alone.

'Help me, Mamma,' she whispered, fingering the portrait in her pocket. There was no answering murmur.

Sinking to her knees, Kumari rested her head against the table. Her cheek rubbed on the golden cloth, ruffling it up. As it did so, she spotted something poking out from underneath, the edge of a wooden chest from which blue satin spilled. She pulled at the satin, revealing a cloak lined in deeper blue, an indigo softness scattered with silver stars that matched a glittering moon on the front. Kumari stroked the silky fabric, sensing the power steeped in every fibre. As she wrapped the cloak around her, a feathered stick fell from its folds.

Kumari raised it in the air, swishing it backwards and forwards. It made a satisfying sound. She could do some damage with this.

'Hey! Careful with that!' said a voice from behind.

That static filled her ears again, like a radio seeking the right station. Kumari whirled round to see Ma standing by the door.

'You be careful,' Ma repeated. 'That's no ordinary feather duster. And the thing you're wearing, that's my ritual cloak. You don't want to mess with that.'

The static cleared; Ma's words began to coalesce and make sense.

'S-sorry,' stuttered Kumari.

Ma's eyes bulged like a bullfrog's. 'Say what? You speak English?'

She advanced upon Kumari, seizing her by the shoulders.

'Come on,' she commanded. 'Say something else.'

Kumari gazed at Ma's mouth, marvelling at the sounds it made. She was still tuning in to this language. Unpractised as she was in the divine arts, Kumari was a goddess, nonetheless. The Gift of Tongues was her birthright. But understanding was one thing. It was much harder to get the words out. She thought for a moment then a smile broke across her face. She remembered something from the talking box, from the yellow boy.

'Eat my shorts,' she said.

Ma threw back her head and guffawed.

'You are one of a kind, girl!'

Gently, she freed the feather duster from Kumari's fingers and unwound the cloak from her shoulders.

'You don't want to go playing with things you don't understand.'

In response, Kumari raised her right hand and extended her little finger. In one swift, chopping motion she sliced the feather duster's handle in half. It was a simple trick, part magic, part martial art. Ma let out a yelp.

'That's my hoodoo duster you broke!'

Kumari took the two halves, pursed her lips and blew upon them. She handed the duster to Ma. It was back in one piece.

Ma's eyebrows nearly hit the ceiling.

'You some kind of witch, girl?'

Kumari smiled and shook her head.

'I . . . goddess,' she said.

'Yeah, goddess. Right.'

Ma was still staring at the duster, trying to figure it out. She was not to know that it was just about Kumari's only trick. Every other charm she tried was so far doomed to fail.

'So, where you from, girl?'

There was no answer to that one. Kumari shrugged her shoulders.

'You telling me you don't know?'

Ma looked at her, incredulous. Kumari shook her head.

'Guess I can't talk,' said Ma. 'Me, I'm from all over the place. Puerto Rican, Irish, Jamaican, you name it. My blood is so mixed up it's a wonder it don't need therapy. My folks moved around so much it just shook it up all some more.

How 'bout your folks, honey? Where are they now?'

Searching desperately for an answer, Kumari had a brain-wave. She whipped Mamma's portrait from her pocket.

'M-mamma,' she stammered.

Ma took it gently in her hands. 'What you saying? That's your mother? So where is she now, honey?'

At that, Kumari crumpled.

'Someone killed her,' she managed to whisper. As the tears trailed down her cheek, Ma's eyes widened in shock and began to well up as she crushed Kumari to her chest.

'There, there, sweetie, you let it out. Everything's going to be just fine.'

Snuffling into the endless acres of Ma's bosom, Kumari knew that this was not the case. It was good to hear it, though, to feel Ma's reassuring pats. They reminded her of her Ayah. She, too, was kind of big. Many a time she had taken Kumari on her lap and told her everything would be all right. The thought of her Ayah only intensified her longing. As her sobs increased, Ma rocked her back and forth. Even if Ma were willing, there was no way she could help. The king-dom had no name, no location on any map. Kumari's one hope was that someone would could come and find her. Right now, it was a possibility that appeared frighteningly remote.

Many thousands of miles away, inside his palace, the god-king paced to and fro. His face was thunderous. The courtiers had never seen him so angry. In point of fact, they had never seen him angry. But this was different. His only child was missing. Vanished without a trace. Somehow she must be in the World Beyond. And he blamed the night guard. Roused from the stupor into which he had sunk, the god-king's face ran with sweat. The very effort was weakening him, but still he raged.

'You should have spotted her,' he cried, as the Ayah wept noisily.

Before him, the guard hung his head. No words would suffice.

Beside the god-king stood the RHM. His eyes bore into the Ayah's. They stared back at him, red-rimmed, glinting with suspicion.

'RHM!'

'Your Excellency?'

The RHM bowed low before his ruler.

'You must be the one to go. You will find my daughter.'

The RHM stiffened momentarily.

'Yes, your excellency,' he murmured.

The RHM's impassive face hid a multitude of emotions. It had been a long time since he had left the kingdom. A lifetime, in fact. He, too, was granted only a year and a day in the World Beyond. He would have to move swiftly. And the king was ailing. It would be foolhardy to leave his side for long. Besides, there was another reason to keep any absence to the minimum. He stared at the Ayah once more. He dared not leave her to her own devices.

The Ayah met the RHM's gaze with equal mistrust then glanced away quickly. His eyes followed hers to the empty throne where once the queen had sat. On it, the queen's portrait, a picture at once lovely and terrible. So much was at stake here; so many possibilities.

Kumari's life.

The royal line.

The very kingdom itself.

KUMARI'S JOURNAL
(TOP SECRET. FOR MY EYES ONLY.
EVERYONE ELSE KEEP OUT!)
THIS MEANS YOU!

The World Beyond
Day 5 – 361 days to go

At least now I've found the moon I can tell precisely how long I've been here. If I climb up and look through the bathroom window I can see it above the lights. Almost a moon's quarter has passed since I left home - Time really does move fast in the World Beyond. It's easier now that I can understand them. It's pretty cool, this Gift of Tongues. Makes me think there's good bits to being a goddess.

I mean, I know there's good bits because Mamma told me so – as did Papa and the Ancient Abbot. The RHM doesn't seem so sure, but then I think he's jealous. Weird how I miss even him. It's not what I expected, being here. I thought the World Beyond would be so exciting, but really it's sort of grey. I don't mean grey in colour – although it is in parts – especially the buildings. I mean it feels grey, like there's a heavy weight pressing down on my shoulders. I think it's because they have no Happiness.

Or at least they don't seem to have a lot of it although Ma is generally always smiling. But I watch the people in the street and they don't look so happy. I guess there is no haze of Happiness and no one tending its fires. When I asked CeeCee and LeeLee they looked at me as if I were mad. They do that quite often. They do things differently in the World Beyond – too many things to list them all.

They have all these amazing machines, for example, they even talk to one another by a machine called the 'phone', which is pretty cool. And they have this thing called a 'computer' which seems to do just about everything. It sits in LeeLee and CeeCee's room and they said they use it to send messages to their friends. What is wrong with just going and talking to their friends, that's what I want to know! Although I wish I could use it to send a message to Papa, to tell him where he can come and get me. That's got to be why no one's come for me – they can't work out where I am.

So many machines and yet they can't stop Time. Makes me think they should have been concentrating on that rather than on coming up with more mechanical things. Weird thing is, they have all these people on the TV who talk about creams which can perform miracles and stop people from ageing. Perform miracles – what a joke! As if a cream can perform a miracle. It's hard enough to perform miracles if you're a goddess and I should know.

I like the TV though, and the people on it – especially Oprah *and* The Simpsons. *The Simpsons are not like any family I have met before – for one thing, they're yellow. Marge, though, is very kind and Homer reminds me of the Ancient Abbot. Not that the Ancient Abbot has the same personality but he does get things wrong. Actually, he isn't much like Homer at all. Homer gets pretty angry. That's the other thing about people's faces here – they all look sort of tight.*

CHAPTER 5

Simon Razzle smiled over the tops of his designer spectacles. He did not strictly need them, but they added a certain *sang-froid*.

'Come, my dear,' he purred. 'There is no need to cry. A little nip here, a tuck there and you'll be restored to your former self.'

Sitting on the opposite side of his imposing desk, the blonde woman dabbed at her eyes with a handkerchief.

'You really think so?' she simpered, blue eyes awash with tears.

'But of course,' insisted Simon. 'You have the bone structure. Your natural assets . . .'

He said the same to all his patients but she was not to know that. She patted her blond curls. Dyed, of course, like her eyelashes. Under them, her forehead stretched too tight, testament to a bad Botox job. Simon was the king of Botox; he knew just where to inject it, along with his impressive range of fillers, smoothers and plumper-uppers. Fake, the lot of them. But now the ultimate cure was in sight. A wholly natural cure for ageing. A way to turn back the clock.

Simon drummed his fingers on the desk, impatient now to get rid of her. When the blonde looked at him, startled, he covered with a smooth smile.

'Finger exercises,' he said. 'Excellent for youthful hands.'

'Oh, really?' she sounded intrigued. 'I must try them some time.'

Surreptitiously, Simon pressed the concealed button located under his antique desk. A moment later, his secretary buzzed through. Simon raised a regretful eyebrow.

'My next client has arrived.'

'Oh, I see,' she fluttered.

Simon smiled and half-rose from his chair. Luckily, she took the hint.

As soon as the woman had gone, Simon picked up the intercom.

'No interruptions until I tell you,' he barked.

'Yes, sir,' came the reply.

Simon sat and stared at the telephone, willing it to ring. This was the most important call of his life; the one that would tell him *she* was here. His eyes almost crossed with the effort; a bead of sweat trickled from his brow. No Botox for

Simon. He preferred a more long-term solution. And if this girl was all that had been promised, she would provide it. The ultimate cure for wrinkles; eternal youth at his fingertips. The passport to billions. Global fame and respect.

So caught up was he in his reverie, Simon jumped a foot when the phone rang. Fumbling, he dropped it, then recovered himself.

'Simon Razzle,' he said, smiling into the receiver. At last, the signal. The girl *was* here!

Thirty seconds later, he was scowling.

'What do you mean they *lost her*?'

Two minutes later, he shouted into the phone. 'You'd better find her, you hear?'

Thrusting his leather chair backwards, Simon leapt to his feet. He kicked his desk once, twice, then slammed down his fist.

'Are you OK, sir?' It was his secretary, full of concern.

'No I am not!' Simon shouted. 'And shut that darn door!'

Throwing himself down on his couch, Simon pounded the cushions. So near and yet so far. They had let the girl slip. Some cock-and-bull story about her running off into the Macy's Parade, then getting picked up by the police and carted off they knew not where. In viciously succinct fashion, Simon had made it clear that was not good enough. He expected a return on his investment. They had to bring him the girl.

Alive, if possible.

But a well-preserved corpse would do.

* * *

Kumari surveyed the Hoodoo Hair salon, taking in the orange walls and silver fittings.

'What do you think?' said Ma proudly.

'*Ay caramba!*' said Kumari.

Kumari had been at the apartment seven days now and her vocabulary was growing, fed by a constant diet of TV and her one-sided chats with Ma. Ma had an opinion on everything. It was what made her such a good hairdresser. People came from miles around to Hoodoo Hair, just to hear what Ma had to say.

'You gotta leave him girl,' she would counsel and the client would nod in relief. It was one thing hearing it from your own mother, quite another getting it straight from Ma. And then there were the potions. Ma mixed them up individually, dispensing them with all the gravitas of a pharmacist and a word of wisdom on each.

'You stir that into his coffee, you'll soon see an improvement. But you mark my words, girl, you gotta change in yourself.'

Kumari watched as the clients nodded gratefully, carefully stowing away the potion until the time was right. Meanwhile, Ma wielded her scissors and wove fantastical creations on their heads. One old lady arrived grey and dowdy and left pink-tinted and permed. Another, younger woman, beamed as Ma transformed a rat's nest into a rivulet of curls. Ma performed magic with her fingers; her potions were superfluous. Entranced, Kumari munched the candy that Ma handed out to her customers, amazed at all the things that buzzed and whirred, at the very fact of electric light.

66

Kumari could not help but flick on and off the switches. Badmash loved it too, once he had figured out that hot light bulbs hurt. Like a heat-seeking missile he had started by dive-bombing them. One bruised beak and a few scorched feathers later, he had learned to leave them well alone. Electricity was only one of the many marvels of the World Beyond. There was the telephone, for instance. Now, how cool was that? Speak into one end and you could talk to someone else miles away! Kumari glanced at it wistfully. She wished she could call home.

'Hey, honey.'

Kumari looked up. Mrs Brinkman was beckoning. The old lady came in every day for a wash and set, it seemed. Ma reckoned she liked the company.

'Ol' Mrs Brinkman,' she would say. 'Been living round here for ever. Her friends, they all gone and died. She 'bout the last one left.'

Kumari liked Mrs Brinkman. She had shrewd eyes that twinkled out of her wrinkled face. Kumari tried hard not to stare at the deep folds that scored her skin. The ravages of Time seemed so unfair.

'This is for you,' said Mrs Brinkman, pressing a candy bar into Kumari's palm. It was as if she knew how much Kumari loved candy. It was the most marvellous thing about the World Beyond. She even loved the gaudy wrappers that encased her sweet treats. Peeling it off with care, Kumari bit through chocolate to the caramel beneath, pausing so she could feel it begin to melt in her mouth, coating the insides of her cheeks. Eyes half-closed in ecstasy, she happened to glance at the mirror. What she saw made her hesitate and lean in for a closer look.

On her chin there was a large pink bump. Kumari had never seen anything like it. In the kingdom, these did not exist. She pressed herself right up to the mirror, examining it in detail. The thing looked angry, volcanic, as if it was about to erupt!

Oh my god, thought Kumari, clapping a hand over her chin. *I have caught some kind of disease! I am going to die. Or at least, be disfigured forever. This thing is disgusting. I can't let anyone see it . . .*

She sat frozen with terror for so long that eventually Ma noticed.

'Kumari, is something wrong?'

Now they were all staring.

'I'm diseased,' Kumari wailed, keeping her hand clamped tight to her chin.

'Have you gone crazy, girl?' Ma was beside her in an instant. Impatiently, she pulled at Kumari's hand, trying to drag it from her face. Finally, she succeeded and stared in puzzlement at her chin.

'Why, you got a zit, girl! Ain't nothing but a pimple.'

A titter ran round the salon. Kumari hung her head, shamefaced. Goddesses did *not* get such things as 'pimples'. Goddesses were perfect.

'You been eating too many of those candy bars,' scolded Ma. 'That's what's given you them zits. You want to give it a rest girl or sure as I'm standing here you'll get more.'

Coming from Ma, this was a little harsh. Kumari stared

morosely at the empty wrapper in her hand. It seemed a high price to pay for a few sweet treats.

'Don't go listening to her,' whispered Mrs Brinkman. 'All of us get zits some time.'

Not me, thought Kumari. It was another disease of the World Beyond. Really, this was a most unhealthy place, what with wrinkles and now pimples. What next, she wondered. Hair that just fell out by itself?

At that moment she glanced up and noticed the man standing by the counter. In the middle, where his hair should have been, the light bounced off shiny skin. Kumari stared so hard that the man noticed and stared back.

'Hey, you're that girl,' said the man, waving the newspaper in his hand.

Kumari dropped her gaze. She had no idea what he was talking about. The man continued, however, his voice rising in excitement.

'It's you, isn't it? That there *Mysssterious* Person.' He gave the 's's such emphasis spittle sprayed from his mouth.

'What you saying?' demanded Ma, striding over to snatch his paper. She read the story once, twice, then looked up, mouth agape. Wordlessly, she held it up and everyone peered round for a closer look. There it was, on page two. A fuzzy picture of Kumari.

'*Manhattan Mystery Girl,*' read out Ma. '*Do you know where she comes from? Police admit they know little about the young girl they rescued from the Macy's Parade . . .*'

Ma's eyes narrowed as she read on, her mind racing as the facts clicked into place.

'*Now residing in the northwest Bronx, the girl speaks very little English. She seems unfamiliar with American customs although she appears to like pizza.*'

'Sonny,' muttered Ma. 'This is Sonny's doin'.'

She stabbed the page with her finger, barely able to contain her rage.

'*One clue to her identity may lie with her constant companion, a baby vulture, although the New York Department of Environmental Conservation confirms that they have no record of the appropriate license.*'

At this, Ma puffed out her cheeks and let out a long, low whistle. Her eyes sparkled dangerously as she glanced up at Kumari.

'You gotta hide that bird, girl,' she declared. 'Else they gonna come take it from you an' kill it.'

A flutter of consternation swept round the room. They all knew what Badmash meant to Kumari.

At that very moment, a white van drew up outside the salon. Mrs Brinkman spotted it first, raising one trembling finger.

'It's them!' she shrieked. 'They got here already.'

Heads full of curlers turned to look. A man got out of the van. Painted on the side of it, the letters, ASPCA. The American Society for Prevention of Cruelty to Animals, aka the animal Feds.

'Qvick,' said Mrs Kowalski, 'you put him here darlink.'

Despite living in the Bronx now for forty years, her accent had never diminished. She was holding out her handbag, stuffed full of bits of wool.

'Forget that,' scoffed Mrs Martinez. 'You put him in here, *mija*.'

She, too, was holding out a bag, this one far more capacious. From the top, a pineapple protruded, next to it a box of cakes. Badmash licked his beak. As far as he was concerned, it was no contest. In a trice, he had hopped in and the top was snapped shut.

By the time the ASPCA agent entered, all was calm in the salon. The ladies stared studiously at their magazines or inspected their nails.

'Ms Hernandez?' The man was polite, slightly nervous even.

'Yeeeees?' demanded Ma, looking him up and down.

The man shuffled his feet.

'We've had a report that you are harbouring a dangerous wild animal at these premises.'

'Say what? A *dangerous wild animal*? Y'all mean my clients?' Ma looked round the salon for reaction. One or two tittered obligingly. Ma stuck her hands on her hips. 'Don't know 'bout you, but I ain't scared of 'em. Now why don't you run along, boy, before one of 'em bites!'

From her hiding place under the towels, Kumari could see only the man's feet. He shuffled them again but still he stood firm. *Oh, please*, she thought. *Please just go before he makes a noise.* A few feet away Badmash was hard at work, pecking open the box of cakes.

'I just need to take a look, ma'am,' insisted the agent, his face reddening slightly. They were all staring at him now and some of them looked pretty fierce. If they were anything like his grandma, these ladies could sure pack a punch. The agent wished with all his heart they had sent someone else.

'Take a look?' repeated Ma. 'Why, sure, you take a look, boy. Where you want to start, honey? Under this here dryer?'

She indicated the hood under which Lola Garcia sat in state. Lola had been quite a girl in her day. Now she leered at the agent. Faced with her gummy grin, the agent took a step backwards.

'That won't be necessary,' he stuttered. 'I'll just . . . take a look round.'

'You do that,' said Ma. 'Tell me if you see a tiger over there by the towels. Or maybe a snake wrapped round those shower heads . . . Might be some kind of *killer mouse* hereabouts! Maybe even a giant roach!'

Kumari held her breath, stifling a nervous giggle. She saw the man shuffle his feet again. Finally, he cleared his throat.

'Ah, actually, it's a bird that we're looking for.'

'A bird? Now, why didn't you say so? We got hundreds of birds, boy. Just you take a look outside. Darn things poop all over the place. I'd be glad if you got rid of 'em. You want a bird, son, you come to the right place.'

The agent cleared his throat again. 'Erm . . . it's a vulture we're after.'

'A vulture?' Ma paused for dramatic effect.

At that moment, Badmash squawked.

The whole place froze for a nanosecond. And then Ma doubled up.

'Awk,' she shrieked, clutching her gut. 'Ark, ark,' she moaned, sinking to the floor. Startled, the agent stared, not knowing what to do.

72

'My pills,' groaned Ma, gesturing. 'Get me my pills, Lola.'

Lola gaped gummily for a moment then leaped from her chair.

'Here you go, honey,' she crowed, cramming Sweetex into Ma's mouth. The agent was already retreating, backing towards the door.

'It's my gut,' Ma called after him. 'I get gas reeeeeeeal bad.'

'Ah, yes,' muttered the agent, not knowing where to look.

'You run along now,' said Ma. 'I'm going to be just fine. I can feel these pills working. Lola, you help me up.'

As she staggered to her feet, Ma let out a giant belch. It was one of her party tricks and, for the agent, the final straw. With one last gulp, he sped out the door and revved his van into action. As the van disappeared towards the expressway, Ma collapsed in hysterics.

'Did you see that boy's face?' she howled, tears of laughter flowing. 'I swear, I thought he was about to faint.' She hiccoughed uncontrollably.

Crawling out from under the towel rack, Kumari retrieved Badmash and clutched him in relief. They were safe, for the moment. She kissed his sticky beak. Mrs Martinez smiled benevolently, unaware of the damage he had inflicted. In her bag lay the evidence – a small pile of crumbs.

Kumari felt tears prick her eyes. She had been so scared that they might take him. Badmash was her last link with home. She could not bear it if he were lost. Catching sight of her face, Ma sobered instantly. Hauling her in for a hug, she held Kumari tight.

'There's nothing to worry about,' she said. 'That man, he's

73

gone now. Ain't nobody going to take your bird. Ain't no one going to take you.'

On the counter sat the newspaper, the picture grainy but distinct. Despite her words, Ma scented trouble.

This was not over yet.

'Ms Hernandez?'

Ma looked up. In front of her stood a stranger. A stranger flanked by two policemen, gazing at her grim-faced.

The stranger waved a piece of paper.

'I'm from ICE. Immigration and Customs Enforcement. This here is a warrant. It orders you to deliver up this child into my protective custody at once.'

Ma's arms tightened around Kumari.

'Over my dead body.'

The stranger nodded to the policemen. They moved to Ma's side.

'You leave me no alternative, Ms Hernandez,' said the stranger. 'I am arresting you for the obstruction of justice.'

And with that, cold steel was clamped around Ma's wrists as Kumari was torn from her grasp.

CHAPTER 6

'The nerve of those people,' said Lisa Anderson, swerving her car into the uptown traffic. Running alongside, the reporter raised his camera. Kumari barely registered its flash.

'Don't you worry, Kumari,' said Lisa. 'I'll have you back home in no time.'

Kumari blinked back a lurking tear. If only it were possible.

It did feel strangely good though, to recognise Ma's block. Better yet to see her face creased up in a big, welcoming smile. She didn't even mind when Ma squeezed her too tight. It had been a long, lonely night.

'You're OK,' Kumari mumbled into Ma's chest.

'Of course I am, child,' said Ma, patting her. 'Ain't no one going to hurt your Ma. I know my rights, Kumari.'

'Your Ma.' It sounded good. Even if it wasn't strictly accurate. Kumari knew who her Mamma was. But Ma made for a good substitute.

'Now, you sit yourself down, girl,' said Ma. 'I got ice cream for you after that pizza.'

Kumari's stomach growled in delight. She'd refused to eat until they released her from yet another holding cell.

'I'll be going now,' said Lisa Anderson. 'You won't forget what we talked about, Ms Hernandez?'

Kumari caught the look that passed between Lisa and Ma. She could almost hear the words before they were said: 'It's for your own good, Kumari.' She'd heard those words from Mamma and from her Ayah and now she could see them hovering on Ma's lips. Except it never was all that good and sometimes downright terrible. And so she ploughed her way through several pizza slices, waiting for the inevitable.

First, however, she could have some fun.

'More ice cream please,' said Kumari.

As Ma ladled out yet another helping of Double Trouble Choc Chip, Kumari smiled with satisfaction.

At the fourth bowl, Ma put her foot down.

'That's enough now, Kumari.'

Beside her, Badmash let out a belch. His feathers were suspiciously sticky. Kumari met Ma's accusing glare with innocence and turned to stare at the TV. Oh goodie, *The*

Weakest Link. She counted the seconds, ten, twenty, thirty. Heard Ma clear her throat. It was coming.

'Kumari, honey . . . '

Kumari pretended not to hear.

'Kumari, listen to me for a second.'

Fixing Ma with her best wide-eyed look, Kumari let her lower lip tremble. A momentary falter but Ma was no fool.

'Kumari, you gotta go to school.' It was said with finality. 'Ms Anderson and I, we promised those Child Protection people. We also had to give our word to the Immigration Services to keep them off our backs. They're not too happy you've been fostered. They'd rather stick you in some institution until they can "process" you, as they call it. OK, I know school is an institution too, but it's better than some prison.'

'Really?' Kumari could feel a rush of delight. 'You mean it? Fab-flippin-tastic!'

'Fab-flippin-tastic' was her new favourite expression along with 'checkitout' and 'hot.' She did not even mind that her efforts reduced Ma's girls to fits of giggles. Kumari could hear them now, clattering through the door. She turned on them with a beaming smile.

'I'm going to school just like you!'

CeeCee looked at LeeLee. As eldest twin, LeeLee tended to speak up. And speak up she did.

'You crazy?' she bellowed at Ma.

Ma's eyes flashed danger. 'Don't you speak to me like that, girl.'

'Someone's got to,' said LeeLee. 'If you plan on sending her to that place. I guess you mean *Moreno*. They'll eat her alive. Rita Moreno Middle School is the worst around. You ask anyone in the 'hood.

'Liliana! That's enough!' growled Ma. 'You're frightening Kumari.'

'Frightening her?' muttered LeeLee, slamming out of the room. 'I'm doing her a favour.'

Two days later, Kumari found herself gazing up at a vast, red-brick building. A steady stream of people sauntered and slouched through its forbidding gates, most of them about her age. Carved above a once-impressive porticoed entrance, the name of this institution. *The Rita Moreno Middle School*, it read.

Kumari glanced at LeeLee and CeeCee, standing protectively alongside her.

'That's it?' she gulped, a sudden frog in her throat.

'That's it,' they echoed.

Kumari shuffled her feet. Suddenly school didn't seem so enticing. Tucked down the front of the new red sweat top she sported under a puffa jacket, she could feel Badmash's heartbeat getting faster. Her feet felt sore in unfamiliar shoes, her calves cold under her thin grey pants. Her legs trembled, itching to run. She had to get out of here.

Panic rose in Kumari's throat. Automatically, she began to chant. She was doing her level best to access Power No 4, the Power to Become Invisible. That way she could hide amongst this herd, this terrifying crowd of adolescents. Oblivious to LeeLee and CeeCee's horrified looks, she chanted louder and louder. OK, so it had never worked before. There was always a first time.

One or two in the crowd shifted their eyes and stared. The majority ignored her. Just another crazy chick. There was one on every corner.

'Shhh!' CeeCee grabbed her arm. 'What are you doing?'

Kumari's eyes snapped open. 'I'm trying to become invisible,' she mumbled.

CeeCee rolled her eyes at LeeLee. 'Invisible, right,' she snorted.

'Never mind invisible,' said LeeLee. 'You just get on in there. And remember, Kumari, don't say nothing to no one except your teachers.'

'It's *anything*,' corrected CeeCee. 'Don't say *anything* to nobody.'

'Whatever,' said LeeLee. 'Good luck. See you later.'

And with that they turned and headed towards their High School. It was only two blocks from the Rita Moreno Middle School but it might as well have been on the moon.

'Can't I come with you?' Kumari yelled after them.

'No way,' shouted LeeLee.

'We'll be rooting for you,' called CeeCee.

Oh, great, thought Kumari.

There was nothing for it but to follow the crowd, now down to a trickle. Up the steps and through the doorway, head up and eyes forward. Past two men sitting at a desk, idly chewing as they chatted. Kumari caught a glimpse of some kind of badge. *Oh no, not more policemen.* On and on she walked, down corridors and up stairways. Picking a likely-looking group, Kumari stuck with them, only finally coming

79

to a halt when they entered what she took to be a classroom.

Everyone was slouched behind a desk. Most were laughing and talking. Someone flicked a rubber band across the room. It landed inches from Kumari. She bent down and picked it up, wondering if she should return it. She looked about for a seat. Not a single one was vacant.

OK, thought Kumari, *now think of something.*

She shuffled her feet, feeling conspicuous. And then she spotted the blackboard. *Excellent!* No one else had yet written the quote for the day. Here was something she could do to look busy. It was what the RHM expected. Each morning before class back home, Kumari would chalk up an appropriate quotation. That way, they could discuss its meaning and the wider implications. Surely her teacher here would appreciate her effort? School was school after all and teachers were pretty much the same, right?

Nervously, Kumari picked up the chalk. She could feel eyes upon her. The odd snigger erupted as she wrote. Looking up, she eyeballed them. Face upon face, staring back. Some confused, some amused, some downright admiring. Then, as one, their eyes flicked to the door, their expressions swiftly changing. Kumari followed suit. A man carrying a pile of books stood there. A man with his lips all screwed up as if he were sucking spaghetti.

Kumari rather liked spaghetti. It was one of the few things Ma cooked that she considered edible. But sucking spaghetti was not a good look. Especially when accompanied by a scowl. The man marched over to the desk and dumped the books on it.

'What do you think you're doing?'

His eyes scanned her careful efforts on the blackboard. *A man should first direct himself in the way he should go. Only then should he instruct others.*

'Today's quote,' said Kumari.

The man glared at her as if he could not work out what she was. Kumari noticed how his nostrils flared. That must be what was making his moustache twitch. That and the little muscle that jumped at the corner of his eye. Really, this man was so uptight. It couldn't be good for his heart.

'You need to calm down,' she said kindly.

'Calm down? Why you . . .' the man took a deep breath. Several, in fact. And then, very quietly, he said, 'Get away from my blackboard, kiddo.'

Kumari could hear the silence that fell. It was as if they were all waiting. Although for what she could not imagine. She must have made some kind of mistake.

'I'm sorry,' she said. 'But you really do need to calm down. It's not good for you, you know. I mean, your face has gone all red.'

Someone tittered in the background. A strange noise emitted from the man's lips. A sort of wheeeeeeeeee sound, like a kettle building up steam. His fingers clenched and unclenched. He appeared to be finding it hard to breathe.

'Twenty years,' he muttered. 'Twenty years dealing with kids like you. Twenty years listening to this kind of stuff. Well, you know what, I've had enough!'

Just as his fist slammed down on the desk, a woman's voice cut over the resultant thud.

81

'Is there a problem, Mr Johnson?'

'Ah, no, Ms LaMotta.'

It was as if all the air had been vacuumed from the room in one collective gasp. As one, the students straightened up. Even Kumari felt her spine stiffen. And then Ms LaMotta turned her laser gaze on her.

'You must be Kumari. Welcome to Rita Moreno. I am the principal, Ms LaMotta, and you are in the wrong classroom.'

Her eyes flicked to the blackboard. The ghost of a smile flitted across her thin face and then it was gone, replaced by a careful blankness.

'Um, yes,' mumbled Kumari, surreptitiously squirming. It was not because of the woman's gaze, more a Badmash situation. Startled by the thud of fist on desk, Badmash had shot down from his hiding place. Right now he was somewhere round her waist, his beak poking out from her puffa jacket. This was not looking good. Ma had begged her not to take him, had even offered to Badmash-sit. But Kumari had been adamant. She was not letting him out of her sight.

'Well, come with me, girl.' Ms LaMotta sounded impatient. Kumari considered her options. It was clear there were not too many.

Hunching over to conceal the telltale beak, Kumari edged towards Ms LaMotta. As she hobbled to the door, she heard the man say, 'Thank *you*!'

Out in the hallway, Ms LaMotta cast her a curious glance. 'Is anything the matter?'

'Uh, no,' said Kumari. What was that shadow on Ms LaMotta's upper lip? Was it, could it be, a *moustache*? Did all

82

grown-ups have one in the World Beyond? No, surely not.

'Aren't you hot in that jacket, dear?'

'No, no.' Why couldn't the woman just back off?

Kumari followed her back down the corridors, which stank of stale sweat and pine cleaning fluid, all the while shoving Badmash back up her top, trying not to breathe in. All at once, she longed for the hillsides of home, the clean smell of the mountains. Fresh air perfumed by real trees, their scent drifting on the wind. Ms LaMotta's voice broke through her thoughts.

'This is your classroom.'

And then she was being shown to yet another desk.

'Ms Martin here is your teacher.'

A face appeared over Ms LaMotta's shoulder, earnest but smiling. Skeleton-shaped earrings dangled incongruously from lobes behind which reddish hair was tucked. Finally, someone who appeared friendly. And moustache-free, thank goodness.

'Hi there, Kumari, I'm Ms Martin. Why don't you make yourself comfortable, take your jacket off?'

'I'm OK,' muttered Kumari. 'My country, it's . . . ah . . . very hot.' She pulled the jacket closer around her as if to emphasise her point, although really it was to keep Badmash still.

'Oh. Sure,' said Ms Martin. 'Well, maybe when you've warmed up.'

'Thank you, Ms Martin,' said Ms LaMotta and with that she swept from the room. Kumari sighed inwardly with relief. Ms Martin seemed much more approachable.

It all began to go wrong again within the space of a few minutes. Ms Martin was conducting a quiz. *Oh, goodie*, thought Kumari. A chance to please her new teacher. The RHM expected her to speak out in her lessons back home. Why should school be any different?

'Name a mammal that can live for over two hundred years,' said Ms Martin.

'My father!' shouted Kumari. A good start. This was easy.

'I don't think so, honey,' said Ms Martin. 'Can someone explain to me the theory of natural selection?'

'Some of us are better than others?'

There was a muffled giggle from the back.

A dangerous glint flashed in Ms Martin's eyes but a tiny twitch of her mouth betrayed amusement.

'*Thank you*, Kumari.'

Jaw set at an angle that meant business, Ms Martin addressed the rest of the class.

'Which appears highest in the periodic table: calcium, magnesium, sodium or copper?'

'Can I go fifty-fifty?'

Ms Martin's voice cracked in exasperation.

'This is not a game show, Kumari.'

Oops. Looked like she'd stressed another teacher out. In Ms Martin's cheeks, the colour was rising. Still, she smiled, in a kind of steely way, her white teeth flashing a warning. Too late, Kumari remembered CeeCee and LeeLee's words of advice.

'I think someone else should have a turn,' said Ms Martin in a tone that brooked no argument.

Except no one wanted to; they were all far too busy gawping.

'You are the weakest link!' someone shouted out to guffaws.

An eraser hit Kumari square on the forehead. Mercifully, at that moment the bell went and everyone immediately leapt up from their desks. Caught up in the surge towards the door, Kumari suffered a couple of sneaky kicks.

'Why don't you shut up, smart-ass?' sneered one large boy.

'Yeah, cut it out,' snarled another.

I've screwed up already, Kumari thought miserably, following the crowd to the next classroom and the next. By now she had learned her lesson. She sat silent, staring at nothing. At lunchtime she tagged along to the cafeteria, walking a careful distance from her classmates. A couple of girls looked back in sympathy but Kumari was too busy pretending that she knew what she was doing to notice.

A line stretched across the cafeteria from a counter on which food was piled high. Here and there it broke as kids bunched up or shoved one another around. Forcing her chin up, Kumari strode to the front, doing her best to appear confident. She could see people in white hats working behind the scenes. Those must be the chefs. Great, this was just like in the palace. OK, so the service was a little slacker. Still, nothing she could not handle. Kumari smiled at the woman behind the counter.

'And what has cook produced today?' she enquired of the bored server.

The server chewed resolutely on her gum, shrugged and said nothing.

'Hey!'

'Hey, you there, you're pushing in!'

'That's her, isn't it, the new kid?'

A crescendo began to build behind Kumari, a chorus of angry cries and hissing.

Somehow she'd got it wrong again. Best to grab a burger and back off.

The server sprang to life. 'Hey, you gotta pay for that!'

Money. She had money. Ma had made her put it somewhere safe. Except that it was no longer there, carefully tucked in her pocket. Which meant she must have dropped it. Or, worse, someone had stolen it. This was not going to plan. OK, dump the burger and make a run for it. But which way to go? The other kids were beginning to crowd in. And then she saw it. Gleaming, beckoning from across the room. A glorious, great big machine thing, its buttons shining with promise, emblazoned across it the word, *Cola*. There was nothing Kumari loved more. Forget about running. This was far too important. She'd just grab a can and go. Nothing too difficult about that.

She could hear them still muttering in her wake, but Kumari did not care. Somewhere in this machine there must be cans of the precious nectar. All she had to do was get one out. Experimentally, she pressed a few buttons. Nothing. She pressed some more. Two, three, then all of them. They continued to flash alluringly. She poked a finger into every opening, peered up the slots, searching. Her throat rasped with thirst. It had been hours since she had drunk anything. She needed one. *Now*.

86

The shiny machine must be broken. She would just help it out a little. Give it a shake. No. OK, time for the direct approach. Raising a leg, Kumari kicked hard. Karali, now that was something she knew about. The ancient martial art had never let her down. This time was no exception. A stream of cans rattled forth, bouncing and rolling across the hard cafeteria floor. Jubilant, Kumari picked one up, popped the tab and drank, smacking her lips.

A few more cans rolled out, dislodged by her efforts.

'Look, guys, free Coke!' yelled a kid and suddenly they were shoving the tables aside, surging across the cafeteria.

'Do that again,' ordered a boy but, shaking her head, Kumari backed off. Thwarted, the boy began to kick the machine, urged on by the others.

Pandemonium grew as the supervisors waded in, shouting at the kids to stop.

'You there,' yelled one at Kumari. 'You stand right where you are.'

Bad idea. The man's face was puce with rage. Kumari kept backing away.

Then she was falling, a stray can bringing her down. As her tail bone hit the floor, Kumari heard a familiar squawk. Jolted out from his hiding place, Badmash shot into the air.

'Ohmygawd look at that!'

'It's a bird! In the cafeteria!'

'Catch it! Bring it down!'

Frantically, Kumari tried to grab Badmash. But freedom was too much fun after hours cooped up under her coat. He fluttered around the cafeteria before spying the food and swooping down. Three passes later, Badmash returned to perch on her shoulder, satisfied. A hot dog sausage dangled from his beak like some oversized worm.

'What's the matter? You never seen a bird before?' demanded Kumari of the gawping crowd. 'You'll hurt his feelings. Stop staring.'

A half-full can shot past her ear, its contents spattering them both.

'Kill it,' came a howl. It was definitely time to leave.

Slamming through the swing doors, Kumari started to run, ignoring the shouts from behind her. Racing blind down the corridors, looking for somewhere to hide. At last she saw an open door and dived inside. A man looked up, startled.

'Hey, this is the men's room!'

'S-sorry,' stuttered Kumari, swiftly backing out.

The shouts faded behind her as she sprinted along. Finally, she slowed to a walk. She'd keep moving all the same. On and on she tramped, along endless passageways. By chance, she stumbled across the entrance lobby, spotted the men in uniform and turned tail. These corridors went on for miles. She could walk around and around all day. That seemed like a good plan, just keep out the way until they opened the gates. Badmash had settled down for a snooze against her chest, once more sated and happy. If she went back to her classroom now, they would definitely take him away. She had so been looking forward to school, but it was nothing like she had expected. The same with the World Beyond. How she longed for home.

Her vision blurred by unshed tears, Kumari trudged on.

It was hopeless. No one challenged her as she wandered past. If this was school, they could keep it. A part of her even missed the RHM, annoying though he could be. At least he cared that she learned *something*. Here, learning was way down the agenda. She had seen the looks on the teachers' faces. They all looked worn down, tired out. Except for Ms Martin. She at least had appeared alive. Actually, this corridor looked familiar. Her classroom was just down there. Lining the walls that lead to it, rows of what appeared to be cupboards. Slouching against these, a group of kids she dimly recognised.

'It's her!' one of them shouted.

Their heads turned as one. *Run!* shrieked the voice in her brain but her tired feet were rooted to the spot.

Rough hands pulled her forward.

'Here, we got something to show you. See, we had a tip off you were coming. So we thought we would welcome you by decorating your locker.'

They were holding open the door of one of the cupboards, sneering as they pointed. The door was festooned with clippings, taken from a newspaper. Kumari's eyes fell on a familiar headline: *Manhattan Mystery Girl*, it screamed.

'That's you, isn't it?' jeered a voice. 'What are you, some kind of weirdo?'

'Yeah, where you come from?' crowed another. 'Says here you don't know.'

'Give us your bird,' said a third, grabbing her by the shoulders. As Kumari began to kick and scream, Badmash was hauled from her embrace. Amid mocking laughter, they shoved her into the cupboard, cramming her in before slamming the door.

'No! Don't hurt him,' cried Kumari as she heard the lock turn. And then she was alone. Her knees were shoved into her chest, the door and walls pressing in. Her arms were jammed by her sides, her amulet digging uselessly into her wrist. She was trapped in this metal box, unable to move a muscle. The dark felt as though it were caving in on her, the air smelt stale and sweaty. Dust choked up her lungs. How long before she suffocated?

'Let me out,' she pleaded but all she heard in response were their jeers. And then silence. Where had they taken Badmash? How would she get out of here? Would anyone even miss her? Suddenly, a rectangle of light as the door was flung open. Before her stood a boy. In his arms was Badmash.

'This your bird?' he asked, as he held him out, smiling. 'Come on,' he said. 'Don't be scared. Let me help you.'

He held out a hand and Kumari took it. The boy had kind eyes. And there was something about his smile.

'Thank you,' she murmured, stroking Badmash's feathers.

'Any time,' he grinned. 'I'm Chico, by the way.'

Chico.

Nice name.

Suddenly, things looked a whole lot better.

In this hell hole of a place, Kumari had found a friend.

KUMARI'S JOURNAL
(TOP SECRET. FOR MY EYES ONLY.
EVERYONE ELSE KEEP OUT!
THIS MEANS YOU!)

The World Beyond
Day 15 (they call this the month of December in the WB) –
351 days to go

OK, I know I don't know where I am or how to get back home but I really do have to get out of here. All the while I'm here I'm not finding out what happened to Mamma. That clock keeps ticking which means Time is passing and soon I won't have any left. It seems to go so fast. Everything happens fast here. Even the people talk fast like they might run out of breath. Which, I reckon, is exactly what happens and how people in the World Beyond die.

Not that the air is any good here – it stinks and it makes me cough. Even Badmash has a cough which makes it really difficult to hide him at school. I have to cough when he coughs and then the teachers look at me like I'm trying to mess around, when really I'm doing my best to listen even when what they say is really dull.

I've realised I need to listen because it's my best chance of getting out of here – the more I know about the World Beyond, the easier it will be to find my way home. I've already looked really hard at every map I can find (waste of time) and CeeCee and LeeLee showed me how to search on the computer so I entered words like *magic+kingdom+*

91

smoke+happiness+goddess but all I came up with was a lot of VERY strange stuff. As Ma said, at least I tried. And I'm going to keep trying. I will *find a way back home*. Imagine how Papa would feel if he knew I finally got motivated. The RHM would probably just say 'about time'. Well, maybe it is.

The trouble is, though, the teachers seem like they've given up, like they don't really want to teach anyway. And the kids act like they don't want to learn all except for one or two. Weird thing is, now I'm listening it's actually kind of interesting sometimes. Although most of my classmates don't seem too happy that I'm making the effort. At least if I go to school they won't lock me up again. That's what Ma says, anyway. She says it will 'keep them off our backs'. I can't imagine why they would want to be on our backs but if Ma says so it must be true. I like Ma very much but she can't replace Mamma.

I know she wants me to think of her like that, like she's my mother in the World Beyond. I suppose she is, in a way, but really I only have one Mamma. I guess that's what the Ayah wanted too, that I'd think of her as a new Mamma. What no one seems to understand is that Mamma is still around. OK, so she's not actually *here* and I don't have any of my magic tools but I still think I can try and summon her. I mean, she's still technically a goddess, right? That means I can summon her anywhere.

CHAPTER 7

The RHM stared up at the starlit sky. Only a thin slice of the moon was visible. It had been fat and full the night Kumari disappeared. Now it barely registered. As reed slim as Kumari herself and just about as powerless. For a second, the RHM felt a flash of guilt. She was nothing more than a child.

He dropped his gaze to the courtyard below, desperately trying to think. Going over it one more time, every detail of that night. Something caught his eye, a faint movement by the fountain. He shrank back behind the shutters, even though his room was in darkness. The RHM preferred it that way, had done ever since things changed at the palace. It was safer to remain unseen, to operate from the shadows. He narrowed his eyes, focusing on the fountain. There it was again, a shape shifting, separating from the great urn that formed the fountain's base.

The shape moved slowly, cautiously, stopping every few feet. The RHM studied it carefully. There was something familiar about its bulk. And then another, smaller shape slinking towards it, a paw reaching out, then swiping. A leg struck out and kicked, sending the palace cat flying through the air. In that moment of temper, the bulk had betrayed itself. The Ayah hated the palace cat and vice versa. Now the RHM's antennae were up.

He had observed the Ayah on more than one occasion sneaking off on some mission. He had no idea what she was up to, but he was determined to find out. Slipping on his heavy cloak, the RHM prepared to follow her. She had been heading in the direction of the temple. He knew a shortcut. At the end of the corridor a great tapestry covered one wall, its golden threads glistening in the light of the butter lamps. The RHM looked over his shoulder then slid behind the tapestry, his fingers reaching for a tiny catch. As he flicked it, a door swung open and he hurriedly descended a flight of steep stone steps. Down and down he ran, following the narrow spiral of the hidden staircase. At last, he reached the ground floor far below and an antechamber. He paused, straining his ears.

Not so much as a murmur. The palace was sleeping. In front of him, another door carved into the wall. Gently, he pressed its catch. As it swung open, he slid out from behind an identical tapestry to the first. He was in the throne room, right next to the temple. The palace holy of holies, guarded day and night by the monks. And yet, there was a way in, if you knew where to look. He could not believe the Ayah had the knowledge, but, then again, anything was possible.

Who would have thought that the queen could have succumbed like that? Let alone that Kumari would have vanished without a trace? While he was pondering these mysteries, the RHM heard a noise, soft but definite. The swish, swish, swish of slippered feet. Crouching low behind the king's throne, he peered out from between the elaborate carvings that crowned it. He saw the Ayah enter the throne room, stop and look round. Satisfied that she was apparently unobserved, the woman began to cross the vast, empty space, heading not for the temple but for the public entrance on the other side.

Puzzled now, the RHM watched as she fiddled with the lock. The door could only be opened from the inside, with a sequence known to a very few. There were just two doors in the kingdom that were ever locked, the temple door being the other. The RHM had urged the king to consider more security measures, but his majesty remained resolute. The locks on these two doors were symbolic, representing the inner sanctum. All other doors would remain open to his people, whom he considered his kin.

Alarmed, the RHM stifled a gasp as the door gave way under the Ayah's fingers. There would be time later to work out how she had discovered the combination. Right now, he must follow and find out what he could. Keeping a decent distance between them, the RHM padded along, eyes fixed firmly on the Ayah's back. It would be disastrous if she caught sight of him. The woman was suspicious enough of him as it was.

To his surprise, she turned away from the streets of the town and headed instead for the path that wound through the lower slopes towards the west. The path was not arduous but the Ayah walked swiftly. Truly, the RHM thought, the woman was remarkably fit. She did not appear so, being squat and rather heavy but her well-padded legs belied muscles that could apparently march for miles.

About an hour later, the Ayah paused. The path abruptly ended at an impassable wall of rock. The Ayah pressed herself up against the stone, scrabbling around with her hands. Then, all of a sudden, she was gone. It was as if she had never been there. Scuttling forward as fast as he dared, the RHM stared at the seemingly impenetrable rock face. Then his eyes fell upon it: the tiniest fissure, a crack barely wider than his hand. The gap was only a few feet deep. There was nowhere she could have hidden. And yet the Ayah had disappeared into the ether.

He shoved his hand into the crack, searching for something that might reveal a concealed tunnel. He tried to squeeze through the gap itself, marvelling at how the Ayah had done it. Even at its widest point, it was perhaps four hand spans, the Ayah considerably wider. Drawing a blank, the RHM paused to think. Logically, there had to be a way in. Or maybe logic had nothing to do with it.

As he pondered the possibilities, realisation struck the

RHM. He was at the western edge of the kingdom. Beyond this rock, the World Beyond and the tribal lands of the fearsome local warlords. What could the Ayah be doing in the World Beyond? Was it something to do with the warlords? If so, that complicated matters. They would have to be eliminated too. Maybe there was some way he could climb up, try to see if he could spot her. The RHM looked up, scanning the ridges that rose above him. There it was: a natural platform, just wide enough to stand on.

Hampered by his heavy cloak, the RHM scrabbled for a toehold. Although he was more agile than he appeared, it was a hard climb. Finally, his fingers found the flat expanse of rock. The RHM heaved himself up on it. Above the platform, the granite pillars dipped low enough for him to see into the World Beyond. The RHM searched the horizon. Stretching before him, a thick forest of mountain spruce. In the distance, more peaks, one shaped oddly, like an eagle's beak. As his eyes adjusted, he noticed something sticking up, slightly higher than all the rest, too regular to be a tree.

By its shape it looked to be a mast. Attached to it, a saucer-shaped object. The object was angled towards the sky, as if trying to catch something. The RHM was no slouch when it came to information. He pored over the scientific papers smuggled in, careful to keep their contents to himself. A little knowledge was a dangerous thing, or so the king believed. His majesty felt that many of the advances made in the World Beyond would threaten the Happiness of his subjects. The RHM disagreed. Many times he had appealed to the king to modernise, so far without success.

Never mind, he had his methods. Although one or two of his contacts were proving troublesome. Only recently he'd needed to deal with one who had grown greedy, foolish enough to believe he would succumb to blackmail. It had been the night Kumari disappeared, in fact. An evil night all round. At least the man would no longer be able to spill his secrets and threaten his position. No point in looking back. The only way was forward. Eventually his time would come, the day he could unveil the World Beyond's advances to the kingdom. And this was clearly one of them, if he was not mistaken. The RHM's curiosity prickled as he stared at the object on the mast.

It appeared to be a satellite dish.

A sudden noise broke his concentration, a sound that the RHM dimly remembered from his childhood. A clatter, distant at first. The roar of an engine. Beneath the stars, a new pinpoint of light, moving ever upwards. This was no shooting star. This thing moved with purpose. Sweat broke out on the RHM's brow despite the chill of the night. He was sure, as he stared at it, that the light was no coincidence. He would guess it was the light of a small aircraft and on it, he would lay his life, sat the Ayah.

What on earth was the woman doing on a plane? And how had she got there? She must have had outside help. One thing he would give her, she was brave. For a citizen of the kingdom to get on an aircraft was astonishing. Technology had not penetrated its borders. It simply was not permitted. For the Ayah to even know aeroplanes existed provided pause for thought. It meant she had access to information. And that was dangerous.

The light soared higher and higher, topping the mountains. And then it was gone, banking round as it bore west. Two things were clear to the RHM: the Ayah was somehow in contact with the World Beyond. Worse, she was even now airborne, heading deep into its heart. The RHM knew his geography. West meant Europe or America. There must be something out there of great importance to pull the Ayah towards it.

Something.

Or someone.

Suddenly, the RHM was certain. The Ayah knew where she was. The Ayah was going for Kumari.

CHAPTER 8

The nightmare was back, only this time she was trapped in a locker, shut up in that tiny space knowing that Mamma was somewhere outside.

'Mamma!' she shouted as she heard her footsteps begin to recede.

'Mamma, wait for me!' But there was no answering cry.

And then there was light flooding her face. Someone must have opened the locker door.

'Chico?' Kumari murmured.

'Kumari, honey, it's Ma. It's OK, sweetheart, it was just a

dream. You were shouting out in your sleep. Hush, now, it's all right. You just lay back down.'

'Ma?' Kumari's eyes focused. She licked her lips. They were dry. She must have been shouting really loud for her throat to feel so sore.

Beside her, Badmash grumbled in his sleep. It started to come back to her. She was not in the palace at all. She was here, in Ma's apartment.

'I thought I heard Mamma,' whispered Kumari. 'They locked me in and I couldn't follow her.'

'You were having a nightmare, Kumari,' said Ma. 'Wasn't nothing but a dream.'

'No!' cried Kumari. 'It's more than that. It's a message. Mamma wants me to help her but as hard as I try I can't.'

At this she began to sob. She could feel Ma's hands begin to stroke her hair.

'There, there, now, Kumari. Your Mamma, she's gone.'

'No, she hasn't!' shouted Kumari. 'She's just stuck, there, in that awful place. She can't go up the Holy Mountain and she can't come back and be a living goddess.'

'Kumari, sweetie, you've got to stop with this goddess stuff.'

'You don't believe me. OK, I'll prove it.'

At that, Kumari sat up and began to chant with all her might.

At first, nothing happened.

'Kumari, you don't have to do this.'

Putting her hands over her ears, Kumari continued her chanting.

101

Suddenly, the window shot open and a blast of wind whirled in, sending the curtains flapping crazily, plastering Ma's hair across her face. Badmash opened one eye, then slid lower beneath the covers. He'd seen it all before. The one Power Kumari had almost got right.

Ma's mouth fell open as the wind intensified, whizzing around her like a miniature twister, whipping her hair up into a beehive, finally sending her spinning above the bed.

'Stop! Stop!' yelled Ma.

At that very moment, the door banged open.

'What is happening here?' said LeeLee, rubbing sleepy eyes.

Startled, Kumari abruptly stopped chanting, sending Ma tumbling down to the floor.

'Just proving I'm a goddess,' said Kumari.

'Whatever. But keep it down. Me and CeeCee, we're trying to sleep here. Can't you two have some consideration?'

As LeeLee stomped off, Ma picked herself up and sat on the bed.

She looked at the window warily. There was not as much as a whisper of a breeze from outside. Seemingly unconvinced, Ma stuck her hand out and waggled it then drew it back in and sighed. The curtains hung still, as did the bedclothes. Only Ma's hairdo hinted at what had occurred.

At the sight of it, Kumari began to giggle.

'You look like Marge Simpson,' she snorted.

Ma glared at her for a second, then her shoulders began to shake. Half-crying, half-laughing she began to hiccough.

'What in the world happened there, child?'

'I used Power No 8. The Power to Have Command Over the Elements. I haven't got it quite right yet.'

'It was good enough for me, girl, I can tell you.'

'So you believe me when I say I'm a goddess?'

'You're certainly something, Kumari. You want to call yourself a goddess, that's fine by me.'

Kumari grabbed the hand nearest to her. 'It's important, Ma. I need you to believe me. If you believe me then you believe in my Mamma. You believe that she still exists.'

Ma's eyes shone with understanding. 'I believe *in* you, Kumari,' she whispered. 'Now get some sleep. We'll talk about it tomorrow.'

'Goodnight, Ma. And Ma?'

'Yeeees?'

'Thank you.'

'You're welcome.'

Ma believed *in* her. For the moment, it was enough.

CHAPTER 9

Kumari held the bottle high. *Potassium Nitrate*, the label read. Looked harmless enough. Now, what was the other stuff Ms Martin had used? She scanned the neat rows of bottles, trying to remember, pulling one down then another, puzzling over the contents. A warning squeak from Badmash made her look up. There was a shadow hovering outside the chem lab door, visible through the frosted glass. Kumari froze, clutching her bottles. There would be big trouble if she was caught.

For one thing, it was recess, when the whole school was forced outside. For another, Badmash was with her when he'd been specifically banned from the building. And for a third, she was not supposed to be here, on her own without her teacher. OK, so she felt bad about that. Ms Martin was pretty cool. But it was important she did this. Kumari had a plan. It had come to her in the night, as all her best ideas did, popping into her head just as she was drifting off, snapping her eyelids apart.

'The chem lab. That's it!' she'd exclaimed as Badmash grumbled sleepily. Things were much tighter at Ma's place than in the palace. Sharing one pillow was hard.

The chem lab. Her favourite classroom, lined with marvellous potions. Ms Martin insisted on calling them by their chemical names but Kumari knew what they really were. These were special ingredients, not for chemistry but alchemy. How else to explain the sparks that flew from the flask Ms Martin held over a flame or the solution that switched colours before their very eyes? While the others yawned or tried to set fire to one another's hair, Kumari looked on, entranced. At last, something in the World Beyond she could understand – good old ritual magic.

The shadow had moved off. Time to set to work. She only had a few more minutes before the bell rang once more. She'd take a chance on the ingredients. After all, she was used to trying and failing. Look what had happened last time. The Great Summoning Ceremony had not exactly ended happily. Somehow, she'd wound up here instead of manifesting Mamma.

Gently, Kumari unwrapped the miniature portrait she had brought in her schoolbag. Placing it on the lab bench, she whispered, 'Hello, Mamma.'

The picture glowed under the harsh strip light, the flesh tones so real it almost seemed to breathe. Kumari traced her Mamma's cheek with one finger. It felt warm to the touch.

'Talk to me,' she pleaded. 'Tell me who did it.' But the picture stayed silent. It was just a painting, after all.

What it needed was a spark of life, a jolt to bring her Mamma back. And Kumari knew just the thing. Or at least, she thought she did. Lighting a Bunsen burner, she then picked up a flask. First the potassium nitrate. How much had Ms Martin used? She tipped in a little bit then added a whole lot more. Her hand hovered over the other bottles she had picked at random. Here was one that looked promising. What was the worst that could happen? A bang, a few puffs of smoke.

'Stop!'

Startled, Kumari dropped the lot into the flask.

'M-ms Martin,' she stammered.

'Move that away from the flame!' said Ms Martin.

Too late. The thing exploded. Louder than Kumari had expected. The smoke, that was the main thing. It seemed to fill the whole room. Coughing and spluttering, Kumari tried to wave it away from her face. Miraculously, it cleared as fast as it had come. She stared around the room, expectant.

'Kumari? What are you doing?'

'Looking for my Mamma.'

'Looking for . . . ? I don't understand.'

'No,' Kumari whispered. 'Nor do I.'

Nothing. *Nada*, as Ma would say. Except another failure to chalk up. Another lost chance to talk to Mamma.

'It's impossible,' said Kumari. 'It's never going to happen.'

Dropping her head to the bench, she sobbed in devastation. After a few seconds, she felt a soft hand patting her shoulder.

'Go ahead,' said Ms Martin. 'Let it out, Kumari. Cry.'

'I can't do it,' wailed Kumari. 'I can't summon up my Mamma. She's stuck in the foothills of the Holy Mountain. I'm stuck here in the World Beyond. Now I'll never find out.'

'Find out? Find out what?' Ms Martin's tone was patient.

Kumari raised a tear-streaked face. 'Find out who killed her, of course.'

'Your mother was murdered?'

Solemnly, Kumari nodded her head. Ms Martin studied her for a moment. Kumari could see that she was thinking. Then her teacher pulled out a handkerchief.

'Here, Kumari, clean yourself up.'

Kumari glanced down at the still smouldering flask and caught sight of her reflection. Her eyes stared out, racoon-like, from her smoke-grimed face. Tear streaks had carved furrows through the soot, adding to the mammalian impression. Kumari grimaced.

'*Ay caramba!*' she said.

'You speak Spanish?' enquired Ms Martin.

'*Simpsons,*' said Kumari.

'Simpsons? Oh, I see,' Ms Martin began to laugh. 'You know, it's quite natural to feel as you do if a parent is . . . ah . . . missing from your life. What about your father? Is he still around?'

'He's back in my kingdom. He runs it, you see. He's a very busy man, my Papa. Sometimes too busy for me.'

'I know how that feels,' said Ms Martin. 'My dad, he heads up a pharmaceutical company. He makes big money, but sometimes I think he feels he missed out on us.'

Ms Martin twisted her hands as she said this, the bitten nails belying her bright smile.

'Do you have brothers and sisters?' asked Kumari.

'One of each. And you?'

Kumari shook her head. 'None. Which means I get to be the only trainee goddess.'

At this, Ms Martin let out a kind of bark of a little laugh. Her earrings waggled as she shook her head. They were shaped like double helixes today.

'You are quite a conundrum, Kumari. A puzzle,' she said. 'I mean, where is this kingdom you come from? I'm not sure I know.'

'I'm not sure either,' said Kumari. 'We just call it our kingdom. Papa told me it's not marked on any map. It's a kind of hidden place.'

Ms Martin frowned. 'You come from some kind of a kingdom without a name? But that's impossible. And what is with this "World Beyond?"'

'*This* is the World Beyond,' said Kumari. Surely Ms Martin knew that? Imagine coming from somewhere and not knowing what it was called. OK, so she could hardly talk. Maybe she could explain it another way.

'You see, I'm a goddess,' she said.

'A goddess. Right.'

Same reaction as Ma had had. What was wrong with these people? Couldn't they recognise a divine being when they saw one?

Ms Martin was looking at her with that special smile on her face. The look grown-ups reserved for when they thought you were nuts.

'And what makes you think you're a goddess?' enquired Ms Martin.

'Well, for one thing, I'm destined to be immortal. Or at least I would have been if I hadn't come *here*,' said Kumari. The thought brought fresh tears flooding down her face. Really, it was all too much. First Mamma. Now her own mortality. It sucked, as Bart Simpson would say. Bart talked a lot of sense.

'Kumari, no one lives forever.' Ms Martin's voice was kind but firm.

'They do where I come from,' muttered Kumari. 'Goddesses don't die. But they can get stuck.'

'Stuck?' Now Ms Martin looked really confused.

'That's what happened to my Mamma. She's stuck in this kind of limbo. She can't ascend the Holy Mountain and she can't cross back to be a living goddess.'

'And why is that?' asked Ms Martin.

'It's because she was murdered. Until I can find out who did it and avenge her death, she can't move on.'

'That's quite a task for a girl like you.'

'It has to be someone of Mamma's blood who avenges her. Which means I'm the only person who can do it. I'm the only one with the right blood. Not even Papa can do it, but

109

in any case he's not well. That's why he hasn't come for me. At least, I think that must be the reason. So it's up to me to get back home and rescue Mamma.'

'But what about your Mamma's parents? Or her brothers and sisters?'

Kumari sighed. OK, it was a little complicated. 'Mamma was not born a goddess. She became one when she married Papa. It's one of the Gifts of the Gods, being able to bestow eternal life. I'm the only one who's both related by blood to Mamma and a living goddess. Which means I'm the only one who can save her and that's what I'm trying to do.'

She looked forlornly at the debris on the lab bench, her gaze drifting to Mamma's portrait.

'May I?' said Ms Martin, picking the picture up for a closer look. 'She's very beautiful,' she said. 'You look like her, Kumari.'

'Uh, thank you,' said Kumari, feeling embarrassed but rather pleased.

'She does look like a goddess,' went on Ms Martin. 'If such a being were to exist.'

'But they do!' exclaimed Kumari. 'We do. I just told you.'

'Telling is one thing. I'm a science major. I need evidence. What does a god or a goddess actually do, for instance?'

'Perform wondrous acts and answer prayers. Shoot thunder bolts across the sky.'

'Can you demonstrate that?' asked Ms Martin.

'Yes. Well, no. I mean, I can when I pass my Powers. Look, I've studied hard to become a goddess. I've been trying to learn my Eight Powers for, like, ever. You know, how to move through mountains. Become invisible. Command spirits. Be invincible.'

'No, I don't know,' said Ms Martin. 'I don't believe in that kind of thing. I know you've been through an awful lot, Kumari. But making up stories does not help.'

Stories? For a second, Kumari thought she might explode with indignation. She'd talked to Ms Martin, trainee goddess to adult. And *this* was her reaction? The one person in this cesspit of a school she thought might actually help her out. The one grown-up besides Ma in whom she had confided.

'I'll show you!' said Kumari. 'Watch this. It's Power No 8.'

She squeezed her eyes shut, clenched her fists and chanted for all she was worth. After a few moments, Ms Martin's voice cut across her efforts.

'What exactly are you trying to do, Kumari?'

'Whip up a whirlwind,' said Kumari.

'It doesn't seem to be working.'

'It doesn't? You're sure?'

Kumari snapped open her eyes.

'I don't understand,' she wailed. 'It's the one Power I can almost manage.'

'Kumari, you have to drop this. It's bordering on the delusional.'

Delusional? And was that *pity* in Ms Martin's eyes?

'Ms Martin, I really *am* a trainee living goddess. These men, they kidnapped me and brought me here. They wouldn't do that to a normal person. My father, he's the god-king. They probably want something from him. Palace treasures, I don't know. But I ran away from them and now I'm lost. All I want to do is get back home.'

The look on Ms Martin's face said it all.

'You've got to believe me,' blurted Kumari. '*Someone's* got to help me get out of here.' She had been so determined not to cry again but, despite herself, her chin wobbled.

'I do believe you're someone special, Kumari,' said Ms Martin. 'I believe everyone is, in their own way. OK, maybe not *everyone*. There are exceptions. But you've got a good mind, you want to learn. That's rare in a school like this. I can see you're really trying. You're an asset to my class.'

'I hate this place,' wailed Kumari. 'I hate being in school. At least when I was at Ma's all day I could watch *Oprah* on TV. Sometimes I'd chat to her, tell her my problems. I know that sounds crazy. But Oprah, she has a nice face. She looks like she really cares. Now I'm home too late to catch her and there's no one else except Ma. Ma, well, she's great, but she's the one that tells me I have to come here. And I so wanted to go to school because, well, I always did. I thought I'd have fun and make lots of friends but this is *bakwas*!'

'Bakwas?'

'It's what we say in my country when something really sucks!'

Ms Martin thought for a moment, then sighed and patted Kumari's arm.

'I'm not going to lie to you, Kumari. Yes, this school *does* suck in a lot of ways. Between you and me, when I first came I wanted to turn tail and run. But there is a lot of good here. Ms LaMotta, she's got big plans, but she's only been here a

112

short while, like me. Things are changing but it takes time. I promise you, in a year you won't recognise this place.'

'I don't have a year,' sniffed Kumari. 'In less than a year I'll be dead.'

'I thought goddesses didn't die?' smiled Ms Martin.

'OK, so I won't technically *die*. But I'll be stuck, just like Mamma. There are only three ways to kill a living goddess and being here too long counts as one. I had a year and a day from the moment I left the kingdom and now I've got 348 left. 348 days measured by *those* things. Those *clocks*.'

Ms Martin glanced up at the clock on the wall then back at Kumari.

'You don't have clocks back home?'

'No way.'

'So how do you measure time?'

'In the cycle of the moons.'

'Well, that's just the same.'

'No, it isn't,' countered Kumari. 'Moons are eternal. Clocks count your time off, tick, tick, tick. Until you have none left.'

'Whatever you might think of them, Kumari, clocks are essential. Right now, for instance, I see it's time for class.'

'No, no,' said Kumari, shrinking back. 'I'm not going in there. The other kids, they all hate me.'

'Nonsense,' said Ms Martin. 'They just don't know you, that's all.'

'I don't want them to know me,' said Kumari. 'I want them to leave me alone.'

'If I promise they won't hurt you will you come to class with me?'

113

'What about Badmash?'

'Badmash can come too. So long as he's quiet and we keep this between ourselves. We wouldn't want Ms LaMotta to find out, would we, Kumari?'

'No,' said Kumari, smiling at her new ally.

The classroom was in chaos, a bunch of kids crowding round something, shouting. Nobody noticed them enter until Ms Martin waded into the group. One boy was pinned to a desk while the others pressed down on his head and arms. Kumari noticed one of the guys who'd shoved her in the locker, practically squishing the boy's chin into his chest. The guy's name was Eddie. He considered himself the big classroom cheese. Come to think of it, he probably was. No one messed with his gang.

'Up, up,' the crowd was chanting, until they saw Ms Martin.

'What do you think you are doing?' she demanded. The boy on the desk looked pretty scared.

'Levitating him, miss,' said Eddie, winking at his cronies.

Levitation, pah! thought Kumari. They didn't know what levitation was.

'I'll levitate you in a minute,' said Ms Martin spinning Eddie round in one swift motion so he landed on a chair.

'You can't do that!' whined Eddie. 'That's child abuse. I'll tell my dad.'

'What are you going to tell him, Eddie? That I helped you sit down?'

At this, the class erupted. Eddie's face took on a fetching shade of red.

'Anyone else like to try out my judo skills?' said Ms Martin. 'I thought not,' she smiled. Kumari glanced at Ms Martin in admiration. For a teacher, that was one excellent move.

After that, the class was eerily silent. Even when Ms Martin later announced a written test on what she had just explained, there was not one single moan. Buoyed up by Ms Martin's earlier words, Kumari went all out to impress, scribbling her answers furiously. So, her spelling was a little erratic. English was not her first language. The Gift of Tongues might be her birthright, but it sometimes skipped on the basics. Even so, when the results were announced, Kumari grinned in jubilation. She had come top out of all the class by a considerable margin.

Beaming, she rose to leave with the rest then felt someone press up against her.

'Read it,' muttered a voice in her ear. A piece of paper dropped on to her desk. As her eyes scanned it, her stomach plunged, landing somewhere around her feet.

Do that again and you're dead, read the note.

Kumari glanced over her shoulder.

Mean eyes stared at her menacingly.

Eddie and his boys were back on her case.

'Hey.'

It was him again, Chico.

'How you doing?'

'Uh, pretty good.'

OK, so that was a lie. She could have done without Eddie and the other weasels. Then again, maybe not a total lie. She felt all the better for seeing him.

'You heading to the cafeteria?' said Chico.

'Um . . . I wasn't planning to.'

'I know what you mean,' he laughed. 'Food's not so hot, is it?'

Hot. One of her new favourite words. Come to think of it, he'd made a little joke. Hot could mean two things. Excellent chance to show her sense of humour.

'Oh, hahahaha,' said Kumari. 'Funny. Not hot. I mean, you know, food can be hot or cold. Or not hot as in not hot.'

Chico looked at her strangely. Embarrassment prickled Kumari's neck. It crawled up her skull, spreading like a rash towards her face. Her inner thermostat had risen by about ten degrees. She had to get out of here before her cheeks gave it away.

'I gotta go,' she mumbled, slinging her bag over one arm.

'Hey, wait,' called Chico. 'Wait a minute, Kumari.'

He was jogging alongside her now.

'Where are you going?'

'I, uh, I don't know,' said Kumari.

'You don't know? Are you lost? This place can be confusing.'

'I, ah, I have to go to the bathroom.'

Why oh why did she have to say that? It had been the first thing to pop into her head. Now he looked embarrassed.

'Oh, sure,' said Chico. 'It's down there. Can't miss it.'

'Great. Thank you,' said Kumari.

Neither of them moved.

'Well, better go,' said Kumari.

He really did have the most gorgeous eyes. Framed by thick, dark lashes.

'Yup,' said Chico, shifting from foot to foot.

'OK, so see you later.'

'Sure. Later.'

Great teeth, too, when he smiled. It lit up his whole face. Somehow it was hard to tear herself away. It was so nice talking to him.

'Want to come with me?' she blurted.

'To the bathroom?'

'Oh, ah, of course not. Just kidding.'

Flashing him a panicky grin, Kumari strode off as fast as she could.

'Kumari,' he called after her but she pretended not to hear.

'Kumari, it's the other way.'

Oh my god. The humiliation.

Well, she wasn't turning back now. Do that and she'd have to walk past him. Let him think she was crazy. He probably did anyway. Resolutely, she kept going, replaying it all in her mind.

Every excruciating detail.

Over and over again.

CHAPTER 10

The RHM sat on his bed at the West Side YMCA, staring at a headline. *Manhattan Mystery Girl Arrest,* it read. Beneath it, a photograph. Although blurred, there was no mistaking her. His contacts had been right. Kumari was here.

The RHM could not believe his luck. It was the break he needed. Had he not flicked through a pile of old magazines and newspapers in the YMCA lounge, he would not have seen it. He had no idea why he had even looked at them. The RHM had no time for newspapers. Since his arrival, he had been busy, taking the bus uptown, midtown, downtown. Looking everywhere for Kumari.

Of course, he did not expect to find her just like that. The RHM was searching for information. Trying to pick up her trail any way he could, sniffing the streets for clues. All he had to go on was the knowledge that she was here, somewhere on the island of Manhattan. The RHM's sources had been 99% sure. And now here was the proof. He read through the article again slowly, absorbing the information.

Child Protection Services confirm that the Manhattan Mystery Girl was taken into custody by Immigration and Customs Enforcement at the University Avenue hair salon owned by her foster parent. It is understood that she is now back in the care of her foster parent. The authorities will not release the girl's name.

'Kumari,' murmured the RHM. He knew, beyond all doubt. Unfolding his map of Manhattan he pored over it. University Avenue was a very long street in the Bronx district, right up in the north-west corner of the island. The RHM was on a tight budget; Manhattan was far more expensive than he had anticipated. It had been hard enough obtaining dollars from his contacts in the first place. Palace treasures did not cut it as currency. Funds were now running low. With no money for a cab, it appeared he would have to brave the subway. The RHM trembled at the thought. The subway ran underground.

Ordinarily, the RHM was tough. He had to be – ruthless, even. But there was one thing the RHM could not bear and that was being underground. It brought him out in a cold sweat. Gripping the rail tightly, he walked down the stairs into the subway station. His train rattled up to the platform and he got on it, watching as the doors shut tight. Closing his eyes, he began to pray as the train shot towards the tunnel, trying to breathe evenly and deeply, the sweat prickling his brow.

'Say, man, you OK?' muttered the man next to him.

'Yes, yes,' answered the RHM, keeping his eyelids shut fast.

Emerging at the 183rd Street station, the RHM tried to forget the rigours of his journey and concentrate on the task in hand. Still, his hands shook uncontrollably as he pulled his cloak about him against the cold. Snow only ever settled on the mountains around the hidden kingdom. New York City was freezing in comparison to the temperate valley he now called home.

Map in hand, the RHM strode towards University Avenue, noting that everything here was built on a slightly more human scale. He passed shops that seemed to sell everything under the sun and restaurants that smelt of their exotic provenance. No one so much as glanced at him. Interesting. Up here, it seemed he fitted in. Hardly anybody stared. Downtown it was different. Downtown they all dressed rather similarly. This Bronx area appeared more diverse. People wore a variety of outfits. He passed a lady in a colourful headdress and bowed a courteous 'good morning.' The lady glared back at him in suspicion.

'Whachoolookin' at?'

His English must be rustier than he thought. He had clearly said something to offend. The RHM hurriedly looked away and pretended to consult his map.

'You need help, man?'

A gentleman was tapping his elbow. Although 'gentleman' may not have been entirely the correct term. The RHM recoiled in alarm.

'I'm fine, thank you,' he said, sidestepping this personage. The man grinned, exposing what few teeth he had and shuffled off.

If this was where Kumari was, he needed to get her out of here, fast. It was time to start making enquiries, knocking on likely-looking doors although it was best to take a softly, softly approach. He would start here, in this shop. It seemed a lively place. The moment he entered, everyone stopped what they were doing and stared. Most clutched pieces of paper in their hands; one man had a stash of dollar bills in his fist.

'You lookin' for somethin'?' enquired the man with the money.

'I am looking for someone,' said the RHM pleasantly.

'Well, they ain't here,' said Mr Dollar Bills.

'How do you know?' asked the RHM.

The shop went very, very quiet. The man took a step towards the RHM.

'Beat it,' he said in a menacing tone.

The RHM cleared his throat.

'Can I just ask you gentlemen if anyone has seen a young girl? She has a pet bird and her, ah, foster parent owns a hairdressing establishment along this road.'

'I said beat it,' growled the money man. The RHM took the hint and retreated through the door, fast.

121

On up the street he went, asking here, there and everywhere, sticking his head through the dodgiest of doors, stopping people in the street. Two hours later, he had made absolutely no progress. University Avenue seemed a very long road and there were so many streets crossing it. The RHM was working along it methodically, but he was beginning to run out of steam. Stopping for a brief rest, he leaned against a low wall and sighed deeply. A head popped up from behind the wall.

'Whatsamatter wichoo?'

Startled, the RHM jumped away from the wall. He could see a man's face poking over it, a face with a cheery grin, crowned with a red woollen hat.

'You don't look so happy,' said the man.

'I'm not,' said the RHM. 'I've walked up and down here for hours and I still can't find her. Kumari.'

'Kumari?' The man wrinkled his nose. 'Can't say as I know no *Koo*-mari.'

'Small girl. About this tall. With a bird. Yes, I know, no one's seen her.'

'You say she has a bird?'

The man hopped over the wall and sat by the RHM. He pulled his hat off his head and scratched it. The RHM noticed he was almost entirely bald.

'Y'know, I *have* seen a girl like that. Over at Ma Hernandez' place. Hoodoo Hair. It's a beauty shop. Couple of blocks from here.'

'That must be it!' The RHM leaped up, tiredness forgotten. 'Which way did you say, kind sir?'

'Two blocks north. You can't miss it. Place is all orange. That Ma, she's quite a gal. Y'know, I thought there was something about that kid. Saw her picture in the paper. Funny, you ain't the first to be tryin' to find her. There was a woman the other day, askin' questions same as you.'

'A woman?'

'Yeah. Big lady but kinda squat. Funny accent, like yours.'

'I see. Thank you,' said the RHM. Alarm bells were ringing.

Hurrying off in the direction the man had indicated, he prayed he was not too late. Sure enough, two blocks later he saw it, a small shop front above which the words *Hoodoo Hair* were emblazoned in silver paint. A snake curled through the letters, which were shaped like chicken feathers. Truly, a remarkable place.

The buzz of conversation stopped when the RHM walked through the door. He smiled and offered his little bow.

'Good morning, ladies.'

A woman dressed splendidly in purple came bustling up.

'Can I help you?' she enquired. The RHM studied her handsome features.

'I hope so,' he said. 'I'm looking for a young girl. She's about this tall, has long, black hair. Her name is Kumari.'

Was it the RHM's imagination or did the silence in the salon deepen? The woman before him, however, did not hesitate.

'Sorry, honey. Never seen her.'

'B-but . . . ' began the RHM, then stopped, ever the diplomat. He looked at a woman under the drier.

'I don't suppose you've come across a girl like that, madam?'

The woman fluttered her lashes and exposed a gummy grin. The RHM smiled into her heavily made-up eyes.

'No, you ain't seen no girl like that, Lola,' the woman in purple interjected. 'Like I said, sweetie, none of us have seen her. Have we girls?'

A chorus of 'no's from the women scattered around the salon, some in rollers, others with bits of silver paper in their hair. The RHM thought the whole thing most bizarre. Especially the woman in purple. She was offering him a bowl now, full of brightly wrapped sweetmeats.

'Here honey, take one with you.'

Then she was holding the door open, smoothly ushering him through it. Almost before the RHM knew where he was, he found himself standing on the sidewalk. Through the plate glass window he could see the women, as one, staring back at him. The woman in purple raised a hand and waved. He noticed she had long, silver-painted nails. Each finger was adorned with a remarkable ring.

They were lying. The RHM could feel it. In his dealings he had learned to be on constant alert and he could smell dishonesty in others. After all, it took one to know one and the RHM was no fool. He could not afford to be; the stakes were too high. So the trail ended here, against the brick wall of their silence. The RHM would simply have to find another way. He was a resourceful man.

He waved back through the window at the purple woman and set off in the direction of the subway. His mind was racing, calculating. There had been a woman trying to hunt down Kumari. He could only hope she had been fobbed off

124

as well. For in his heart of hearts, he knew it was the Ayah.
It meant she was definitely here, in New York.

And she had a head start.

CHAPTER 11

Kumari slapped her school bag against her legs as she walked. It made a good sound, sort of rhythmic. Thursdays she walked home alone. LeeLee and CeeCee had chess club. It felt good to be on her own; it gave her time to think without interruption. One thing she had noticed about the World Beyond was that there was far too much going on.

What with TV and school and Ma's constant chatter, she never had much time to think, let alone feel sorry for herself. Actually, feeling sorry for herself was something she rarely did. It was better to take action. Find some kind of way out of whatever mess she was in, although this time she was stumped. It appeared there was no way back from the World Beyond and no means to summon Mamma. And all the while, the sands of Time were running fast. It was enough to depress even the most resilient goddess.

On the plus side, things at school were looking up. Two of the girls had asked her to sit with them at lunch break. Charley and Hannah were their names. They seemed pretty nice. Badmash liked them too. Well, he would do – they fed him doughnuts. And at least Hannah and Charley talked to her as if she was normal, unlike the others who acted as if she were some kind of fruitcake.

'Hey, pigeon-girl!' the gang would call.

'He's a vulture,' Kumari would answer.

The gang seemed pretty stupid, all in all. Maybe that was why they picked on her.

Turning the corner, Kumari decided to cut down the alley-way. CeeCee and LeeLee had taken her that way once or twice – it shaved a few minutes off the walk. Trouble was, there was more than one alleyway and what she thought was the right one turned out not to be. Halfway down, Kumari could see a row of trash cans blocking the end. *Ay caramba!* She'd have to retrace her steps.

'Well, if it isn't pigeon-girl.'

Oh no, Eddie's gang. They must have followed her from school. Five or six of them, blocking her route. This time there was no escape. She would simply have to fight her way out. Except that fighting was a last resort, or so the Ancient Abbot had instructed. Besides, there were lots of them. The odds were not good.

127

'Come on, pigeon-girl, hand over the bird. I'm thinking it'd make a nice sandwich.'

Eddie mimed eating Badmash. The rest fell about laughing. Kumari noticed he had a rash of pustules on his cheeks.

'No way, zit boy,' she countered.

Big mistake. Huge mistake. Suddenly, the gang wasn't laughing. Eddie thrust his chin inches from hers.

'What did you call me?' he demanded.

Kumari stared into his mean eyes. He took a step towards her, then another. The gang was closing in, her way was blocked. This called for drastic action. Whipping round to face the end of the alleyway, Kumari started chanting, frantically running through the Powers in her mind, settling on No 7. Power No 7 – the Power to Move Through Solid Walls.

'OM BEMA TARE SENDARA
LOKA WASHUM KURU SOHA . . .'

Focus, Kumari, focus. She could only hope this was working. *Think goddess big time,* she told herself, as she charged for the trash cans.

There was a *whoosh* and a *splat* as she put the brakes on just in time. The trash was rising up from the cans, whizzing round and round like a whirlwind. Over Kumari's head it soared, twirling and spinning towards the hapless gang, a spiral of orange peel, empty tins and unidentifiable gloop. Gaping at it, open-mouthed, Kumari forgot all about her chant. For endless seconds the trash hovered over the gang before cascading down, covering them from head to toe in filth.

Eddie spat dried dog food from his mouth. Rotten eggs dripped from his earlobes. The others were in a similar state.

Badmash started cackling at the sight.

'Shut your bird up!' Eddie snarled. 'Or I'll . . . '

'Or you'll what?' said Kumari.

'Yeah, you'll what?' echoed a familiar voice. She looked up and saw Chico.

'What you going to do about it?' repeated Chico, sauntering forward until he stood between Eddie and Kumari. Behind him was a whole bunch of kids from school, most of whom were laughing.

'Looks to me, Eddie, like you need a bath,' continued Chico.

Eddie said nothing. Kumari noticed he was looking at Chico with something approaching respect.

'So what was with that tornado thing?' piped up one of Eddie's sidekicks.

'Yeah, that was *weird*,' said another.

'*She* did it!' said a third. '*Her*. She was, like, singing or something.'

All eyes turned to Kumari. She took a deep breath. She could see the questions in Chico's eyes, the doubts written across other faces. Ever so casually, she shrugged.

'Search me,' she said. 'Must have been some freak weather thing. Kind of like the stuff we did in class the other day. You know, global warming.'

She caught sight of one or two of her classmates nodding in agreement. Looked like she had got away with it. At least for now. She wasn't so sure about Chico, though. His expression was unreadable. Right now, he was looking with narrowed eyes at Eddie.

'Go on, scram,' said Chico. 'This is the second time I

caught you bothering Kumari. You don't get a third chance, Eddie. Bother her, it bothers me.'

Without another word, Eddie walked, his cohorts trailing behind him. The other kids parted to let them pass, giggling and holding their noses at the stink.

'Are you OK?' Chico asked.

'I'm fine,' mumbled Kumari. 'Really, I'll just be getting along now.'

'I'll walk you home,' said Chico. 'Make sure you get there OK.'

'Uh, OK,' said Kumari. Great. Another chance to humiliate herself. The bathroom incident still burned. It made her feel hot just thinking about it.

All the way home, Chico said nothing. It was beginning to make Kumari nervous. She wished he'd just spit it out. There was obviously something on his mind. She could tell by the way his lips pressed together. The RHM did that all the time, as did her Papa. She was dying to ask him what it was but there was something that stopped her, this weird shyness that fell on her when Chico was around, like she was all too aware she might be a *klutz*.

Klutz. Now that was a good word. Mrs Brinkman said it quite a lot. Along with *schmuck*, *schlep* and *kvetch*. The World Beyond certainly had a rich and colourful language. Tum tee tum. Twiddly dee. Keep talking, Kumari, in your head. Anything to fill that awful silence. *Is he ever going to speak?*

'This is it,' said Kumari, stopping in front of Ma's apartment building. 'Well ... erm ... see you at school tomorrow, I guess.'

Hope you get a tongue transplant in the meantime.

'Hey, wait a minute,' said Chico.

Oh, good. Surgery won't be necessary.

'I . . . I wanted to tell you something.'

This could be interesting.

'Those guys, you don't want to be afraid of them. If they know you're afraid, they'll just come after you more. You see, I used to be like them. You know, in a gang. Soon realised it's just for cowards. It was my grandpa told me that. I live with them. My grandparents. My mom, she's . . . not well.'

'Oh, OK,' said Kumari. Silence. *Now what do I say?*

'My dad, he's sick, too,' she offered.

'Uh, right. That's too bad.'

'That's how he lost his Powers which is why he can't help me. And it means he can't keep National Happiness at Maximum or do anything about Mamma's death.' Oh no, she was burbling. *Stop it, Kumari. Too late.* He was looking at her like she'd lost her mind, as indeed he might.

'Your Mamma's dead?'

'Kind of. Long story. She's sort of stuck, you see.' He obviously didn't.

Chico took a step back and shook his head. 'You are one strange girl.'

'Gee, thanks,' said Kumari but he was already walking away. She watched him go, her heart heavy. This was not how it was supposed to be. What she wanted more than anything was to fit in, to be normal just like the other kids. It was what she had always wanted, even back home.

Being a goddess was not all it was cracked up to be. All those hours spent on her own or with the Ancient Abbot,

131

trying to master the Eight Powers. All those lessons with the RHM, attempting to learn the higher arts. And when it came down to it, none of that knowledge was any use. Certainly not here in the World Beyond, where, if anything her results were worse than ever. Take today, for instance. *Total wipeout.* A magic mess. OK, so she had talked her way out of it *this* time. But what about next time and the next? It was tough being different. The other kids, they noticed. Chico certainly knew something was up. He'd called her *strange*, for heaven's sake.

And, actually, he had a point. She *was* strange compared to him. Chico fitted in the World Beyond. So did Charley and Hannah. This was their home. This was where they belonged. Kumari wanted to belong too, at least for the moment. Of course, she would not always be here. She'd figure something out, very soon. She didn't want to think about the alternative: that she might be stuck here forever. Or, worse, until her Time ran out. Quite literally. The End.

Then again, there was another option. She could choose to become 100% mortal. Ridiculous idea! She shoved it immediately from her mind. The thought stayed with her, though, all the way up the stairs to Ma's apartment. It dogged her footsteps as she cursed the broken elevator and stalked her to Ma's door.

Not even Badmash's somersaults could lift her spirits. He tried every circus trick he knew but still he could not raise a smile.

'It's no use, Badmash,' Kumari whispered. 'Something has got to give.'

Badmash belly-flopped to the floor and sighed.

Happiness was a long, long way off.

KUMARI'S JOURNAL
(TOP SECRET. FOR MY EYES ONLY.
EVERYONE ELSE KEEP OUT!
THIS MEANS YOU!)

The World Beyond
Still December – 345 days to go

Would it be such a bad thing, not being a goddess? They don't even believe in them in the World Beyond. It's not like I get any special treatment – quite the opposite, in fact. I've had about as much success in summoning Mamma here as back home, which means a big, fat zero. But then again, if I give up being a goddess I am never going to save Mamma.

I have to face facts. That's what Papa would say, at any rate. Not sure how you do that. Face facts, I mean. It doesn't look like anyone is coming to rescue me. They would have surely been here by now. Maybe no one has noticed that I'm missing. No, that's stupid. Of course they would. So if they know I'm missing why has no one come for me? It must mean they can't or they don't want to, in which case I'm as good as dead. OK, in limbo, whatever. Thing is, it wouldn't even be the same limbo place as Mamma – limbo has to be endured alone, which would really suck.

Maybe if I can become mortal I can buy enough time to find the kingdom somehow. That way I get more than a year and a day and I haven't even got that much left. A whole moon cycle has passed since I came here. That means only eleven moons left. And I don't even know where to start to find my kingdom. Maps are totally useless. Googling doesn't get me anywhere. I need more time to work on it.

I can't take too much time, though. Do that and I'll get old and die anyway. I'll kind of shrink and get all wrinkled. I don't want to think about it. Either way I die so I have to do something. At least if I'm mortal I'll fit in better. Someone might want to be my friend. Right now they all think I'm weird, especially Chico. He might even think I was weird if I was mortal but I guess that's the risk. OK, I'll do it. No, I won't. Yes, I will. I know, I'll make a list for and against.

Being Mortal	Being a Goddess
Live longer in World Beyond	Have eleven more moons in the World Beyond
Make friends	Have people think I'm weird
Possibly get old/wrinkly	Stay young forever
Be normal	Have Powers (theoretically)
Unable to summon Mamma	Can summon Mamma (but see above)
Mamma still stuck	Mamma still stuck

CHAPTER 12

Kumari sat on her bed that night, gazing at the stars twinkling in the puddles. At least, they looked like stars, shimmering wetly on the city streets. In reality, they shone from the buildings all around and from the cars rushing up and down the street. They reminded Kumari of the dragons of old, belching poisonous clouds as they passed. Their headlamps swept the streets like eyes, their bumpers smiling dangerously. Their tyres squashed anything that dared get underfoot. Truly, they were terrifying.

Her breath formed mist on the windowpane. Idly, she drew with her finger, sketching out a mountain far away, clouds of Happiness drifting beneath. It was cold enough to snow, or so Ma said. There might even be a white Christmas. Not that she knew what Christmas was. She guessed it had something to do with all the gaudy decorations adorning every building. Ma had stuck a flashing display above the salon door, complete with a chubby guy dressed in red.

'Who's that?' Kumari had asked. The man looked familiar.

'That's Santa Claus,' said Ma, fiddling with the bulb in a reindeer's nose. 'You mean to tell me you never seen Santa Claus before?'

Come to think of it, she had, that first day when she had run right through the parade. It felt like forever since she had begged the man in red for help. In fact, it was only a few weeks. She had sloped down to Hoodoo Hair about an hour after Chico left, slipping in the back door as Ma now insisted.

'But why?' Kumari had asked. Was there some problem coming in the front?

'Never you mind, Kumari,' said Ma. 'Just do as I ask.'

She kept the blinds down now in the salon as well, so no one could see in. Actually, it looked even funkier, seeing as the blinds were silver Lurex. One thing about Ma – she had her own unique taste.

In the salon, all was light and bustle. Kumari instantly felt better. The apartment was dark and lonely in comparison. Here, she could chat to the clients.

'Mrs Brinkman,' said Kumari. 'Do you think it's important to, you know, fit in?'

Mrs Brinkman considered her question carefully. 'Sometimes yes, sometimes no. You see, Kumari, it's most important to be true to yourself. If that means you are different, then so be it.'

Kumari looked into her wise old eyes. Mrs Brinkman had a point.

'Yes, but it's hard being different.'

'Nothing important is ever easy.'

Kumari thought this through for a moment. It reminded her of the Ancient Abbot.

'I guess you're right, Mrs Brinkman. If something was easy, everyone would do it.'

'Exactly,' said Mrs Brinkman. 'Here, take this,' she smiled conspiratorially. Pressing a few dollars in Kumari's hand, she added, 'Go buy yourself something nice. A Christmas present, something pretty.'

Kumari stared at the dollars in her hand. She had never bought herself anything. Well, OK, she bought her lunch every day with money from Ma but this was different. Back in the kingdom, everything was provided for her. The girl goddess wanted for nothing. Here, she had to admit, it was much the same, although frankly standards had slipped.

Not that she wanted to appear ungrateful. But there was now a distinct lack of gold thread, not to mention fine silks and jewels and slippers tailored to her feet. Instead, she wore CeeCee and LeeLee's hand-me-downs when not in school uniform. Sometimes Ma would let her borrow her favourite pink cap just to add a flash of sequins. When it came to clothes, she was worse off than she had ever been.

Thanking Mrs Brinkman, Kumari had skipped back home, stopping to gaze in every window. There was nothing much to look at, though – a couple of grocery stores, a hardware outlet. Somehow a bunch of bananas didn't cut it as a pretty present. Nor, for that matter, did a plastic bucket. Defeated yet again, Kumari's mood faded fast. Shutting the door to her tiny bedroom, she sat on her bed for A Think.

And here she was, several hours later, journal open beside her on her pillow, Badmash curled up, asleep, feet twitching, the bedroom lights turned out. Actually, she had never turned them on. It felt better to sit in darkness. Kind of matched her state of mind, made her feel like she was truly suffering. It was hard work suffering – hungry, too, as it involved refusing food. That bit was especially tough when enchiladas were on the menu.

Ma had shrugged her shoulders.

'You'll eat when you're hungry.'

CeeCee and LeeLee, too, had left her alone, after the twentieth time of asking. Now that they had, it didn't feel so good. Suffering was becoming boring. She could hear the TV through the wall. It was *South Park*, one of her favourites. Sighing, Kumari stared out the window some more. Might as well suffer properly.

She stared out the window often. Couldn't avoid it, seeing as her bed was squashed right up against it. From here she had a grandstand view of the sidewalk two storeys below. Tonight, though, the sidewalk was empty. Nothing to gaze at but the puddles. Everyone must be indoors, sheltering from the rain. And then she saw it, a sudden movement in the shadows. Had she not been staring so hard at nothing much she might have totally missed it.

Craning forward, she kept her nose a few inches from the window pane. That way, she reasoned, she stayed out of sight. There it was, once more, a shape scuttling along under the street light. As Kumari peered, it bobbed up and down again. Now this was really interesting. There was someone out there trying to hide.

The shape was crouched down behind some cars. She wished she could see through them. Then it occurred to her, maybe she could. There was always Power No 2. *Oh, yeah, right, Kumari. And I'm so good at my Powers.* Still, it was worth a try. After all, it was the Power of Extraordinary Sight. She would take this one carefully, really concentrate on getting it right.

'Don't rush at it, Kumari,' the Ancient Abbot always said. For once she would take his advice.

At first, she thought that, as usual, nothing was going to happen. And then she could feel it, something whizzing up through her. Her cheeks felt hot, her whole head tingled. Opening her eyes, Kumari blinked once or twice. She squinted at the cars down below. She could clearly see two shapes now crouched behind the cars, then another and another. She was actually seeing through metal. Which meant her Powers had worked!

Hardly daring to believe it, Kumari kept looking. The more she looked, the more she could see. This was one cool Power. There were four men, all dark-haired, bent over so she could not see their faces. Now, if she could only read what they were thinking . . . no, her Powers were not yet that refined. Then one turned his head and Kumari gasped. She

139

recognised him at once; it was the kidnapper who had held her, the one who had helped her out of the car when she pretended to be sick. Another also turned and, seeing him, she knew for certain. The kidnappers were back on her trail.

And they knew roughly where she lived.

This called for immediate action. Tiptoeing into the hallway, Kumari grabbed the phone. She'd learned a few things in the weeks she'd been in the World Beyond. Time to put them into action.

'I want to report an emergency,' said Kumari when the 911 operator answered. 'There's a gang of men trying to break into cars. Corner of Rosa Parks Place and Grand Avenue. They're kind of suspicious looking. I think they might have guns. And I have reason to believe they are illegal aliens. No, I can't tell you how.'

Slamming the phone down, Kumari skipped to the window and waited.

'Come on,' she muttered under her breath. After what felt an age, she heard sirens.

'Watch this, Badmash,' she said as, in the street below, four heads popped up and looked about. Too late, they spotted the flashing light of the police car which stopped a few feet from them.

'Hands up,' shouted a policeman, just like in the movies.

Humming softly to herself, Kumari smiled as the four were taken into custody. Another few weeks locked away would do them good. More importantly, it would buy her time. Time she desperately needed.

* * *

140

Simon Razzle licked his lips. He could taste blood at one corner.

'Not so handsome, now, huh?' smiled the goon. 'You wanna get cosmetic surgery, doc.'

His accomplice giggled.

'Cosmetic surgery. Hey, that's funny. Him being like a surgeon and all I mean . . . '

'Yeah, yeah, OK, we get it.'

The first goon leaned forward. His breath assaulted Simon's bloodied nose. It smelt of garlic, more garlic and a touch of oregano.

'You got one week to find the money, doc. $30,000. One week and I'm being generous. Mr Paolozzi, he's a patient man, but your time is running out.'

The goon made for the door, shoving his accomplice before him.

'OK, OK,' mumbled Simon. He could feel his lips swelling. Some of his patients would pay good money for that kissable, puffed up look. He half-smiled then winced in pain.

'Something amusing you, doc?'

'No, no,' said Simon.

'That's good,' said the goon. 'Me, I got no sense of humour.'

'You can say that again,' muttered Simon as soon as the coast was clear.

Sitting down heavily at his desk, he sank his battered head into bruised hands. He had begged them not to touch his fingers, on account of his work. This was a bad situation. There was no getting round it. He had to come up with the money in just one week or he was mincemeat. If only he had left the casinos well alone, he would not be in this mess. All right, so he had been stupid. Gambling was for mugs. And now he owed Paolozzi big bucks. His line of credit had finally run out. There was no getting out of this one, not even with the famous Razzle charm.

Opening up his laptop, he tapped out a slow, painful email. *The deal is off*, it read, *unless you deliver the girl within three days.*

Pressing 'Send', Simon tried not to whimper. Those goons had meant business. It was time for Simon, too, to get tough. He gazed at his precious hands. The bones were not broken. Yet. Fail to come up with the money and he could kiss good-bye to his livelihood. There was no way he could perform intricate procedures with hands that had been mashed to a pulp. As a matter of fact, there was no way he would be doing anything if he wound up dead.

He had clawed his way this far and there was no chance he was going back. *Simon Razzle, Surgeon to the Stars*. His eyes flicked to his instruments, laid out neatly on a table. The razor-sharp scalpel glistened under the surgery lights. The sight of it made him catch his breath. The girl, she was the key. He glanced at the clippings on his desk, taken from the newspapers. The ones the broker had sent to prove that the girl was indeed out there. Somewhere. He gazed harder at the blurry picture. The secret of eternal youth flowed through those pretty veins. Secreted somewhere inside that slender body, the source of endless billions. Find it, extract it and Simon would be saved. He could name his price, ensure his fame. Pay the goons. Save his life.

But all that would take time and time was not on Simon's side. Three days were all he had before he had to think of something else. And think of something else he did. When the stakes were this high, loyalties meant nothing. He would cut out the broker – find the girl for himself. That way, all the rewards were his and he would need every penny. Simon might be on the verge of making billions but his lifestyle was hardly cheap.

Come to that, why not make some extra? The secret of eternal youth was just one source of funds. There was another, quicker way, to make some cash. He could literally sell the girl's looks. Find her, slice her up and his troubles would be over. And luckily for Simon he had the perfect customer in mind.

Punching an unlisted number into his cell phone, Simon forced his mouth into a smile. It helped to smile when making such an important call. Added that crucial air of confidence.

'Hello? Simon Razzle here. I have an interesting proposition. All I need from you is a small deposit. Say $30,000.'

So many ageing clients. So many desperate women. And this one was more desperate than most.

She would literally buy a new face.

KUMARI'S JOURNAL
(TOP SECRET. FOR MY EYES ONLY.
EVERYONE ELSE KEEP OUT!
THIS MEANS YOU!)

The World Beyond
January 28th – 306 days to go

I've done it. I told them – Hannah and Charley. About the kidnappers and everything. They were really sweet and said I should have told them before and I mustn't ever be on my own. OK so I didn't tell them everything – they'd freak at the goddess stuff. I still have to sort that out, but at least now my friends know about the other thing.

I just read that back. Unbelievable! 'My friends.' I actually have some! I think Badmash is a bit jealous. He is sulking - a lot. It's not like I love him any less, but I've never had real friends before just like me. Well, OK, not just like me, but they're my age and everything. We talk and we hang out and we have so much fun it's amazing. I never knew you could have such a good time just talking about stuff. I guess this is what it feels like to be normal.

We talk about school, Ms LaMotta's moustache (Charley thinks she should wax it), boys and our parents. I don't really tell them much about Mamma and Papa – they just think I live with my foster family. Ma, CeeCee and LeeLee really are like family now – sometimes it feels like I've always lived with them. And they don't care about that Manhattan Mystery Girl stuff which kind of died down, thank goodness. I mean, it's not like reporters hang around or anything. They got bored with me pretty quickly. Once they realised I couldn't tell them anything then that was it really.

The authorities, too – they've kind of given up. It's not like I'm going to suddenly remember something crucial. I've told them I don't know where the Kingdom is or how to get there. I can tell they think I'm crazy but there's not a lot they can do. In any case it's easier for them just to forget about me. They've got too much paperwork. That's what Ma says at any rate – I'm just another statistic.

Anyway, Charley and Hannah were cool about the kidnappers. They wanted to know why some men were after me and I said I didn't know. Then I said OK my Papa is an important person and then they got really excited and wanted to know who he is. I had to act all grown-up and say that it's better they don't know and then they started making really wild guesses like he's a reclusive billionaire or something. Then they guessed he might be an Indian prince. That was getting too close so I looked really bored at that idea.

They gave up after their third guess when I started to look a bit upset. I mean, the idea of Papa being a Bollywood star was slightly insulting. Papa would never embarrass himself in such a way although, come to think of it, it would be kind of cool. But I started to think of him blown up big on screen and imagining his face. It reminded me of how I miss him and that's why I started to look upset and then Hannah and Charley were upset too and they stopped their guessing. I'm glad I've told them, though. It's so great to have friends. Friends. I have friends. I am normal. Almost.

CHAPTER 13

'Mind if I join you?'

'Who, me?'

'Yes, you.'

Good start, Kumari. Like he doesn't think you're a klutz already.

'So, how's it going?' said Chico. Kumari sneaked a peek over his shoulder. The cafeteria line stretched forever. Hannah and Charley would be ages.

'It's . . . better,' she smiled.

OK, so the clock was still ticking and she was still stuck *here* while Mamma was stuck *there*, but despite that, all things considered, life *was* getting better. Even more so since Chico had sat down, come to think of it. Oh no, better not think of it. Cheeks on red alert.

'So . . .'

'So . . .'

She noticed his leg was jiggling. Could he actually be nervous too? Not Chico. No way. Then again, maybe.

'Um . . . how's your grandpa?' said Kumari. 'I heard he was in the hospital.'

Chico's eyes darkened for a moment. She felt her heart twist.

'He's doing good, thanks. They just wanted to keep him in to make sure. He had this kind of dizzy spell but he's OK now. It's my grandma I've got to worry about. She won't leave the old guy alone. Keeps telling him to rest. Like my grandpa would ever sit still. The minute her back's turned, he's up and out the door.'

'He sounds great,' smiled Kumari. Poor Chico. Beneath his upbeat manner, he couldn't hide his concern.

'He is. A really good guy. How 'bout you? You got a grandpa?'

'Um, no,' said Kumari. *That's it, keep a lid on it. For once don't freak him out. Keep the weird family stuff to yourself. At least for now.*

'That's too bad,' said Chico. 'My grandpa, he's taught me such a lot.'

'Like about the gang stuff?'

'The gang stuff and other things. He's a wise old guy. And generous. Him and grandma took me and my little sister in

148

when we had no place to go. I mean, they should be sitting back by now but instead they brought us up. Put us on the right path.'

Kumari had never seen him this serious. His grandparents obviously meant the world to him.

'He must be a wonderful person.'

'He is.'

Chico flashed her *that* grin and she felt her stomach go into spin cycle. Round and round and round, just like at the Laundromat. Come to think of it, she liked the Laundromat. It was kind of fun watching the clothes go round. *Concentrate, Kumari. This guy is gorgeous.*

'So you want to grab a soda sometime?'

'Uh, sure, that would be nice.' *Nice? For goodness' sake. He asks you out and you say that would be 'nice'? Does 'grabbing a soda' class as being asked out? Aarrgh – this is so complicated.*

'Hey there.' It was Hannah, behind her a smirking Charley.

'Room for us?' asked Charley.

'I was just going,' said Chico.

A parting smile for Kumari.

'Later.'

'Uh, later.'

Don't, she begged silently. *Don't you two start. Pleeeeease.*

And they didn't. At least, not for thirty whole seconds. By which time Chico was safely across the cafeteria and out of earshot.

'So he said he'd see you later?' giggled Hannah.

'Like, how much later?' snorted Charley.

'I have no idea,' said Kumari loftily. 'Whenever. You know.'

'No, we *don't* know,' sniggered Charley.

'But we sure would like to,' added Hannah. And with that they were off again, chortling as they munched their sandwiches.

Kumari could not help but join in. Their laughter was infectious. Every time one of them started, it set the other two off. It was true what she'd said to Chico. Despite everything, life was surprisingly good.

So good that sometimes she even forgot the clock ticking away in her head. Or the fact that she was so far from home.

KUMARI'S JOURNAL
(TOP SECRET. FOR MY EYES ONLY.
EVERYONE ELSE KEEP OUT!
THIS MEANS YOU!)

The World Beyond
April 1st – 243 days to go

It's the first day of April today in the World Beyond and they have this really weird custom where everyone plays jokes on one another. At least, they say they're jokes but some of them are not exactly amusing. Whoever put plastic wrap over the toilets was pretty lame and most people think it was Eddie. We got him back, though – me, Hannah and Charley – we super glued some coins to the ground near where he sneaks off to have his filthy cigarettes. Then we hid and watched as he tried to pick them up. He broke his fingernails trying – too funny!

Hannah has come up with a really great idea and at first the teachers thought this, too, was a joke. She suggested we all wear the same Yankees beanie hat in case the kidnappers suddenly reappear. That way, they won't know which one is me, especially if we pull them low over our foreheads. It's pretty hard to tell who someone is in a beanie, even harder if they wear a scarf. Anyway at first it was just me, Charley and Hannah but suddenly it caught on. Everyone assumed it was a fashion thing until Charley told Chico. Once Chico started wearing one, the whole school followed. Even those people who don't support the Yankees, which is pretty cool.

I sort of wish Charley hadn't told Chico in a way – it's just one other reason for him to think I'm strange. But it's a really nice thing for him to do and it shows he cares. On the other hand, maybe it's not such a good thing. I don't want him to think I'm some kind of sad case. Charley says guys like girls who are perky and smile a lot. I don't really do perky. Anyway, it's better he likes me for who I am. At least, that's what I think.

LeeLee said the same thing this evening. Not that I told her about Chico specifically – we were talking about boys in general. And not because I started the conversation. It was because we'd been watching Dream Date on TV and I said I thought they were all really gross and it kind of went from there. CeeCee didn't say much. I think it's because she likes this guy at her high school but he doesn't like her. If he doesn't like CeeCee he must be an idiot and why would you want to go out with an idiot, anyway, is what I said. Then CeeCee went really, really quiet and LeeLee kicked me so I shut up. Still, I think it's good advice: Always be yourself.

Anyway, all of this is what Ms Martin would call hypothetical. Good word. I like that. We have to produce a hypothesis about our science fair projects. Mine is that magic can defy the laws of physics. I'm still working on it. Ms Martin gave me that look she does, the one where she raises one eyebrow and stares right at you. Then she kind of smiled and said, 'I can't wait, Kumari.' Me neither – I mean, my magic hit rate is not exactly high.

CHAPTER 14

The sidewalk was icy. Squealing, the girls clutched on to one another.

'Heeeeeeeeeeeelp!' shrieked Hannah.

Too late, she skidded, knocking the other two down. They landed in a heap, laughing, Kumari loudest of them all. She glimpsed the sky, blue despite the cold, and thought *I'm happy*. How weird.

Spring was late in coming. The big freeze showed no signs of letting up. Which suited Kumari perfectly as she was having the time of her life. Back home, snow sat on mountains, looking pretty. Here you goofed around in it.

And there was nothing Kumari and her posse liked more than to goof around, except perhaps hang out and talk *stuff*.

Kumari sat up on the sidewalk. 'Hey, isn't that Daniel?'

'Get up, get up!' hissed Hannah, adjusting her beanie hat. She was already on her feet, cheeks pink.

Charley and Kumari looked at one another. 'Hi, Daniel,' they chorused.

'Hey,' Daniel mumbled, sloping by. 'How you doin', Hannah?'

They waited a full ten seconds after he passed before collapsing in giggles. Hannah flapped her hands in mortification.

'Stop it! Stop it, he'll hear!'

'Hey, Hannah, we're sorry,' said Kumari. 'We didn't mean to upset you.'

'She's not upset.' Charley grinned wickedly. '*Daniel* said hello. To Hannah.'

'It was "hey," actually,' said Hannah. 'Not that I noticed.'

'Uh, right.' Kumari winked at Charley. It was *fantabulizmous* having friends.

Especially today. Today was an important day. The minute the bell sounded, the girls headed for the subway. Today they were going shopping Downtown. It was Charley's idea. She could not believe Kumari had never so much as seen the big stores. And with Ma's birthday coming up, it seemed the perfect excuse.

Kumari patted her purse one more time. In it, her earnings. Twenty dollars and fifty eight cents exactly. How impressive was that? It had taken weeks of sweeping up at the salon on Saturdays with a few shampoos thrown in. That was until she picked up the wrong bottle by mistake and turned Lola's hair a fetching shade of green. Lola had still tipped her, insisting she liked it, but Ma had taken Kumari off shampoo duty that instant and given her back her broom.

She still had a couple of blisters on her hands as a souvenir. Actually, she was kind of proud of those blisters. She had worked hard for them, darn it. She paused to pick at them and a headline at the newsstand caught her eye:

Hollywood Star Adopts Orphan, it read.

So that was their latest victim. Kumari shook her head. The *Manhattan Mystery Girl* thing was forgotten and that was just the way she liked it. The papers moved on quickly. Being old news made her feel safer. She pulled down her Yankees beanie hat. It was like a sea of confusion bobbing in and out of the school gates and so far it had worked. Even so, she glanced around before descending into the subway. She had no idea if the kidnappers were still in custody. It was best to make sure.

'You OK, Kumari?' asked Hannah.

'You bet,' said Kumari, smiling at her friends.

'Quick, the Badmash Bag,' said Charley. They were nearly at the turnstiles. Kumari crammed Badmash into his special carrier, complete with chocolate treats. Now that he was getting bigger, Badmash was harder to conceal. Another problem with being in the World Beyond – Badmash was growing quicker. Back home he'd be a baby vulture for ages – out here it was different. It was Hannah again who had come up with the solution: a Kate Spade tote stolen from her aunt.

'I borrowed it,' Hannah insisted. 'Besides, she'll never notice.'

Hannah's aunt lived on the Upper East Side and wore more labels than a baggage carousel. She worked for some fancy magazine and considered Hannah's mom 'a failure'. Only failure wasn't the word she used; it was more like 'disappointment'. Kumari thought Hannah's mom was lovely – she had wild hair and read a lot.

The bag was the perfect size. Badmash liked to snooze in its cosy confines. Kumari left its zipper open a little, afraid he would suffocate. It certainly got him past Ms LaMotta, who was no big fan of Badmash. Actually, Ms LaMotta was no big fan of anyone. She ruled the school with a rod of iron. At least, she tried to rule with a rod of iron. At Rita Moreno its effect was more that of a rusty nail. Only that morning she had stopped Kumari in the corridor.

'Show me your hall pass, Kumari.'

'My hall pass?' Oh yes, *those* things. Kumari shrugged.

Ms LaMotta looked at her and sighed. 'I'll let it go this time, Kumari. Oh and Kumari . . . '

'Yes, Ms LaMotta?'

'Good work on your science fair entry.'

'Uh, thanks, Ms LaMotta.' She'd noticed! *Oh my god.*

A great big glow filled Kumari as she relived the moment.

'What are you smiling at?' asked Hannah and then she leapt up. 'We're here!'

As they emerged onto Fifth Avenue, Kumari craned her neck. Concrete citadels, stretching skywards. Suddenly she was back there, running through the crowd.

156

'I can't *believe* you've never been Downtown,' said Hannah.

Actually, she had but that was another story she was keeping to herself. Her desperate race through the parade. That thing with Santa Claus.

'Are you OK?' asked Charley. 'You've got, like, this funny look on your face.'

Kumari grinned at Charley. 'Not as funny as *your* face, girlfriend.'

Laughing at one another, they linked arms and strode along. A few steps later, Kumari stopped dead.

'Wow! What is this?'

'That's FAO Schwarz. It's a *toy store*,' said Hannah.

A toy store? It was more like a palace. The place glistened with expense. Inside, she could see the ceiling twinkling blue. There were even two soldiers guarding the entrance.

Nodding to them, Kumari swept through the gleaming glass doors, Hannah and Charley giggling behind. Once inside, she stared in amazement. This was no toy store. This was paradise. Mile upon mile of *things* arrayed enticingly all around. Enormous stuffed jungle animals looking on benignly from behind thick ropes. A life-size snow leopard stretched out, its eyes all too real. It reminded Kumari of home. She swallowed the thought. A delicious smell wafted towards her. Following it, she found an ice cream parlour to die for; alongside it, more candy than she had ever seen, acres of shiny wrappers.

Even Hannah and Charley were getting excited, now they had forgotten about acting cool. Stuffing candy into paper sacks, they gorged as they drifted round the shop.

157

'Oh my god, moving stairs!' said Kumari.

Hannah and Charley exchanged another look. 'That's an *escalator*,' said Hannah kindly.

'I knew that!' said Kumari.

She could hear music from the top of the moving stairs. Stepping onto them gingerly, she held on tight. At the top, she gasped in astonishment. There was a piano so big that people were dancing across it! It looked so much fun she just had to join in. Leaping aboard, she started to twirl round on the keys. A dancer tapped up to her.

'This is *our* show, sweetie,' he spat as, deftly, he tripped her up.

A man in a blue jacket grabbed her and hauled her down. Hannah and Charley were doubled up, in fits.

'You get to dance on the piano *after* the performance,' growled the man.

'Come on,' said Charley. 'Let's split.'

Another wobbly ride on the escalator back through the wonderland of toys. On the way out, Kumari spotted something: a box with *Magic Set* written across it, a rabbit adorning the lid. What had rabbits got to do with magic? She'd never come across anything quite so stupid.

'A magic set? Boring,' said Charley.

'My brother had one,' offered Hannah.

'Magic? That's not magic,' declared Kumari.

'You some kind of expert?' said Charley.

Actually, I am, thought Kumari. *But I must not, cannot tell them that. Otherwise they won't be my friends. They'll think I'm totally weird.*

Out loud, she said, 'Nah! Just think it looks dumb, that's all. Come to think of it, that rabbit looks a bit like Mr Johnson.'

She pulled a Jabba Johnson face and the other two collapsed. Still giggling, they burst out through the glass doors and skipped together down the street, skidding to an abrupt halt outside another fancy store as Charley shouted, 'In here!'

She disappeared through the revolving door and Kumari attempted to follow suit. Somehow she ended up back on the street.

'Whoops! Must have pushed too hard.'

'You are a *lunatic*,' grinned Hannah.

Phew, she'd got away with that one too. First the escalator, now the revolving door. The World Beyond was still full of obstacles, most of them designed to trip her up. Kumari looked for Charley. She was heading for the cosmetic counters, running the gauntlet of women with perfume sprays. They looked decidedly scary.

'Try this,' said a woman, dowsing Kumari in a smelly cloud.

'Eugh!' said Kumari. 'That stinks.'

The woman glared.

'It's *Divine*,' she said.

'Whatever,' said Kumari. The woman didn't know the meaning of the word.

The woman stared at her blankly, her red-glossed lips slack.

Ahead, Charley was sticking her fingers into little pots,

159

rubbing all sorts of colours on her face. As Kumari and Hannah approached, a saleswoman glided up and skewered Charley with a patronising stare.

'Can I help you?'

To Kumari's ears, it sounded like she meant the opposite. Behind her glacial smile was an icy tone that said, *Beat it, teen scum.*

Charley took it in her stride. 'I'd like a makeover,' she announced.

The saleswoman raised a perfectly plucked brow.

'We're not doing those today.'

'But it says here you are,' said Charley, pointing to a placard on the counter.

'Well we're not,' snapped the saleswoman. 'Can I help you with anything else?'

'Come on, Charley,' said Hannah. 'Let's just get out of here.'

Charley's mouth took on the stubborn pout Kumari knew all too well.

'I'd like a M.A.K.E.O.V.E.R. please,' she said, very slowly and clearly. The saleswoman did not flinch.

'Go away, little girl.'

Little girl?! Kumari could not believe her ears. She saw the flush rise up Charley's cheeks. Worse, she saw her shoulders droop in defeat and her eyes fill with tears. How dare this person humiliate her friend? She'd show her humiliation. Without thinking, Kumari raised her arm, closed her eyes and began to chant. Power No 8, she could do that. Maybe it was a sugar rush from the candy but she forgot all about *fitting in*. All she knew was that Charley was hurt. And no one did that to her friends.

'Oh. My. God,' she heard Hannah gasp.

She could feel the whirlwind begin to rise, stirring the hairs on the back of her neck. Opening her eyes, Kumari saw cosmetics darting through the air, whizzing towards the saleswoman's face. Mascara scored black lines down her cheeks, lipstick smeared scarlet streaks across her chin. A pot of cream dumped itself all over her hair. Green shadow applied itself to her ears. A fluffy brush inserted itself into the woman's gaping mouth and stuck out like a squirrel's tail. A huge can of hairspray whipped round and round then covered her in its contents like glue.

Excellent – it had worked. Almost too well, in fact. For a split second Kumari felt a pang of guilt. But the woman had been really mean. And then, like a large, fluffy dart, Badmash came flying. Somehow he had worked his way out of the bag and was intent on adding the final touch. Snatching a tub of glitter from the counter, he hurled it into the air. It flew up and then drifted down, covering the saleswoman in a rainbow layer of sparkle. It might have looked pretty on its own but, with the rest, it was a disaster.

The saleswoman let out a muffled, 'Gnnnh!'

All around, people were staring. With a sick feeling, Kumari realised what she'd done. All those months of acting normal, hoping to fit in, wasted for a few seconds of revenge. The chant died in her throat as she dropped her arm. Instantly, the cosmetics fell back down. One or two customers clapped and cheered. Grabbing Badmash, she shoved him back in his bag.

'Come on,' she said, 'we're leaving.'

They left the saleswoman looking like some kind of crazy clown and raced for the exit. All the way out, the other two said nothing. She could feel them darting her worried looks. Once on the sidewalk, she stopped.

'Look, I'm a goddess,' she announced.

'A *goddess*?!' Charley snorted.

'Oh, come *on*,' said Hannah.

She looked at them steadily. Charley's face began to cloud.

'You mean it, don't you?' she said. 'You really think you're a goddess.'

'I *am* a goddess,' said Kumari.

'Sure you are,' said Hannah. 'Just like I'm a supermodel.'

They both looked at Hannah, all curvaceous five foot two of her.

'See what I mean?' Hannah shrugged.

'You mean you're, like, a sex goddess?' said Charley. 'Y'know, like in all the magazines. *How to be a Sex Goddess. Let Your Inner Goddess Out.*'

'No,' said Kumari. 'I mean, like I'm a real goddess.'

'Oh, come on,' said Charley. 'What are you, some kind of street magician?'

'I told you,' said Kumari, exasperated. Not even her best friends would believe her!

They trudged to the subway in silence. Neither of them would meet her eye. All the way uptown, they studiously stared at their hands. As they exited at their stop, Kumari tried one last time.

'We can still be friends, right?'

'Uh, s-sure,' stammered Hannah. Charley said nothing. Kumari watched them walk away and felt a pain shoot through her heart. The pain stayed in her chest, aching as she wandered home. Dismally, she realised she had broken her rule. She was all alone. Luckily, no kidnappers appeared. Instead, she saw someone else. Someone who also thought she was weird. *Chico.* And he, too, was on his own.

'Hey . . . ' Kumari half-smiled.

Chico kind of mumbled something about just seeing Hannah and Charley. Then he was gone, passing her by. Just like all her other friends. Fat tears rolled up from under her eyelids and spilled down her ashen face. All her life she had wanted friends and now they were lost. She was friendless once more. She simply could not bear it. A muffled squawk sounded from the bag.

'At least I've got you,' whispered Kumari.

But, as much as she loved Badmash, it was no longer enough. She needed her friends back. Apart from Ma and the girls, they were all she had. And then it came to her in a flash, a bolt of lightning to the brain. She knew what she had to do. Had known for a long time, in fact.

What was the use in being a goddess if she was never going to get back home? *Face it, Kumari. There is no way back to the Kingdom. The World Beyond is your world now. You have to make your life here.* At least if she chose to become 100% mortal she could live out a normal span. And *be* normal. Truly fit in, just like she'd always wanted. She was sick of being different from her friends. Today's slip-up made her feel more alone than ever. If she became mortal,

163

she could finally be one of them. She could stop pretending, because she really would be just like them, and just like the people who had become her family. CeeCee and LeeLee were like the sisters she had never had and Ma did her best to be her mother.

Renouncing her Powers would be one huge step. Vast. Immense. Scary. But things could not go on as they were. She needed her friends.

Before she could change her mind, Kumari turned and ran back to the subway. She still had time before Ma got home. She could just about get there and back. All the way back Downtown, she talked to herself non-stop to keep the doubts at bay. Not out loud, of course. Couldn't risk anyone else thinking she was nuts. Fa la la la la. Fiddly dee. At last, here was her stop.

34th Street for the Empire State Building. She gazed up and up.

The tallest building in Manhattan, it was perfect for her purposes. She rode the elevator to the Observatory. The ticket cost nearly all the money she had left. This was so important, though. She hoped Ma would forgive her. She would just have to sweep some more floors, buy Ma a late birthday present. Stepping out on to the promenade, the view swam, dizzying, towards her.

New York City, laid out beneath her feet. It felt like she was on top of the world. No time to waste, though. She would have to find a quiet corner. Groups of people came and went. Finding a moment alone seemed impossible. A party of tourists snapped away, taking endless pictures. At

164

last, they wandered off to the next photo-op. All of a sudden, she was on her own.

Seizing her chance, Kumari threw open both arms and howled to the heavens. The Renunciation Rite had been drummed into her since she was a child, in case of emergencies. Not even she could mess it up. Or at least she hoped not.

'TYAGA, TYAGA
SARVA TYAGA KARI
NIJA DHARMA YAYA
TYAGA KARI !'

Stamping her feet and shaking her tail, Kumari gave it all she'd got, crying out to the elements, demanding they do her bidding. She could feel a blast of sunlight upon her face. *Oh good, she'd got that one right.* Then the wind started to whip up, first a breeze then a blast. Dimly she heard a man's voice.

'They said it was changeable, but this is ridiculous!'

The sound of footsteps running for shelter as the wind tried to lift her off her feet. She clung on to the balustrade, determined to see this through at all costs, sinking deeper and deeper into herself, at one with her chant. A crack of thunder snapped her out of her trance. There was rain falling on her face. What had been clear skies were angry and grey. A flash of lightning ripped through the clouds. Then another and another. All at once, a fork shot forth, a rod of fire aimed at her heart.

It was as if it was meant for her her, an arrow from the heavens. She knew then she had made a terrible mistake. The gods were infuriated. One of their own had rejected them. It was an unforgivable act. Horrified, Kumari realised what she had done. But it was too late to reverse it. At the last moment, the lightning struck her amulet and bounced harmlessly off. She felt its energy sizzle and dissipate. As quickly as it came, the storm died away. All that was left was the rain, mingling with the tears on her face. Brushing them aside, she patted Badmash.

'I'm free,' she whispered.

Somehow the words rang hollow.

Strange that it should be her amulet that saved her. Almost like it was a message from Mamma.

She could not remember anything of her journey home nor of her subsequent trudge from the subway. It was only when she saw the person waiting on her doorstep that the brain fug cleared.

'Chico! What are you doing here?'

She was too tired to care what he thought of her.

'I came to see you,' said Chico. 'Thought you might like to have that soda with me.'

'With you? Um, OK.'

Had it had been worth it?

From now on, she would be one of them. Mortal. No longer a goddess. *Normal.*

Trying to smile, she said, 'I'd love a soda.'

Things would never be the same.

KUMARI'S JOURNAL
(TOP SECRET. FOR MY EYES ONLY.
EVERYONE ELSE KEEP OUT!
THIS MEANS YOU!)

The World Beyond
June 3rd – 180 days to go

Funny, but I still keep counting down the days, even though it doesn't matter any more. I mean, I'm mortal now. I have no idea how long I have left. That is so weird – not knowing how long you have to live. It's like what Ma says – 'death don't make no appointments'. Anyway, I feel different. At least, I think I do. It's kind of strange and at times I feel sad but it's also like a weight's been lifted from me. Like I don't have to try so hard but just be as in, be normal. As in, be me, Kumari. Now I do normal things the same as everyone else.

Like we went to Orchard Beach this weekend and it was INCREDIBLE. I loved the sand, I loved the sea, I loved everything about it. We took the train all the way out there, to this place called Pelham Bay Park, me, CeeCee and LeeLee. Ma had to work, of course, Saturday being her busiest day. So CeeCee and LeeLee were in charge, which meant they basically let me do what I liked. They sat and read while I fooled around in the sea, ate ice creams and had the best time. The sea was weird but great – salty so it helps you float!

I'm going to ask Ms Martin about that tomorrow. How come salt helps you float? I mean, it's not like if you eat lots of it you float better in the bath. At least, I don't think so. Anyway, the sea certainly beats swimming in a freezing lake, although it is a lot busier. There were so many people there – lots of them just lying on the sand. When I asked CeeCee and Leelee what they were doing they said, 'Sunbathing'. Sunbathing?! You don't bathe in the sun. I mean, ridiculous!

But everyone was doing it, taking off as many clothes as they could. I wondered if it was some kind of ritual they practised here on the first really hot day, like a sun salutation, but I didn't want to ask in case I looked stupid. Not that LeeLee and CeeCee would have called me stupid – they kind of treat me as their personal pet. Like I'm a little odd, but they indulge me all the same and throw me lots of treats.

I don't think I'd even try to tell them about the goddess thing. Not that it would bother them. Nothing really bothers LeeLee and CeeCee. They'd probably just say, 'Whatever'. Anyway, the goddess thing is over. Finito. For good. And it's already working. Hannah, Charley and I are once again hanging out. It was really simple in the end – I mean I'm normal now so it's easier to act it. It was Hannah who came up and said 'You coming to Jimmy Jazz?' and we all went just like that. Maybe they can see that I'm different and just like them now. Whatever, it's worked. I have my friends back.

I wish Hannah and Charley had been at the beach with me. It would have been a real blast having them around. We could have giggled at the guys flexing their pecs and the girls trying to act like they didn't care. There was one guy who looked a bit like Chico, kind of moody in a good way. He *kept his shades on all the time and was just staring into space. His friends were laughing and kidding around, but this guy was really cool. It made him seem ten times older than the others – like he was more sophisticated. I wonder what he was thinking about. Probably nothing! He could have been cool and then again he could have been really dumb. It's sometimes hard to tell.*

Chico is not dumb – not at all. He's really smart, but in a good way. Like he doesn't show it off – he just knows things and talks about them. When we went for that soda and he talked about his grandpa some more, that was so interesting – all the stuff about what his grandpa teaches him and what he did when he was young. Turns out his grandpa was a boxer, but he doesn't believe in violence. He says it's not the way to work things out. That's why Chico tries never to use his fists.

It was so great sitting there talking to him but then we both had to go. Ma was due home and Chico had to go help his grandma cook. Now, how cool is that – a guy who likes cooking! He said he'd make me something some day. I don't know if that was an invitation or not. And then I told him I can't cook and he said he'd teach me. Double, double cool – Chico giving me cooking lessons!! But then we both had to rush, seeing as we spent so long saying goodbye and now I'm not sure if he meant any of it. I hope so, I really do.

CHAPTER 15

'Class, I have an announcement,' said Ms Martin. 'This year, for the first time, we are entering the Future Thinkers Essay Contest. This year's title is: No Place Like Home. The best entry goes through to the state round. You have plenty of time to think about it as the closing date for entries is not until September which means, I'm sure, you will put in plenty of work over the summer break.'

Ms Martin stared especially hard at Eddie as she said this, whose response was to sneer and ostentatiously pick his nose. Kumari's ears pricked. She had never entered a competition. She immediately began to Think. She was still Thinking as they spilled out of school.

'See you guys later,' she said to Hannah and Charley.

'You not coming to Jimmy Jazz?' asked Hannah.

'Not today. Got to Think.'

'You've got to think?' echoed Charley. 'You can't think and shop at same time?'

Jimmy Jazz was just their favourite place to go and try on stuff after school. They hardly ever bought anything but the sales assistants didn't seem to mind.

'I've got a *lot* of Thinking to do,' said Kumari with a grin. 'You should try it some time.'

'Fun*ny*. OK, see you later, you weirdo.'

'Less of the weirdo stuff,' retorted Kumari.

'OK, see you later Ms *Normal*.'

They tripped away down the road, waving and giggling. Normal. That was nice. She wished for a moment she had gone with them. No, this was important. For some reason, she really, really wanted to do well in the essay contest. She would have to come up with something extra special if she was to stand any chance. Today was a Thursday which meant CeeCee and LeeLee were at chess club. The perfect opportunity to Think, although it meant walking alone.

Walking alone was not so good. It was too warm for beanies now so she was more conspicuous. A baseball cap didn't work as well as she couldn't tuck her hair into it. But it was such a glorious day, too nice to be cooped up in the apartment. Maybe she'd stop off on the way home. Do some Thinking in her park. The park was the perfect place for Thinking, seeing as it required lots of concentration. She had never really believed the RHM when he said that but it turned out it was true.

No one else came to the park, probably because it was not really a park at all but more like a tiny patch of wasteland where some kind of building had once stood. Now, weeds poked up through bits of old wall and wound their way over burnt-out timbers. Kumari rather liked the weeds. At least they proved that something green could grow.

OK, so it was not Central Park. Or even the Bronx Zoo. They both had lots of green, but Central Park meant a subway ride. There were other parks closer by but in them she always felt like the city was still on top of her. As for the Zoo, she couldn't go back after the Badmash incident with the cute female cockatiel. Although that wasn't exactly Badmash's fault. How was he to know he wasn't supposed to let her out? Vultures had feelings too. Boy, Thinking was hard. All these other thoughts kept rushing in. Come on, Kumari, concentrate.

No Place Like Home.

And there wasn't really, was there? Every day she tried to kid herself. Trying to find things she liked about the World Beyond when in truth things here were getting worse. And all the while her heart was somewhere else, somewhere she would never see again.

'Enough, Kumari,' she whispered fiercely. *No more tears. Remember what Mamma said.*

'I miss you,' she cried aloud although there was no one around to hear. The constant hum of traffic blurred out most

172

sounds. This was an oasis in a concrete jungle. A jungle that was nothing like the frangipani fields back home. Back in the hidden kingdom . . .

Simon Razzle smiled in jubilation. Finally, he had spotted her. The girl was a mere fifty metres away in that patch of scrubby wasteland. Pulling in, he parked. Finding the kid had proved a challenge. He couldn't risk hiring a private detective. With what he planned to do, the stakes were just too high. The simplest thing had seemed to be to go and look for her, drive round and round the neighbourhood. After all, he had a rough idea thanks to the newspaper clippings helpfully sent by the broker.

Only now that same broker was proving troublesome, refusing to take no for an answer. Business was business. They still wanted their cut. There had been only one thing to do and that was to get his hands on the girl first. Otherwise, they could demand any price if Kumari fell into their clutches. So far they had failed but he had not been able not risk it any longer. And now he had found her, he had to act fast.

'Aark! Aarrk!'
'Badmash! You made me jump.'
'Aaaaark, aaaaaaaaaaark!'
'Badmash, what's the matter?'
From nowhere, they appeared. The kidnappers. Oh my god, they were out.
'Hey, goddess,' sneered the first. She recognised him, the one that she had kicked.

'Time to go,' said the second. It was his buddy from behind the car.

'Stay away from me!' yelled Kumari. 'Touch me and I'll turn you all to stone.'

'Go ahead,' said the first. 'Show us what you can do, *goddess*.'

Clearly he had never forgiven her for the kick. There was a nasty glint in his eyes now. Kumari's fingers felt for her amulet. *Mamma. If only you could hear me.*

'I'm waiting,' he said. 'Come on, baby. Petrify me.'

His cronies sniggered and moved towards her, closing in. Kumari stared at them, helpless. Renouncing her Powers had been a big mistake. But there was no going back now. Maybe she could bluff it out. Convince them she was still dangerous.

'This is your last warning,' she said. 'Come any closer and you're concrete.'

Above her head, Badmash kept up his din, frantically flapping and cawing.

'Shut your bird up!' snapped Kidnapper No 1.

'Make me,' said Kumari. Inside her guts felt like chewed gum, but there was no way she'd let them see that. Dropping into a Karali stance, she kicked out with her leg. Satisfyingly, it contacted, right on the bone again. The crack sounded like a whiplash. Pain contorted the man's face.

Infuriated, the kidnapper lunged for her.

'Let's go now, girlie.'

'She's not going anywhere,' came a shout. Kumari whipped her head round. Chico! Behind him, the entire baseball team on their way back from practice.

Wow, it was like her amulet had actually worked. If only.

'These guys bothering you?' demanded Chico.

'Oh, yes!' said Kumari.

'Leave her alone,' snarled Chico to the main man.

'Get lost, kid,' the kidnapper snapped back.

With that, they piled in, bats flying everywhere. The fight was short but bloody. Finally, the kidnappers beat a retreat, heavily outnumbered.

'We're not through with you!' yelled Kidnapper No 1. 'We're coming back for you, *goddess.*'

His bedraggled band did not look so brave as they were chased away. Still, Kumari shivered as they disappeared from sight. Those men had brought her here, to the World Beyond. They had stolen her from her home, from Happiness. And for what? Why? She was still none the wiser. Even as Kumari wracked her brains, she was distracted by a shout.

'Chico, man, are you OK?'

Two of his team mates tried to grab him. Too late, he swayed and slumped to the ground.

'Chico! Oh no . . . '

Kumari fell to her knees beside him.

His face was pale, the bruises already beginning to form. Kumari bent forward. He was muttering something. And then his eyes flicked open and he stared into hers.

'That guy, he called you *goddess.*'

'Don't try to talk,' Kumari said. 'Has somebody called an ambulance?'

She felt doubly bad as she gazed at his damaged face.

Chico hated to fight.

In the distance, sirens could be heard, getting closer and closer. Suddenly, there was a squeal of brakes, then someone shouting, 'Stay where you are.'

A couple of the team members appeared, panting, from the street.

'It's the cops.'

'They got those guys.'

'Hang on, Chico man, here's the ambulance.'

None of them noticed the fancy car parked a short distance away or the man crouched low in the driver's seat.

Simon Razzle watched the commotion in his rear mirror, grim-faced. So, he hadn't managed to snatch the girl. At least the competition was out of the way for now. But it meant more watching and waiting thanks to those fools. His one sighting of his prey and those idiots had spoiled everything. It had been a lucky break to spot her at all, wandering into that wasteland. And then *they* had appeared, the broker's hired hands. If it wasn't for those hoodlums, he'd have her by now.

Simon was sick of waiting. All these months, prepping for this moment. Researching, practising techniques. Refining his methods. He could not afford to get it wrong and kill off the golden goose and so he had taken his time, making sure everything would work. His client's deposit had held the goons at bay but now he needed to make his big bucks. And before his very eyes the opportunity had slid from his grasp.

Still, the appearance of the boys carrying baseball bats had been an unexpected bonus. The girl remained free for the taking. The competition was foiled for the moment. And he'd managed to identify the girl's exact habitat, although no doubt she'd now be on the alert. Things were getting complicated. It was time to get someone else to do his dirty work. Preferably someone the girl trusted. That way he could avoid any messy business. The cops appearing again, for instance. After all, he had a reputation to protect, unlike those hoods. As the cuffs were snapped on to their wrists, Simon gave thanks for serendipity. There was more than one way to skin a cat.

Or, in this case, a goddess.

CHAPTER 16

Sonny Hernandez read the card twice.
Know where she is? Call this number. Reward offered.

Above the card, the picture from the *Daily News*, the one that went with the *Manhattan Mystery Girl* story.

He had seen several cards like this one all over the 'hood. Seemed like someone was very interested in Kumari. And where there was interest there was bound to be profit. Sonny considered himself a natural-born businessman. Dialling the number, he hummed a few beats to himself. He also liked to think of himself as a musician. His Ma, she never took his talents seriously. Well, he'd show her that he wasn't some two-bit street punk.

'Hello?' The voice was expensive, Sonny could tell that at once.

'I'm callin' 'bout your card in the phone booth.'

'Oh, yes?'

Sonny smiled. The guy couldn't keep the excitement out of his voice. This had to be worth one hell of a pay day.

'Do you know where she is?' the man asked.

'I do, for a price,' answered Sonny.

'Can you bring her to me? Even if she's . . . reluctant?'

'You come meet me first so we can, like, negotiate.'

'Meet you where?'

'The Bronx. That's where I hang out.'

The man hesitated.

'No, that would not be suitable. You call me when you have her. Bring her to the place I specify. For that I will pay you $5,000.'

Five thousand bucks? This guy wanted her bad.

'I'll do it for $10,000,' said Sonny.

'$8,000,' said the man.

'Eight thousand five hundred, it's a deal. Hey, man, what's your name?'

'You don't need to know that right now.'

'OK, OK,' said Sonny. For that money he could call himself Mickey Mouse for all Sonny cared.

'There's just a couple of conditions,' said the man. 'You must deliver her alive and unblemished.'

'Unblemished?'

'Unmarked. In perfect condition.'

179

Jeez, now the guy was talking like Kumari was a sofa or something.

'No problem,' said Sonny. 'I'll call you.'

The money was practically his.

A whole lifestyle away in Manhattan, Simon Razzle smiled as he snapped his phone shut. His inner cash register went *kerching*! At last, things were coming together. The girl would soon be his to sell. And this time he could name his price. Having cut out the broker, he stood to gain even more.

His contact was out of a customer. Simon had a better prospect lined up. Two bangs for his buck. Double the profit margin.

From her 33rd floor hotel room, she could practically touch the Manhattan skyline, a million lights glittering under a blood-red moon, the Empire State Building the proudest symbol of them all. She was not, however, interested in pretty lights. She was staring at the screen in front of her on which a message had just popped up.

Reading through it, the Ayah clenched her fist then slowly relaxed her fingers. One more dead end. She would find Kumari somehow. She had to, before the RHM did. It was time to turn up the heat. Tonight she had to catch a plane back to the borderlands of the Kingdom. There would be no more excuses or second chances. This time they would get it right.

Picking up the phone, she rapped out orders, her newly streaked hair bobbing as she spoke.

180

'This is your last chance to find the girl. You have twenty-four hours. Or else.'

Slamming down the phone, she stared blankly out the window.

The lights twinkled ever brighter.

But she did not see a single one.

CHAPTER 17

Chico was off school for three days. Three days in which to make a decision. She could not risk anyone else suffering. It was time to cut loose. People around her got hurt. First Mamma, then Papa brought to his knees. Ma arrested by those people. Now Chico, battered in her defence. And she was the one common factor. Which meant she must somehow be causing all this pain. She was bad news, rotten karma. The curse of Kumari. Who knew where it would strike next?

From now on, it would just be her and Badmash. Same as the good old days, except they were not actually all that good. As soon as she made up her mind, she put it into practice. It was so hard, that first time, walking right past her friends to another table in the cafeteria.

'Hey, Kumari, I saved you a place.'

'No thanks, I'll sit here.'

'Kumari? It's me, Charley.'

'Nothing personal, you guys, but just leave me alone.'

She could see the hurt on their faces, the looks of bewilderment. Her guts wrenched, but she stayed firm. It was better that way. At home, she didn't say much, just the basics like 'yes' and 'thank you'. In the evenings, she went to her room to read instead of sitting together watching TV.

'What's up with you, Kumari?' Ma asked.

'Nothing,' said Kumari.

'You want something to eat?'

'No, thank you. I'm fine.'

'Teenage stuff,' she heard Ma whisper to CeeCee and LeeLee. 'Best leave her alone.'

Fine, if that was what they wanted to think. She was doing this for their own good. It was easier to be alone than feel guilty. Safer to keep her head down in class and avoid Ms Martin's eye. Besides, it was easy to tune out of class when all she could think about was Chico, wondering how he was, hoping he was OK. For all of that, when the time came she would have to cut loose from him too. Still, when Chico finally reappeared, swathed in bandages, it took all her resolve to ignore him. But Kumari was nothing if not strong. She had to be, for all their sakes. She was Trouble with a capital T. Everyone stay away.

Once she began to skip class, it became easier and easier. But forged sick notes only did it for so long. Simplest to stay away, period. She hit on a new trick: double back once CeeCee and LeeLee had dropped her off. Duck out the school gates, take a roundabout route in case the kidnappers showed up. Once safe in the apartment, she would turn on the TV, settle Badmash in her lap and feed him his favourite snacks. If she could not hang with her real friends at least the old gang were still there. She reacquainted herself with *Jerry Springer*, caught up with *Scooby-Doo*, shouted out the answers to game shows and sighed over the soaps. There was a whole lot you could learn from TV. In some ways, it was better than school. Just who was she trying to kid? She missed school, missed her friends.

She had never thought she would say it, but Rita Moreno was not so bad. With Ms LaMotta in charge, things were getting better all the time. And then there was the essay competition. She had really, really wanted to win it. No chance of doing that now. How long before she got expelled? Or worse, Child Protection came knocking? Whichever way she worked it, someone got in trouble. Maybe she should just disappear. Do everyone a favour.

And then, on the sixth day of cutting school, she came home to find she was not alone. Ma was waiting in the hall, arms folded, a stern look on her face. It stopped Kumari in her tracks. Ma never looked like that. Even yelling and hollering she never looked so *serious*.

'What you think you're doin' child?'

'I, uh, I forgot something.'

'You *forgot* something?' Ma raised an eyebrow. 'What you forgot is your mind.'

Dumbstruck, Kumari stared at Ma. Someone must have told her.

'Well, come on then, speak, Kumari. Cat got your tongue or somethin'? Ms Martin tells me you not been in class all week. Got somethin' better to do, I expect.'

'I . . . ah . . .'

'Go on, spit it out. You tell me what's so important. Must be somethin' *really* special to keep you here instead of school.'

'I can't go to school,' Kumari whispered.

'Say what? Come on, speak up.'

'I can't go to school, Ma. People keep getting hurt.'

Ma raised both eyebrows.

'Is someone picking on you Kumari? Because if they are, you just tell me.'

'No. The other way round. People keep getting hurt around me. I mean, I'm the common factor. First Mamma. Then Papa. You getting arrested. Now Chico. It's like Ms Martin says. I'm the *constant*.' Kumari's voice cracked, her eyes filled. 'I'm scared they'll hurt someone else. I mean, all this can't be a *coincidence*. I knew whoever killed Mamma would try to get me. But it's like everyone else is getting hurt along the way.'

'*Who's* going to hurt someone else?' Ma's eyes brimmed with concern.

'I . . . I . . .'

It was too much. Ma could be, probably would be next.

185

She had been so kind and that was the problem. She was in danger just because she cared. There was only one thing Kumari could do and that was put distance between them. Whipping round, she slid the latch and was off, running down the stairs. Echoing round the stairwell, Ma's voice calling after her, pleading.

'Kumari, come back. Kumari! Let me help.'

'You can't help,' muttered Kumari. 'No one can. I'm bad luck.'

The Badmash Bag swung from her shoulder as she jogged. Suddenly she heard a retching noise.

'Oh, Badmash, I'm sorry' said Kumari, stopping to lift him out. 'See, I can't even look after you. Did I make you feel sick?'

She cuddled him for a second against her chest. Boy, he was getting heavy.

'How's your bird?'

It was Sonny, appearing out of nowhere, a stupid grin plastered to his face. He leant over and tried to pat Badmash.

'Ow!'

Sonny snatched his hand back. For a second there, she saw his fist clench. And then he unfurled his fingers.

'Who's a naughty bird, then?'

'*Who's a naughty bird, then?*' *Had Sonny morphed into a boy scout?*

'What do you want?' asked Kumari.

'Now, that's not very friendly, is it?'

The hurt in his eyes appeared genuine, but Kumari knew better. Sonny Hernandez was about as genuine as a fake fingernail and not nearly so convincing.

186

'I gotta be going,' she said.

'I'll tag along with you.'

'You don't even know where I'm headed.'

'Doesn't matter. I need the company.'

Kumari kept walking. Sonny kept pace beside her. She stopped outside the corner store. Sonny stopped too.

'I need a Coke,' she muttered. What was with this super-friendly *schtick*? Any moment now he'd be offering to carry her bag or help her across the road.

'Can I carry your bag?' asked Sonny. 'Must be kind of heavy.'

'I can manage,' said Kumari. 'Haven't you got something better to do?'

'What could be better than this?' said Sonny.

Oh barf! Still, super-smooth for him. Which was not saying much. Sonny was hardly Mr Slick.

'Whatever,' said Kumari.

Inside the store, she grabbed herself a can of Coke.

'Coke. Good idea,' said Sonny.

My, he had upped the interesting stakes.

'OK, well I'll see you,' said Kumari, clutching at the Badmash Bag as it slid awkwardly from her shoulder.

'Here, let me help,' said Sonny. 'I'll hold your Coke.'

'Uh, thanks,' said Kumari. 'Come on, Badmash, settle down.' For some reason he was really agitated, making the bag swing around.

Grabbing her Coke back, she took a gulp, anticipating the hit to her brain. When it didn't happen, she took another. Weird, her mind felt all fuzzy. Usually it felt . . . sharp. Now it was kind of woozy . . .

187

And with that, Kumari slumped into Sonny's arms, her Coke spilling across the sidewalk.

Half-dragging, half-carrying, her, Sonny tried to hail a cab – no easy task in a neighbourhood where cabs were as rare as a white dude with rhythm. Finally, he stopped one by the simple trick of throwing himself in front of it.

'Park Avenue,' he snapped at the driver, dumping Kumari on the back seat. He hauled the Badmash Bag from her shoulder and hurled it into the gutter. Badmash shot from the bag into the air, wings flapping furiously. Ignoring his angry squawks, Sonny slammed the cab door.

'She drunk?' demanded the driver.

'Just drive,' snarled Sonny. The stuff he had slipped into her Coke should keep her quiet, but for how long he could not be sure.

As they drew up outside Simon Razzle's address, Kumari began to stir. Dragging her from the cab, Sonny got her into the building fast. Hand her over, get the money. Then she was Razzle's problem. A couple of other people were in the elevator. A well-dressed woman threw Sonny a look.

'My friend's got bird flu,' said Sonny.

Instantly, the woman shrank into the corner. Sonny sniggered to himself. Bird flu. Pretty funny, considering what he'd just done to Badmash. Bird flu. Bird flew. He should have been a poet. Sonny was still sniggering as he staggered into reception, Kumari hanging from his arms, apparently dead to the world.

Depositing her on a leather sofa, Sonny strutted up to the receptionist.

'Tell Mr Razzle Sonny's here.'

The woman looked at him in distaste.

The other clients in the waiting room barely glanced up from their glossy magazines. Either this was an everyday occurrence or they just did not care. Suddenly, Simon shot from his surgery.

'What are you doing, you imbecile?' he hissed. 'You're far too early.'

'Hey, man, don't call me that,' said Sonny, trying to work out what imbecile meant.

'Just bring her in here. Quickly,' snapped Simon, casting an anxious look at his clients.

'Won't be long, ladies,' he cooed.

They smiled back, thinly. Everything about Simon's clients was thin, except for their plumped-up lips post procedure.

'Through here,' said Simon, as Sonny lugged Kumari into the surgery. He was holding another door open, one that led to a smaller ante-room. In it, Sonny could see a bed, instruments laid out beside it. The place looked like something out of *ER*, right down to the rubber gloves.

'What you gonna do to her?' Sonny asked, dumping Kumari on the bed as indicated.

'Never you mind,' said Simon, handing Sonny a wad of notes. 'Here's your money,' he added. 'Now beat it. I don't want to see your face again.'

'You're the boss,' said Sonny. 'Nice doin' business with you.'

Hustling him out the door, Simon breathed a sigh of relief.

'Whaaaa . . . ?'

From the other room he heard the girl. Instantly, he was by her side, needle poised. As he plunged it into a vein, she did not so much as wince. The sedative Sonny had slipped her had done its work. For now, it was best to keep her nice and quiet. At least until his client was ready. Wouldn't want to damage that lovely face. It represented pure profit. As Simon stared down at her, he felt a flicker of something. Not remorse, not even regret. But the sweet tingle of big bucks.

Groggily, Kumari tried to focus. The ceiling kept swimming away from her, rippling round in a wobbly whirlpool, dipping and diving like she was on a boat. She had only been on a boat once, on the lake near the summer palace. Papa had rocked it side to side to make her laugh. She generally laughed when she was scared. Mamma had stayed on the shore. Come to think of it, maybe she was still on the boat. Kumari tried to turn her head to see Mamma, but somehow it would not move.

'Ma . . . ' she tried to say, but her lips could not form the word. Everything was swaying so much she could hardly think. Wait a second, this was no boat. She remembered now, she was in the World Beyond. It was Sonny who had brought her here. There was that other man, the guy in glasses. The one with the smooth, shiny face.

The same face that was bending over her now, staring into her eyes, freaking her out. She had to push him away, get out of here. Why would nothing move? Her limbs felt so heavy, her body would not obey her brain.

He was murmuring something. She stared up at him, stricken.

'Where are you?' he muttered. 'Heart? Lungs? Brain? In the blood?'

The guy was crazy, that much was obvious. He was looking at her like she was a lump of meat he was about cut up.

'I'll find you,' he said. 'If I have to extract every organ.'

Oh my god, she'd been right – this was a human abattoir.

She tried to scream but of course it was useless. She was paralysed, helpless. Then she felt a sharp prick in her arm, followed by a dull ache. He was holding up a syringe. In it, her blood, ruby red.

'You're in there somewhere,' he said, gazing at it. 'The secret of eternal youth.'

The guy was practically salivating. *You've got it wrong!* she wanted to yell out. *I am no longer a goddess. I will age just like you. I am mortal now.* But instead she lay there, aware but immobilised. Another jab to her arm and she drifted back down into sleep.

Some time later, it felt like she was swimming from the bottom of a lake, up to the surface. Was this day or was this night? Was she alive or dead? How long had she lain here, alone in this white, white room? Who was the man who kept terrorising her with his needles? Then, all at once he was back again, bending over her. Beside his, a woman's face. She looked weird, her features somehow stretched. They were leaning so close that she could feel their breath. The woman's eyes were unlined, but so very, very old.

'She's perfect,' said the woman.

'I told you,' said the man.

And then, to her horror, the woman stroked her cheek with one wizened hand.

'This is the face I want,' said the woman.

'It's yours. For the right price. There's a small matter of paying the balance on your deposit.'

The woman smiled. Her tombstone-like teeth stuck out of ageing gums.

'Simon, darling, I'll pay whatever it takes. But I want this face and soon.'

'Patience, darling. I have to make sure the donor tissue is absolutely ready. Rejection is a possibility with any transplant. She needs to be primed and prepped.'

They were talking about her face as if it were on sale. But this was *insane*. You couldn't buy a face like a pair of shoes. What on earth was happening? She could feel Simon's fingertips now, tracing her jaw line.

'I'll cut here and here,' he said. 'There'll hardly be any scarring. Face transplants take very well, as long as you keep up the drug regime.'

Cut here and here? Transplant? He meant it. He actually meant he was going to cut off her face and sew it on to this old woman!

These people were freaks. She had to get out of here. *Come on, arm, move! Kick, legs, get going*. Nothing, not a twitch. She heard the groan come deep from within her chest. And then another painful jab and she was falling back.

Slipping under into sleep.

CHAPTER 18

Ma read the headline one more time. *Manhattan Mystery Girl Vanishes.* For once she was glad to see it in the news. Maybe this would help find her.

'Here, honey, take my handkerchief.' Mrs Brinkman was offering a scrap of lace.

'*Ay, amiga,*' Mrs Martinez sighed.

Lola simply held out a glass of brandy.

On the counter, Badmash perched, staring out the window. Ma had found him on the doorstep four days before. Without Kumari. He was so distraught she did not like to leave him alone. He had sat on the counter ever since. His feathers flat, his belly thin, Badmash was desolate. Refusing to eat or even sleep, he kept watch for his mistress. Ma's heart broke every time she looked at him, for herself and for Badmash. She went over and over the last time she saw Kumari in her mind. How she wished she'd run after her.

'I should have stopped her!' she would wail at intervals over the days that followed. The police said they were doing their best, but Ma did not have much faith.

'This is not like her,' she would insist. The officers' expressions spoke volumes. Seemed like the kid had had problems at school. No doubt they'd pick her up Downtown.

But as time went on, it became clear this was serious. Ma's one consolation was that Sonny could not have been involved. He'd been fishing upstate with a friend the day Kumari disappeared.

'You think this'll help?' gulped Ma, holding the paper up for the whole salon to see.

'Sure it will,' said Lola staunchly.

'*I* vouldn't be so sure,' said Mrs Brinkman.

Ma sighed. They were right, both of them. No one had any answers. All they could do was hope and wait. She'd tried everything else. Or maybe not *everything*. A germ of an idea lodged in Ma's mind. By the time seven o'clock came, it was a fully-fledged disease.

'Goodnight,' said Ma, shooing Lola out the door. 'You stay safe now, you hear?'

Lola grinned in her lopsided way and lurched off down the street.

Locking the door and pulling the blind, Ma reached into

her towel cupboard. There it was, at the back. Her precious hoodoo duster. She whirled it round her head.

'Come on, baby, let's rock!' crowed Ma.

Suddenly there came a tap at the door. Must be that darn Lola. She was always forgetting something. She'd forget her own head if it wasn't stuck to her.

'Lord save us, Lola,' said Ma, throwing open the door. 'What is it this time?'

Except it wasn't Lola that stood there but a young man. Cute face. Latino look. Kind of familiar, in fact.

'Yeeeeeees?' said Ma. Couldn't be too careful. Especially not in this neighbourhood, on your own after dark.

'Hi, I'm Chico,' said the young man. 'I'm a friend of Kumari's.'

'Ohhhh. *That* Chico. Well, come on in, honey.'

He looked tired, pale despite his olive skin. There were dark rings under his hazel eyes.

'You want somethin' to drink, Chico?'

'No, thank you, I'm fine.'

He stood there awkwardly, hands shoved in his pockets. He cleared his throat and Ma smiled encouragement.

'I was, ah, just wondering if there's been any news about Kumari?'

'No, honey, there ain't. Here, why don't you sit down?'

The faint hope on his face crushed, Ma thought he might crumble any minute. This was the boy Kumari had talked about and it was obvious he cared deeply for her.

'There must be something we can do,' he muttered. '*Something.* Anything. I've been looking everywhere, you

195

know. Anywhere she might be.'

'I know,' said Ma. His mouth was trembling. The boy was on the verge of tears. She so wanted to tell him it would be all right. For both their sakes she wanted to fix this. For Badmash, sitting still as stone on the counter. The boy's eyes followed her gaze.

'Oh Badmash,' he said softly. 'You poor thing. You miss her, don't you? I miss her too, man. I can't tell you how much.'

That was when Ma made up her mind. This was no time for pussyfooting. She had been about to start her hoodoo when the boy showed up. She would carry on, whatever he thought and perform the Vision Spell.

'There is something we could do,' said Ma. 'Or rather, that I could do.'

Hope lit up his face like a thousand birthday candles.

'What is it? I'll try anything.'

Ma flourished her duster. She would have to go carefully. Most folks thought this a little crazy, never mind some young dude.

'You know anything about magic?' she asked.

'You mean like conjuring?'

'Ha, conjuring's for kids. I mean real magic. Hoodoo.'

Chico shrugged his shoulders.

'Dunno. Guess I never thought about it. Except when Kumari . . . '

'Yeeeeeees?'

'Oh, nothing. Doesn't matter.'

Ma gave him a long look, but the boy kept his mouth shut.

'OK, Chico,' she said. 'You can help me out.'

Handing him the duster, she reached back into the towel cupboard. Pulling out a bunch of roots, a red flannel bag and a jar of powder she also passed them to Chico. From the wardrobe, she retrieved a purple robe, which she wriggled into with some difficulty.

'Suffering rattlesnakes,' said Ma. 'Stupid thing must have shrunk.'

When at last she was ready, she took the duster from Chico.

'Listen to what I say,' she said. 'And follow my instructions *exactly*.'

'OK,' said Chico.

The boy was cool. She liked that.

And now to business. Wishing with all her might, Ma lit a candle. Then, planting her feet wide apart, she raised both arms above her head.

'Come to me,' she called out. 'Show me where Kumari is.'

Whisking the duster round and round, she chanted it again and again. 'Show me, show me where she is . . . '

Whisk, whisk, whisk.

'The powder,' she commanded.

Hastily, Chico unscrewed the top of the jar. It had once contained face cream but now the jar was full of what looked like dust.

'Throw it over me,' said Ma, never dropping her duster rhythm. Whisk, whisk, whisk. Trying to conjure answers from the air.

'OK,' said Chico, chucking it full in her face.

197

'I said *over* me,' spluttered Ma. 'Not rat splat in my mouth!'

'S-sorry,' stuttered Chico.

'Never mind. Hand me the roots, boy, and the bag.'

Shoving the roots into the bag, she added seven beans from her pocket.

'Wishing beans,' she said, in answer to Chico's look. Then, holding the bag up high she rattled it hard.

'Come on, come on,' she muttered, dancing on the spot. 'Work, just this one time.'

Out of the corner of her eye she could see Chico, mouth open, staring. Letting out one last caterwaul, Ma sank to her knees, exhausted.

'Help me up, son,' she gasped. 'This is not going to work.'

'You can say that again,' said Chico, trying with all his might to haul her off her knees.

Slumped in her chair, Ma sagged in disappointment. *Nada mas.* Never again. She was a rootin', tootin' hoodoo hex-up. And then her gaze fell on something, a photograph of a small boy scowling. A picture of Sonny in the old days before he turned really bad.

'Sonny!' she snarled. 'This is Sonny's doing.'

'You saw that?' asked Chico.

'Nope. I didn't need to. That picture says it all. Sonny said he was away the day Kumari disappeared. Some cock-and-bull story about fishing upstate with a friend. That picture was taken the day Sonny's uncle took him fishing when he was eight. The kid hated it and has done ever since. How could I have been so blind?'

'How can you be absolutely sure he was involved?'

'He's got these brand new sneakers. Lots of bling. Which means he got money from somewhere. And when Sonny gets money it's never legit. Now I think about it, it all makes sense. Sonny is involved somehow. Someone might even have paid him to take her. After all, she was kidnapped once. Could be the same people behind this. Find Sonny, you find Kumari. It stands to reason.'

'Where's Sonny now?' demanded Chico.

'I don't know. But I'll track him down.'

'Let me,' begged Chico. 'He might tell me stuff he'd never tell you.'

What he said made sense.

'OK but you be careful,' said Ma. 'He hangs out round Fordham Road. Got a friend down there sells sunglasses. Sonny sometimes helps him out. They work a stand outside the kebab shop. If they ain't there it's 'cause the cops showed up. Those boys, they don't have no street licence. If he ain't there, I don't know where he is. Boy is a law unto himself.'

'Thank you, thank you,' said Chico, flinging his arms around Ma.

'Aw shutterbugs,' said Ma. 'I can see why Kumari's sweet on you.'

'She is?' said Chico. 'Well, thanks for that, too.'

Chico strolled down Fordham Road, scoping it out from behind his shades. Over there was the kebab shop. He could see a stand out front, two guys hawking stuff. Ambling over, he pretended to take a look. Fake designer sunglasses, logoed wallets.

'You got anything else?' he asked, dangling a pair. Neither of these guys looked like Sonny's photo. Then again, neither of these guys were eight years old. He tried to make out some resemblance to Ma but that too was tough. She had one unique look. Chico squinted at the pair again. Maybe the one on the left.

'Anythin' else?' said one with heavy emphasis.

'Yeah, like, you know, other stuff. I mean the real deal, man. The solid gold. You know what I'm saying?'

The pair behind the stand looked at one another. The one on the left moved to Chico's side.

'I can get you anythin' you want. You pay up front. No questions asked.'

'It's for an *acquaintance*,' said Chico. 'An associate of mine. Said I could rely on you to come up with the goods. Told me you'd do it for a price.'

The guy's eyes sharpened, narrowing at the scent of cash. *Bingo!* Thought Chico.

'Who told you this, man?'

'A mutual friend. He told me to come here, find Sonny.'

There it was again, that gleam. Looked like his gamble had paid off. It was obvious someone had hired Sonny to do whatever he did. Guys like Sonny were never the boss.

Taking another wild guess, Chico plunged on.

'My friend, he says you did good last time. With the girl. He'd be willing to pay the same for a similar job. Know what I'm talking about, brother?'

'Razzle said that? He thinks I did good? Well, you tell *Simon* the price, it just went up. It ain't so easy

200

snatchin' someone just like that. Who's he got in mind this time?'

'Oh just some chick, you know,' said Chico, heart beating fast.

'Yeah,' Sonny sniggered. 'Simon, he likes the chicks. Says he "appreciates their aesthetic".'

'Weird, huh?' said Chico. 'Wonder why he said that.'

'Well, he's some kind of cosmetic surgeon, ain't he?'

'Oh yeah, yeah, I know,' said Chico. 'What I mean is, "aesthetic", that's kind of a long word don't you think?'

'That's what you get when you hang out on Park Avenue.'

'Guess so,' said Chico. 'Look, I gotta split. Meeting Simon. You know, to talk business.'

'Sure,' said Sonny. 'You give him my regards.'

'Oh, I will,' said Chico. 'Big time.' *Sucker.*

Heading for the subway as fast as he could, Chico called Assistance for Razzle's number. His receptionist answered on the third ring, in a deeply shallow sing song tone.

'Simon Razzle, Surgeon to the Stars, Mindy speaking *may-ihelpyou*?'

'Yeah. Got a delivery for Mr Razzle. Just checking I got the address right.'

'431 Park Avenue.' Slam. The phone went down. Chico smiled despite her rudeness.

'Hang on, Kumari,' he muttered. 'I'm on my way.'

He could only hope he was not too late.

Someone was banging and crashing around. Or maybe she was dreaming. Painfully, she tried to open her eyes. The

201

white light scorched her pupils. There it was again, another bang. Then a shout, sounding very far away. Suddenly the sound exploded into the room. There was one almighty slam.

'Kumari!'

She knew that voice. *Now, where on earth had she heard it?*

'Kumari, it's me Chico,' it said.

Chico? Who was Chico?

'Kumari, look at me. What have they done to you, sweetheart?'

Sweetheart. Now that was nice. Woozily, she tried to smile in his direction.

'Come on, Kumari, we have to go.'

He was pulling her away from her pillow.

'No, no,' she protested. 'Got to sleep.'

She tried to snuggle back down. Suddenly her cheek was stinging, the blood racing to her skin. What a nerve. He had slapped her!

'Ow,' she cried, trying to hit him back.

'That's my girl,' said Chico.

Somewhere in the background she heard a groan.

'Ignore that. Come on, Kumari, we're outta here.'

He could not have said anything nicer. She tried to stand, swayed and fell. Instantly, he had caught her, sweeping her up in his arms. As they exited the ante-room, Chico stepped over something on the surgery floor. Through the mist that fogged her mind, Kumari saw it was the crazy guy with the needle.

'Don't worry about him,' said Chico. 'He's out for the count.'

As he carried her out the door, the world spun faster and faster.

'My hero,' she murmured.

And then she threw up, all over Chico's shirt.

It was the last thing she remembered.

And the first when she woke up.

KUMARI'S JOURNAL
(TOP SECRET. FOR MY EYES ONLY.
EVERYONE ELSE KEEP OUT!
THIS MEANS YOU!)

The World Beyond
June 20th - 163 days to go (got to drop this counting thing)

Ever since he rescued me Chico has been super nice. It's like he's forgotten all about me being weird and actually wants to be my friend. I just have to try to forget that I threw up all over him. I mean, how embarrassing is that?! But he's been really nice about it. Said that it was no wonder I was sick considering the stuff Razzle was pumping into me. Told me he'd have done the same (although I'm sure he wouldn't). Anyway, he saved my life. Simple as that. I will never, ever forget that and I told him so (urk!).

Even better, Hannah and Charley came round to see me and we ordered in pizza from Giovanni's. Giovanni's is just the best and Ma even let us eat it in my room. It was kind of tight – Hannah sat on my bed and Charley on the chest of drawers – but Ma said I wasn't to get up even to sit on the sofa. The doctor told her I had to rest and she's taking that very seriously.

Thing is, I feel fine. I mean, it's not like I've broken anything. I had this really big headache for a day or two that the doc said was from all the drugs. OK – I cry sometimes. Ma says that's to be expected. She says anyone who's gone through what I've gone through would feel all mixed up for a bit. But Hannah and Charley don't think I'm mixed up – at least, no more than normal. They even said they don't care about the freaky goddess stuff – they're just happy I'm OK. I did try to tell them about being mortal but they started to get those looks on their faces again so I dropped it. I guess it is confusing, one minute me saying I'm a goddess then I'm not. I'm confused, for heaven's sake, never mind Hannah and Charley!

Chico's been to see me a couple of times. He gets on really well with Ma. In fact, I saw her wink at him the other day. I wonder what that was all about. In fact, so much for resting – my room's more like Grand Central Station. Just after Hannah and Charley left, Ms Martin appeared. Ms Martin actually came to my house! It was weird seeing her out of school and she sat on my bed and everything. Actually, once we'd been talking for a bit I kind of forgot she's my teacher. She even brought me some candy and told me not to worry about it being unhealthy. And then she told me about this cool trick you can do where you drop mints into Coke and it shoots up really high. She said it was OK to tell me as it was of scientific interest. Somehow I don't think that will wash with Ma if I try it out in the kitchen.

Then, just before Ms Martin left, she gave me a notepad and a pen. She said I might like to start thinking about the essay competition – maybe make a few notes. When she said that, these big tears just fell out of my eyes. I mean, how embarrassing (again!). But Ms Martin was really cool and just said it was good to cry. In fact, she said she cries whenever she watches It's a Wonderful Life but not to tell anyone as it might blow her cover. I promised I wouldn't breathe a word although I'm not absolutely sure what she meant.

Anyway, here I am. I have the notepad beside me. But all I can think about is that crazy man's shiny face and the way he looked at me. It was like I was this specimen, like all I was to him was an experiment. And he went on and on about finding the secret of eternal youth. I wanted to shout out that he was wasting his time but my mouth felt like it was full of cotton wool. I can still see the bruises on my arm where he kept sticking in his needles. Boy did they hurt. Most of all, I remember that woman's voice. The woman who wanted to buy my face.

Sometimes I think it must have been a dream and then I look at the bruises and see it wasn't. The police also seem to think it was a dream – at least, they're not taking me seriously. OK, so they questioned Razzle, but that was three days after the event. No wonder they didn't find any evidence. Like Ma said, he got rid of it. As for Sonny – he's disappeared. Even Ma said 'good riddance'. And when I tried to tell them about the woman who wanted to buy my face they really started to look at me like I was a lunatic. That was when Ma got me out of there in case they tried to lock me up in some other institution.

Park Avenue's a world away from the Bronx, that's what Ma told me. Apparently it's a whole different ball game when you've got a fancy address and a medical certificate. So it looks like Razzle will get away with it and I'll just have to forget it ever happened. Except I can't forget. I see it every night when I close my eyes. That horrible little room with the white light and nothing else. The hard bed he kept me strapped to. The tubes sticking out of my arm. I'm not even sleeping and I'm having nightmares. This is far worse than when I dream of Mamma. At least then I wake up. One thing I do know, if I can survive that I can survive anything.

Ma says I should try to think of something else – keep my mind busy. I think that's why Ms Martin brought me the notepad and talked about the essay contest. I bet Ma called her up. Maybe it's not such a bad idea. I mean, I really wanted to enter it before. Before everything happened. 'No Place Like Home.' Good title. I like it. I was thinking about it after Ms Martin left. About home, I mean. I could really see it in my mind – like I was standing up on the mountain. I could see the palace down below and Papa's chimney and my window. Thinking about it now, I can almost smell the wood smoke on the wind. Almost but not quite.

CHAPTER 19

'And finally, Kumari.'

Ms Martin smiled encouragement. Kumari stood up and cleared her throat. The audience had sat through all the other entries until her turn. This was going to be tough.

'*No Place Like Home*,' she squeaked, then stopped. *Come on, take a deep breath, get going.* She caught sight of Chico in the audience, Ms LaMotta sitting up front. The entire school was crammed into the auditorium. She did not dare look for Charley and Hannah. They would only make her explode into nervous giggles. In fact, summer seemed to have been one long giggle, Charley and Hannah determined to keep her cheerful.

Along with Chico, they'd filled her days with so much fun that Razzle felt like a distant memory. But now summer was over. They had all fallen back into the rhythm of school. Most insistent of all, the approaching deadline of the essay competition. And at last the day was here. Kumari breathed in long and slow, just the way Ma had shown her. When she spoke again it was with more authority although her knees still shook.

'My home is a place far away, although I am not sure of the exact distance. You will not see it on any map and it does not have a name. We know it as our Kingdom and my father is its ruler. I was in training to be his successor but instead I ended up here, in the World Beyond. Although I wish for it more than anything, I do not know if I will ever return.'

Her voice broke over this last sentence. *Steady*, thought Kumari. *Keep reading nice and clear. You want this so much. You know this is important.*

'In my homeland, the most important thing of all is Maximum National Happiness. It is my father's job to stoke its fires and to send its sacred smoke over the entire kingdom. That smoke spreads the magic which keeps the kingdom content. Everything we think and do is judged in terms of Happiness. If something will not make the people Happy, then we consider it *bakwas*, which is not to be confused with *Badmash* which means "naughty", in our language.'

She looked up and smiled. Badmash was safe in his new bag under Ms Martin's seat. Little did Ms LaMotta know she was but a few feet from That Bird.

'Happiness to us,' continued Kumari, 'comes from inside,

from the heart. We believe that health, true wealth, love and expressing yourself are all you need to be truly Happy. The haze of Happiness my father sends out over the kingdom helps to maintain all of these, giving the people the confidence that they are cared about and taken seriously at all times.'

Momentarily, Kumari hesitated. Taking another deep breath, she plunged on.

'Here, in the World Beyond, things are very different. Happiness is not nurtured and so people have to look outside themselves for contentment. Here, people go to gyms and swallow pills and yet they cannot fight the curse of Time. In my country, no one wrinkles up, goes bald or has grey hair. They simply fade away gracefully when it is time to die.'

She looked straight at Chico. He dropped her a slow wink. A surge of confidence shot through Kumari. They were all listening intently.

'We have no radio, no news. No telephone, no TV. Yet, somehow we are happy. Maybe it is because, without these things, we are forced to listen to and trust ourselves. We are not slaves to gadgets. People from the World Beyond might consider my country primitive. It is true we do not have many of the things that make life here easy. We do not even have electricity. Instead, we have butter lamps. Although electricity is marvellous, there is something magical about a candle flame. Indeed, there is something magical about my kingdom as a whole. It is the special ingredient that keeps us young. More than that, it keeps us Happy. No one knows where it comes from or how the magic happens but it is my

209

father's sacred duty to maintain it by tending the holy fires.'

She glanced up from her paper. You could have heard a pin drop.

'I think the people in the World Beyond could learn a lot from my homeland. My people have peace and security – they are proud to be themselves. Each person has fulfilling work and every family looks out for one another. We have no wars and no poverty. We are self-sufficient and complete. We know that true wealth is not about gathering endless objects. It is about having enough for your needs and feeling grateful for what you have got. In the World Beyond, there is a constant scrabble to succeed. It is a race in which there are no winners. People have lost sight of what is important and yet everyone seeks more and more. Real success is not about what you have. It is not about who people think you are. Success is living the life that suits you best. It is being your truest self.'

Her throat was dry. She clutched the lectern. Not so much as a sigh from the assembled faces. She had expected cries of protest, maybe the odd 'boo'. But not this, a shimmering silence.

'I miss my homeland very much. I miss the beauty of the mountains. I miss seeing the stars at night and living by the cycles of the moon. I wish that people in the World Beyond could break free of Time's tyranny. I would love to share with you the magic of longevity and lasting youth. I would like everyone to know the freedom that comes from living in tune with nature's rhythm. Above all, I wish you could know what only we in my homeland can experience, the gift of

Maximum National Happiness.'

Another long pause. She looked across the rows of upturned faces. Taking a deep breath, she straightened her shoulders. She'd saved the best for last.

'In my time here I have learned that there truly is no place like home. Although I may never again see the Holy Mountain, I can picture it in my mind. I can still smell the sweetness of the air, see the sun light up the valleys. I feel the touch of my Mamma's hand, hear Papa call my name. I carry my home with me in my heart as I walk through this World Beyond. I know that although Time will claim me, my love for it will never die.'

She gulped, looked up from her papers and shuffled them nervously together. No reaction. Not even polite applause. They had obviously hated it.

And then they were clapping, one or two whistling and cheering. She saw Ms LaMotta wipe her eyes. Ms LaMotta, of all people. Shakily, she made her way back to her seat. They were urging her to turn round, to go back up on to the stage. The result had been announced

'The judges are unanimous,' said Ms Martin, trying to make herself heard above the din. 'We have a winner. Kumari.'

Oh my god, thought Kumari.

It would be hard to be happier than this.

KUMARI'S JOURNAL
(TOP SECRET. FOR MY EYES ONLY.
EVERYONE ELSE KEEP OUT!
THIS MEANS YOU!)

The World Beyond

October 5th – 56 days to go (why can't I break this habit?)

I still can't believe it. Me winning the essay contest. I've never won anything before in my life, although I suppose I've never actually entered any competitions. Anyway, I have the plaque so it must be real and they're going to engrave my name on it. Best of all, it's my essay that goes through to the state round. My essay. Unreal!!

Although it's going to be tough standing up in front of all those people. It was bad enough reading it aloud in front of everyone at Rita Moreno. Imagine what it's going to be like standing up at the Humanitarian Institute. That's where the final takes place, in this grand building Downtown. Hannah, Charley and I Googled it but we couldn't find out too much other than the Institute is run by some company called Humanity Inc. who are sponsoring the state contest. Its official title is the Future Thinkers Essay Contest. Hannah did her snorty laugh thing at that bit. I mean, me a Future Thinker! It is pretty funny.

Anyway, first prize is $1,000! That would really help Ma out. She'd be able to buy thing she's needed for ages or pay off some bills. Not that I'm going to win it. I mean, I'd like to win it, but that really would be surreal. There are bound to be hundreds of entries. Ma says she's so proud of me just winning this round she's fit to burst and even CeeCee and LeeLee got all excited. They never get excited about anything so it really must be a big deal. And you know what . . . I'm *proud* of me. I really feel like I've achieved something here. I did it all by myself and I won on my own merit.

It's not like they gave me the prize because I'm the girl-goddess. They gave it to me because I wrote the best essay. I mean, back home everyone is nice to me because they have to be. In the World Beyond they don't care who I am. Mostly, they don't even know. Anyway, what is there to know? I gave up being a goddess. In a weird way that disappoints Hannah and Charley – they keep asking me if I'm sure. Of course I'm sure. I'd know if I was still a goddess. And it's not so different – I couldn't do much when I was one. I hadn't got any of my Powers right. Those I could sort of do didn't work all the way. At least now I don't even try. It's less stressful being mortal! OK, it's not less stressful. It's just different. But I'm not different, I fit in. That's what I want, isn't it?

CHAPTER 20

'And this year's winner of the Future Thinkers Essay Contest, sponsored by Humanity Inc., is . . . Kumari . . . there's no surname here . . . oh, OK, just Kumari!'

The woman on the podium looked flustered. Someone pushed Kumari forward. Then she was walking on to the stage, beaming, blinking into the lights.

'Congratulations.'

A man was shaking her hand, half-turned towards her, his other, best side angled towards the cameras which were flashing away like crazy.

'Thank you.' She smiled up at him. The man's eyes disturbed

her. He was looking at her the same way Badmash gazed at a doughnut just before he tore it to bits. All of a sudden, the man reached out an arm and pulled her in to him, close.

'Turn for the cameras, sweetie.'

His arm was clamped around her shoulders, the flashes bouncing off his blinding white teeth.

'How's the campaign, Mr Raider?' a reporter shouted.

'It's going great.' The man grinned, his grip tightening on her collarbone.

At last he let her go. Instantly, she was forgotten. Mr Raider, whoever he was, was swept off to one side. Kumari was led off the other, still in a daze of disbelief. To have actually won the State Essay Contest. It was incredible. Just wait until she could tell Charley and Hannah. The squeals would be deafening.

'Kumari!' she turned. Ma was bustling up the backstage corridor. Behind her Ms Martin, both of them wreathed in smiles, and behind her CeeCee and LeeLee.

'I am so proud of you,' said Ma, enveloping her in a huge hug.

'We all are,' said Ms Martin. 'You've done this for the whole school.'

Kumari pressed the cheque into Ma's hand.

'$1,000! I can't accept this!'

'Of course you can,' said Kumari. 'Think of it as a late birthday present.'

Another camera flashed nearby. 'Hey, isn't that the Manhattan Mystery Girl?' said someone.

'Time to go,' said Ms Martin, making a most un-teacher-

215

like gesture at the *Daily News* reporter.

Kumari threw her a look of admiration. Ms Martin really rocked.

Jack Raider threw down the paper.

'I can't believe you screwed this up.'

He was gesturing at the headline: *Manhattan Mystery Girl Wins Essay Contest.*

His PR person looked scared, as well she might when faced with Jack in this state. Jack Raider hated to miss an opportunity, especially when it involved the mayoral race.

'I pay you to keep me in the papers,' he went on. 'To enhance my profile. Isn't that what your job entails? Or am I missing something here?'

The PR's mouth flapped in fish-like fashion. Jack ignored it and carried on.

'This kid is gold dust. How come no one knew she was the Manhattan Mystery Girl? She's young, ethnic, beautiful. Even her essay was perfect for us. She talks about happiness being the meaning of life. I mean, how much more on-message can she be? And I'm not even paying *her*!'

He looked significantly at the PR. Jack rated VFM alongside JFM. Value for Money. Jack for Mayor. He was an acronym kind of guy. It played well with the kids and if it played well with them it chimed with the moms. He was all for getting the mom vote. It had worked for Clinton, hadn't it? So this was just the mayoral race. One day mayor, next day president. He liked to drum it into his people at all times: one opportunity leads to another, leads to another (or OOLALA!).

'So how about we call up the kid?' he said kindly. Kindness generally made people feel worse. It was a little trick he purveyed at his self-help seminars, although he liked to think of them more as 'help yourself'. The self-improvement industry had certainly worked for Jack. Humanity Inc. reaped him millions. Luckily for him, none of his customers was aware of his less than scrupulous past.

'I'll get right on it, Mr Raider.'

'You do that,' said Jack, baring his dazzling teeth and giving his PR a little pat.

Kumari. He liked it. Even her name was perfect.

'You want me to go on TV? With you?'

Kumari could not believe her ears. Her fingers clenched around the telephone as she listened to Jack Raider talk.

'I'm sorry but I don't think I can do that. On *Oprah?* Oh, I see . . . Sure, I understand Mr Raider. Of course I think the world should be a better place. You liked my essay that much? Really? That's very kind of you to say . . . Uh, yeah, I think my school would like that very much. I mean, they could really do with some more money. You want me to what? Wear a badge? And a T-shirt? Um, I guess that wouldn't be a problem. You're going to call your campaign HUNK? "Happiness: the Ultimate New Knowledge." Ah, sure, I think that's snappy. Of course I know what an acronym is. You want me to help you bring Happiness to the planet? I don't really know what I can . . . well, yes, I know I wrote all about it. "On-message." What does that mean? Oh, I see, kind of like saying the right

217

stuff. Well, I guess it *is* for the good of mankind, as you say. Peoplekind. Ha ha. Very funny. Oh no, I absolutely support equality. You say you've spoken to Ma? And the car will pick me up and take me to the airport? Of course I'll be ready, Mr Raider. Just one thing, can I bring Badmash? Badmash. My pet vulture. He's very concerned about Happiness. I can bring my pet cockroach for all you care? Great, I'll see you there!'

She stared at the receiver still in her hand. UNBELIEV-ABLE. Totally BIZARRE. She was going to be on Oprah with some wannabe mayor guy.

Oprah.

Unreal.

KUMARI'S JOURNAL
(TOP SECRET. FOR MY EYES ONLY.
EVERYONE ELSE KEEP OUT!
THIS MEANS YOU!)

The World Beyond
October 29th – 32 days to go (stop counting, Kumari!)

Some days I wish I had never heard of Oprah. I mean, going on her show was a blast, although Badmash took the plane ride very badly. A machine that can fly better than him – not good for his self-esteem. Although I thought it was really cool,

218

seeing as it was the first time I'd been on a plane. Or at least the first time I remember being on a plane. I guess the kidnappers must have brought me here on one. At least, that was one of Ms Martin's theories once she actually decided I must come from somewhere so why not a nameless kingdom? Anyway, all her enquiries came to nothing so it's academic, as she'd say.

Anyway, I was so looking forward to seeing Ms Martin and my friends and telling them all about it. But ever since we got back, some people at school have been mean, especially Eddie. The day after the show aired I walked back in and I was really tired after the flight back and everything so I kind of kept my head down and didn't say much and some people took that to be attitude. It was like, oh suddenly she's all snobby because she's been on some TV show, and it wasn't that at all. I was just tired.

Hannah and Charley said to ignore them, that they were just jealous. Like Eddie is ever going to be on Oprah – in his dreams! And some of the other kids just came up and said, 'saw you on TV – you were cool'. The teachers were OK about it too but that was probably because I mentioned that I was at Rita Moreno Middle School. Ms LaMotta actually smiled and said, 'Well done' and Ms Martin winked at me. After that, though, she carried on as normal and boy was I grateful. I could already see Eddie working up a head of steam, flicking me the evil eye.

Anyway, Chico told me he thought I looked great on TV which made me feel a whole lot better. Then he asked me if I was going to the Halloween Ball and said he'd see me there.

He's going to see me there. Now, what does that mean? Does it mean I'm sort of going to the ball with him or does it mean just what it sounds like and he'll see me there? This boyspeak is very confusing and Hannah and Charley weren't much help either. They just said, 'So, he'll see you there,' and then burst out giggling.

Ma says I can stay out until 10pm but no later and then said CeeCee and LeeLee would come get me. I said I could get home on my own but she gave me that look. Since Oprah, Ma's been all excited, telling everyone at the salon how I'm now a Celebriteee – she says it like that with a great big smile on her face. Being a Celebriteee obviously isn't enough to let me stay out late, though. I mean, the ball finishes at 11pm so it would only be an extra hour.

Oh great – one more reason for Eddie and his gang to make fun of me. Eddie gets to stay out as late as he likes but that's because no one cares where he is. At least, that's what Ma said and she's probably right but I could do without any extra ammunition for him and his weasely friends. Maybe the ball's not such a good idea. I don't even have a costume. And if Chico really wanted me to go with him he'd have asked me exactly that. Then again, I really ought to go, seeing as Jack Raider's sponsoring it. Aargh – I don't know what to do. Why is life so complicated?

CHAPTER 21

Halloween, schmalloween. Kumari didn't want to go to the ball in any case. What was so great about wearing some supposedly scary costume? Totally ridiculous. She'd done her bit, secured sponsorship. Raider was only too happy to cough up the dough. Another opportunity for him to look good, supporting the underclass. Well, she was above all that. She would stay home, reading her book. Avoiding Eddie and the like.

Except that the more she thought about the Halloween Ball, the more it seemed like it would be a blast. And besides, Chico would be there. Not that she cared one way or another.

'Hey you,' she said to Badmash. 'How about we dress up, just the two of us, in scary costumes?'

Badmash looked straight through her, nodding his beak in time. He was busy listening to LeeLee's iPod. *Birdman*. Interesting.

'Great,' sighed Kumari, flopping back on her pillow. 'Even my bird has abandoned me.'

She flicked through the magazine she'd borrowed from Ma. So many glossy advertisements. Jack loved it when she came out with that stuff, about how *things* did not make you happy. But some things do, she thought. Does that make me a hypocrite? Really, it was all so confusing.

Whatever. At least her school got Raider's money and she got to spread her message. Maybe she really could bring more Happiness to the World Beyond. Now, that would be satisfying.

'Surprise!'

Kumari nearly jumped a foot. Bursting into her bedroom were Hannah and Charley, dressed up in their Halloween outfits. In their arms, carrier bags galore, behind them a beaming Ma brandishing a hot brush.

'We've brought your costume,' said Hannah.

'And your make-up,' said Charley.

'And I am going to style you up a storm,' added Ma.

Ohmygoodnessfabugosh. It was the girl posse. She must have died and gone to Halloween heaven.

'Arms up,' ordered Hannah, swapping Kumari's sweat-top for a silver number.

'Legs out!' demanded Charley, replacing Kumari's jeans with spider web fishnets.

As Ma worked away at her hair, the two of them applied her make-up, turning her into a gorgeous ghoul. She pouted, blinked and smiled to command, all the while basking in the warmth of their friendship. When they had finished, Hannah dragged her to the mirror.

'What do you think?' she said.

'I . . . ah . . . '

'What's the matter? Don't you like it?'

They were all looking at her now, concerned.

Kumari grinned. 'I love it!' Then she burst into tears.

'I knew it!' said Hannah. 'I said she'd hate it.'

'It's not that,' gulped Kumari. 'It's just that I can't believe you made me look so good.'

'How about the hair?' asked Ma, uncharacteristically anxious.

Kumari gazed at herself, at the soft tumble of waves that framed her face. She felt a surge of confidence, of strength. More herself than ever.

'The hair is *fatte*,' said Kumari. 'That's "awesome", to you guys!'

A huge grin lit up Ma's face. 'Time to move,' she said. 'Off you go, girls. Knock 'em dead. I'll babysit Badmash.'

One last look in the mirror. It was time to hit the party trail.

As Kumari shimmied past she heard Ma murmur, 'Well, you sure look like a goddess tonight.'

'You think so?' asked Kumari.

'I think so,' said Ma. 'Now you go shake your heavenly *fatte* booty.'

'You betcha,' said Kumari.

223

The gym was heaving with ghouls, some scarier than others. They caught sight of Eddie in his usual gear.

'Nice costume,' said Kumari.

'Looks like you lost your boyfriend,' he sneered.

He was jerking his head in the general direction of the dance floor. It was one undulating mass of bodies, most of them wearing masks. No way she would spot anyone there, never mind Chico. Not that she was looking, just generally checking things out.

'I don't know what you're talking about,' said Kumari.

It was hard to adopt a lofty tone when you were shouting. The music was so loud it sent shockwaves up her spine. Hips swaying, arms swinging, she began to dance with Hannah and Charley. Hair whipping round their faces they whirled into the centre of the crowd. It was hot, steamy, sweaty, lights flashing, the beat pulsating. They were holding hands, whizzing round faster and faster, heads back, laughing, dizzy. She let go and stumbled back into someone.

'Oops, sorry,' she said.

And then she saw him. Dancing up close to another girl. She'd know the back of his neck anywhere. He turned and she felt sick. They were practically glued together.

'Hey, there's Chico,' said Hannah.

'I know,' mumbled Kumari.

'Isn't that Maria he's dancing with?' added Charley.

Maria. If they'd had a Homecoming Queen at Rita Moreno she would have been it. Miss Cheerleader. Miss Great Legs. Miss Perfect. *Chico's Miss.*

224

Suddenly Kumari wanted to be anywhere else but here. She started to push her way through the crowd, off the dance floor.

'Excuse me, excuse me,' she muttered, not like anyone could hear.

Ahead, she spied a door. Great. An escape route. Stumbling through it, Kumari found herself out in the cold and dark. All at once, light sliced across her face. She was not alone any more.

'Hey Kumari.'

'Chico.'

'What are you doing out here in the cold?'

'I, uh, needed fresh air.'

'Come and dance.'

'No thanks.'

She could feel rather than see his confusion. It really was very dark out there.

'Shouldn't you be getting back?' she said. 'Maria will be wondering where you are.'

'MARIA?!' He grinned. 'Come on, I want to show you something.'

There was no resisting Chico, especially when he was dragging her by the hand. Wall to wall sound hit her as he pulled her through the door. Her eyes took a moment to adjust. When they did, she saw where Chico was pointing. There was Maria, locking lips with some other guy.

'Her boyfriend, Joe. My cousin,' said Chico. His breath tickled her ear, sending a butterfly fluttering down her spine.

His cousin. Right.

'Joe asked me to look after her until he could get here.'

Well, he'd certainly been doing that. Kumari gave him another long, assessing look.

'What's the matter? You don't believe me?'

All of a sudden, she had a flash. A certain knowledge that he was telling the truth. It was as if she could see right into his mind and heart and read what was there. It was all there, in Technicolour. Bizarre. But undeniable. Written large in black and white. *It's the truth. If she believes me, she'll take my hand again.*

'Actually, I do,' said Kumari, interlacing her fingers with his. Chico threw her a startled look, then smiled and squeezed her hand.

Now, what had that flash been all about? It had almost felt like Power No 2, the Power of Extraordinary Sight. Impossible, though. Her Powers were well and truly renounced. Must have been her instincts, then. Or maybe just desire.

'Now, do you want to dance?' said Chico.

'Uh, sure,' mumbled Kumari.

Kind of late to try to act cool. In any case, the heat was building, radiating between them with every move. Still they danced apart. It was as if they touched, they might combust. As she spun round she caught sight of Charley, upthisclose with some cute guy. And then she saw Hannah, dreamily smiling, her head against Daniel's chest.

'Let's go outside,' Kumari said, grabbing Chico's hand. The answering glint in his eye sent those butterflies into orbit all over again. *Ignore them*, she told herself. She had to talk to him and now.

226

'I need to tell you something,' she blurted, the minute they were out the door.

'I'm listening.'

Was it her imagination or was he breathing a little faster?

'That thing you heard the day you rescued me in the park. What you said before you passed out. It's all true. I am a living goddess. A trainee one. Or at least I was.'

'And?'

'And, well, that's it. Except I'm not one any more, so it's all OK. I'm like you, like everyone else. Normal. Well, almost. I know I scared you off because I acted kind of strange, but it's fine now. I fit in. No more goddess stuff.'

Now she was gabbling. Slow down. Gabbling is not cool. It's not even remotely sexy. SEXY? Ohmigosh. Where did that come from? He's looking at me like, I dunno, like something. Breathe, Kumari.

'Let me get this straight. You were a goddess but now you're not?'

'That's it!' She beamed. 'The tornado thing – that was me practising my Powers. And Simon Razzle, that was all about eternal youth. Goddesses get to live forever you see. Not that I will now that I have chosen to become mortal. But he doesn't know that. He thinks I'm still a goddess. I tried to tell him but he wouldn't listen. That's why he tried to cut me up.'

'Uh huh?' said Chico, a smile playing round his lips. Clearly he thought she was crazy.

'You see, I was kidnapped,' she went on. Might as well spit it all out. 'That's how I was brought here from my kingdom.

227

Those guys you beat off, they were my kidnappers. That stuff in my essay, that wasn't all of it. My father's not just a king, he's a living god. My mother, she's a living goddess too except right now she's kind of stuck.'

She stopped to draw breath. Was he getting any of this? By the expression on his face she had clearly just blown it. Then he was reaching out, pulling her to him. His lips met hers and the world stopped. So this was what it felt like. Melting. Electric. Like fireworks made liquid, white hot, spreading through her limbs. No clashing of noses. Somehow, it all just fitted.

'Hey,' he murmured. 'I don't care what you are or were. It's *you* I care about. Kumari. You know, that crazy girl who's funny and, yes, kind of strange. But I like that. I like that you're different.'

'You do?' she said. Now this was a revelation.

'You didn't scare me off, Kumari, I did that. I scared me. Like that day I just walked past you in the street? I didn't know what to say. It's because I liked you so much I couldn't act normal around you. You have this *strange* effect on me.'

'I do?' she asked. Whoops, she was beginning to sound like a parrot.

And then it didn't matter any more what she said because he was kissing her again and when he did that words were superfluous. She kissed him right back. It felt natural. It felt *right*.

Not strange at all. Just gloriously fantastic.

The World Beyond
October 31st – very late – 30 days to go

He kissed me. I can't believe it. He actually kissed me. Even better, I kissed him back and it was so easy. We didn't knock noses or clash teeth and I managed not to bite his tongue or slobber and it felt like, well, right, like we were meant to be doing it. In fact, it felt so good we carried on back inside. I didn't even care that everyone could see us. Actually, I forgot everybody else was there although that's not going to work in reverse. Knowing how things are at Moreno, I'll never hear the end of it.

When I looked up, Charley was grinning at me and then I saw Maria staring and I swear she actually turned green. Maybe she's not so into Joe after all – maybe it really is Chico she's after. In any case, I know Chico's not into her so that's OK. Tee hee. Although that was weird how that happened. Somehow I just knew.

Best of all, though, Chico doesn't think I'm strange. Well, he does but he doesn't care. He likes the fact I'm different. 'Stay exactly the way you are,' he said and then we kissed again. And again, quite a lot, before CeeCee and LeeLee appeared to drag me away. By then, I didn't even care that Eddie saw although it still sucked I was leaving early. But

*that was only because I could have gone on dancing and kiss-
ing Chico all night although, if I had, my lips might feel even
more tingly than they do now. And my chin is a little raw but
it was so worth it. So, so worth it.*

*Eugh – get a grip Kumari. You kissed a boy, so what? People
kiss every day. It doesn't mean anything. But, actually, it did –
mean something to me, I mean. Whoops – too many 'means' in
one sentence. Ms Martin would not be impressed. OK, what I
mean is – aaargh there I go again! What I want to say is that it
felt really good and kind of significant but ultimately I'm still
the same person.*

*I tried to say that to Hannah and Charley in the restroom
when we all took a break together – Hannah did her hand
flapping thing to signal we had to leave the dance floor and
meet up. Very subtle. Anyway, they pounced on me as soon as
I got in there and demanded to know everything. How I felt,
who kissed who first (or is that whom?) – every single detail.
And I said the bit about still being the same person and they
both burst out laughing and then gave me a hug. I still have
no idea why they laughed but it doesn't matter – they still
love me. They said as much when they finally stopped laughing. Friends! I couldn't be without them.*

CHAPTER 22

The butter lamps flickered, casting shadows across the picture. Instinctively, the king looked over his shoulder. There was no one there. Nothing but an empty throne room in a sleeping palace. He turned his attention back to the portrait.

'Help me,' he whispered. 'Give me a sign. I cannot bear to lose you both. I am so lonely.'

But the portrait stayed silent. It was, after all, just a picture. A picture in a kingdom immersed in sadness. It was partly the king's fault. He could barely bring himself to tend the fires, to create the haze of Happiness for himself and his people.

231

Instead, he spent hours in here, gazing at the image of his dead queen, thinking about the daughter he had lost, wondering where in the World Beyond she could be.

'What should I do?' he asked the portrait again. The queen looked back at him, enigmatic as ever. 'Should I send someone else?' he persisted. 'Someone other than the RHM?'

Silly question. The RHM was the best person for the task. It was so hard, though, to sit and wait. To be powerless for once.

'Perhaps I should go myself,' mused the king, instantly dismissing the very notion. If he went there would be no one to rule the people. Duty came above all else. Take one step into the World Beyond and he, too, would be lost. Sometimes it was hard to be in charge. Especially when you were ill and weak and had apparently lost all your Powers.

'A year and a day,' he murmured. The sweat prickled on his forehead.

A year and a day. And her time was nearly up. Kumari was out there, alone, at the mercy of the ticking clock.

'We have to find her,' he cried to the heavens. 'We have to find her,' he told the portrait.

And all the while his queen stared serenely from within the gilded frame, her features etched in fine brush strokes.

'You cannot talk,' said the king. 'How could you? I am a fool. A fool rattling around alone inside this palace. Perhaps the Ayah is right. I should take another queen. After all, you are never coming back, either of you. Should I do that? I don't know.'

The king let out a deep sigh. At least he had the Ayah to

232

comfort him. She had proved herself a tower of strength in between her trips to tend her sick aunt. Mercifully, she only ever went for a few days, insisting she did not want to leave him alone too long. Although when she reappeared this time she had done something rather strange to her hair. It had turned shades of yellow. How on earth could that have happened? Something to do with her aunt's illness? The mysteries of the feminine were imponderable. The king stared into space.

The butter lamps flickered again. He thought he saw something glisten. The king shuffled closer to the picture. There it was, without a doubt, a tear. A droplet forming in the corner of one eye, spilling, coursing down the canvas. The message that he'd hoped for all these long and lonesome months. Reaching out a hand, the king scooped it up and licked his trembling finger.

It tasted of salt, of blood, of love. It was a resounding 'no'.

'Thank you,' he sobbed. 'Oh thank you, thank you.'

At last, his queen had spoken. He must never give up hope.

Some day he would be reunited with them both. Until then, he would wait.

From her hiding place, the Ayah watched, teeth clenched in rage. Wretched portrait! How she had hated that woman. Her *sister*. She had had it all: king, country, child. Everything the Ayah secretly wanted for herself. And would still have, whatever it took. Kidnap, extortion. Double-dealing. Even murder. All right, so forget the child. King and country would suffice.

In his weakened state, the king was the perfect puppet for her plans. She had been careful to act as his confidante, to induce the sense of dependence she desired. Despite all her efforts, however, he still preferred to talk to the portrait of his dead queen. It was galling but no matter. She would get there in the end. She needed the king alive to ensure the docility of the people. Their loyalty to him remained absolute despite the absence of Maximum National Happiness. It would be far easier to take the country with the king under her thumb. Simpler to subdue a nation whose figurehead was almost helpless.

Slipping out the door, the Ayah headed for the hills. This time there was no RHM to follow her. She had known he was there, of course, but the man was easy to evade. Besides, he would never find his way through the labyrinth within the rock. And him thinking himself so clever. The stone maze could only be navigated by those who knew it was there. Otherwise, it appeared impenetrable, nothing more than a wall of granite. But the Ayah had played here since she was a tiny child, had explored it with her sister.

Her sister.

Curses on her. How she wished she had never been born. The green claws of jealousy had clutched the Ayah from the moment she set eyes on her sibling: beautiful, good. Perfect. Nothing like the Ayah in any way. And then her sister had gone on to marry the king and jealousy had turned to hatred. Then she had had the child to compound everything. The day Kumari had been born the Ayah again cursed the gods.

She could still remember her sister begging her to come to

the palace although it was strictly forbidden. Once elevated to royal status, all contact with immediate family was lost. Posing as a distant cousin had been the one way she could be smuggled in. Much as it rankled at the time, it had been too good a chance to miss.

For the Ayah had spotted her opportunity and had already begun to plan. The Kingdom was there for the taking, slumbering on as it had forever, its citizens stupefied by Happiness, the god-king a gentle ruler. Seize the reins and it would all be hers, along with all the wealth and glory. Then people would bow down to her, would tremble in her presence. Once she had suppressed them, of course. Shown them who was boss.

All she had to do was proceed with cunning; stealth, for now, was the best way forward. It had enabled her to remove her sister and then her child without anyone being able to point the finger. Once they had disappeared, the king was a sitting duck, victory almost a foregone conclusion. Prudently, however, the Ayah also preferred to take the long view. Which was why she had decided to use Kumari to raise funds for her ultimate mission. She would need money to pay the warlords, to get them to help her take the Kingdom and suppress it. Then she would be its absolute ruler with access to all the Kingdom's secrets and riches.

She would even force the king to use one of his Great Gifts and grant her eternal life. Despite this, she still needed the warlords; it was unlikely the palace would fall without a fight. Too many loyal supporters of the god-king and his family. Although she did not count the RHM amongst them.

The man had his own agenda. For that very reason she had never left the kingdom for too long, despite the urgent need to find Kumari.

To leave was to lay the way open for the RHM and he clearly felt the same way about her. Angrily, the Ayah pressed on, resentment fuelling her footsteps. Emerging from the rocks, she marched over to the trees, thrusting her way through until she reached the clearing and the old shepherd's hut. The door to the hut was never locked. There was no need; no one ever came near here. Inside, she powered up the generator and switched on her laptop.

Connection to the satellite was instant. She scrolled through her messages. Nothing. Furious, she slammed the laptop shut. What were those idiots playing at? They seemed to have dropped off the planet. There had been no communication from them for weeks now. Surely they could not have got themselves incarcerated again? Could they really be that stupid?

Time was running out, for her and for Kumari. Razzle would only pay up if he found the secret of eternal life. For that, Kumari had to be alive or freshly dead and her year and a day was nearly up. There was nothing for it; she would have to go herself, back once more to Manhattan. Spin the king that line again about her ailing aunt. In the meantime, she might as well do some work. The Ayah was nothing if not diligent.

It was how she had found Razzle, through relentless searching on the internet. Googling endlessly until she found the paper he had written on 'The Cosmetic Holy Grail:

Eternal Youth'. The minute she saw that, Kumari's fate was sealed. It was clear the man would pay anything for such a prize. And so it had proved, once she had initiated contact. All she had to do was deliver and the money was hers. With it, she could put her plans into action. Insurrection was expensive.

'*I can get the girl myself.*' Imagine! He would never have known about Kumari if it wasn't for her. Well, they would see who got there first. Simon Razzle was a surgeon, not a sleuth. After all, the girl had slipped through his fingers yet again.

Calmer now, the Ayah reopened her laptop. It paid to keep a cool head, to think down the line. After all, she'd been planning this for ever. Or at least since the day that child was born. The Ayah might not have been so favoured by the gods but she had made the most of what she'd got. Education, that was the key. Especially for the ugly sister, for the one who was not destined to marry a king. Knowledge had been her weapon and she had wielded it well.

Logging in to her online English course, the Ayah picked up the day's assignment. *Families*. What could be more appropriate?

'Mother, sister, brother . . . ' she recited.

'Uncle, aunt, niece . . . '

She stopped, choking on the words, snapping the laptop shut a final time. Forget this. Forget procrastination.

It was time for Plan B, for action.

KUMARI'S JOURNAL
(TOP SECRET. FOR MY EYES ONLY.
EVERYONE ELSE KEEP OUT!
THIS MEANS YOU!)

The World Beyond
November 21st – very, very late – 9 days to go
(stop it, Kumari, just stop it!)

I don't know what to write. I'm so confused I don't know where to start. It's 1am and I can't sleep. I just keep staring at Mamma's picture and thinking. Badmash looks so cute all tucked up, but when I look at him it makes me think even more. I mean, he's stuck here too, like me. We're all stuck, me, Mamma and Badmash, in one place or another.

It all started with this TV show on the Geography Channel. We had to watch the Geography Channel on account of CeeCee's project. She's doing a whole thing about some place called Borneo, where she says the people used to be headhunters. I found that rather hard to believe so I double checked with Ms Martin. Turns out, not only is it true but Ms Martin has actually lived there! She says it was when she served with the Peace Corps and helped set up a jungle school.

I mean, respect! It's kind of hard to imagine Ms Martin in the jungle, what with her A-line skirts and all, but she said she'd show me the photos of her with the Iban in their long-houses (that's the people who used to be the headhunters). She said in the old days the District Officer used to have to count the heads to make sure a new one hadn't appeared! Come to think of it, Ms Martin does wear skeleton earrings so maybe she's cool with bones. Whatever. I suppose she must be. She is a science teacher after all.

Anyway, CeeCee is doing her project about the same place so Ms Martin said she'd give her some information, but in the meantime to watch this show tonight on the Geography Channel which is what we were doing when suddenly these mountains appeared. Turns out it was the show before the one we were supposed to be watching and it was all about this mountain range and I swear I recognised the peak of one. I'm sure I saw it once, back home, in the distance.

I remember because it was when Mamma took me on a walk to show me where she had played as a kid and we climbed up these rocks and looked out towards the distant mountains. One had a peak just like a bird's beak and when I said that Mamma laughed and told me that's what she used to call it: Eagle Beak Mountain, although that was not its real name. And that got me thinking – I suppose there could be more than one mountain in the world shaped like that. Of course there must be. But it reminded me of home so much that it physically hurt.

I had that sudden flash of Mamma. It was like I could hear her voice all over again. 'Eagle Beak Mountain,' she said and then she laughed and took my hand. I had to leave the room I was so shaken up. I suddenly realised I had forgotten Mamma there for a bit. I suppose that's because I've learned to look after myself instead of expecting Mamma to do it. I've worked out things Mamma would have explained – things like why people are sometimes mean. Or how often they can

239

be really kind just when you don't expect it. Then all the stuff about friends and boys – Mamma would have really liked Chico, I'm sure. I know I've had help along the way, from Ma and Ms Martin and my friends. Those people weren't there before – it was just me, Badmash, Papa and Mamma. So how could I forget about her when she's still stuck in that awful limbo place? There must be something I can do to help. I mean, what am I doing here?

CHAPTER 23

'Ms Martin?'
      'Yes, Kumari.'
'I don't know what to do.'
'Read through the chapter and then answer the questions
at the end.'
'I don't mean my homework assignment, I mean my life.'
Ms Martin looked up from the papers she was supposed
to be marking although Kumari could see the crossword
half-concealed in the pile in case Ms LaMotta appeared. Ms
Martin hastily shuffled the papers together and gestured to
a chair.

'Sit down, Kumari,' she said. 'Why don't you tell me about it?'

Trouble was, she didn't know where to begin. There was the kiss; that changed everything. Or maybe it didn't. And then the fact she was friends again with Hannah and Charley. Plus the essay contest, HUNK and the benefit concert coming up. That was going to be amazing – Deranged were playing. Not to mention the improvements at Rita Moreno. OK, so she wasn't responsible for that, although Ms Martin said she partly was. Something about being an inspiration. But all things considered and despite all of the above she couldn't help but feel pretty miserable.

'Kumari?'

Ms Martin was waiting. Still she could not find the words. How do you explain what you don't understand? Especially when what you don't understand is yourself and everything is so mixed up.

'It's OK,' said Kumari. 'I'm sorry to bother you.'

'Wait. Come on, Kumari, sit back down. I can see there's something on your mind. Why don't you tell me what it is? Maybe we can solve the problem together.'

'I don't think so, Ms Martin. You see, I have to go home. I still need to find out who murdered Mamma. There's so much here for me now but it's just not enough. And the thing is, going home, it's impossible. That's my problem. I'm stuck here when I should be there and there's nothing I can do.'

'I see,' said Ms Martin. 'Is there anything else that's bothering you?'

How did she know? Sometimes Ms Martin was really smart.

'Um, yes, actually, there is. The Happiness thing, well, I'm not. Happy, I mean. And I feel such a fraud when I tell people about it. How can I preach Happiness when I'm miserable in my heart? How can I tell people what to do when I'm unhappy myself?'

Ms Martin thought for a moment. Then her eyes lit up.

'I've had an idea Kumari,' she said. 'Something that's just connected in my mind. There might be another way to locate your kingdom. A kind of indirect route. My father told me only last night of someone who is trialling a new technique, even more exciting than DNA-mapping. If it worked we could find out where in the world you come from. Or at least get very close. That would make you happy, wouldn't it? Then your problems might be solved.'

'You mean it? When can we start?'

'I'll call him right away. And Kumari, don't worry.'

'I won't,' Kumari lied.

The minute the man produced the needle it brought it all rushing back: Simon Razzle, endless injections. Terror and pain.

'Kumari, that's a pretty name,' he said.

'It means "goddess" in my country.' Kumari looked nervously at Ms Martin, who gave her a reassuring nod. Badmash puffed up his feathers and fixed the man with a beady look.

'My name's Theodore. But you can call me Theo. There we go, all done.'

Kumari looked at her arm. There was the tiniest mark which he proceeded to cover with an elastoplast. She saw the syringe laid in a dish.

'Is that my blood?'

'Certainly is. Hopefully this will tell me all I need to know. Well done, Kumari. You were very brave.'

At this, Badmash settled his ruffled tail feathers. He had obviously decided Theo was OK.

'You can relax now, buddy,' smiled Theo. 'I like your bird,' he said to Kumari. 'What is he, a *Gyps* vulture?'

'Um ... I'm not sure,' said Kumari. 'He's just Badmash to me.'

'Well, he's a pretty cool character, whatever he is. And he obviously loves you to death.'

He nodded to Ms Martin.

'I'll give you a call when I find something.'

At the door, Kumari turned.

'Does this mean you'll be able to locate my homeland?'

'I hope to, Kumari. I'll give it my best shot.'

His smile lit up his whole face. Kumari noticed the way Ms Martin glanced at him.

'Thank you,' said Kumari. 'By the way, what does Theo mean?'

'Theo means "God's gift".'

Kumari giggled. Ms Martin actually blushed.

'These markers, what do they mean?' Ms Martin peered down the microscope.

'They mean Kumari is someone very unusual. I've never seen anything like these.'

Theo glanced at the clock. Almost midnight and they still had a way to go. He'd had to call her over when he found the markers, though. Or at least that was what he told himself.

'Can I get you a coffee, Ms Martin? It could be a long night.'

'I'm fine, thank you. And my name is Helen.'

Great smile, thought Theo.

'You know, Helen,' he said. 'The evidence does indicate something extraordinary is going on here. There are more things on heaven and earth, as Bill Shakespeare said, than you or I could ever dream of.'

'"There are more things on heaven and earth, Horatio, than are dreamt of in your philosophy." *Hamlet*: Act One. Sorry, I've slipped into teacher mode.'

'No need to be sorry. It suits you. I'm sure you're a fine teacher. Now, shall we cross-match these results with the geographical index, see what we get?'

A few moments later, Theo sighed.

'I'm getting nothing.'

He sat, tapping his teeth with his pen. There had to be some way of doing this. Her markers did not relate to anywhere. Officially, Kumari was off the map. All of a sudden, he sprang to his feet.

'The bird!' he cried out. Rifling his bookcase, he pulled out a fat tome. Skimming through it, he landed on a page.

'There it is.' He held it up triumphantly. 'The *Gyps* vulture, now only found in a handful of places. Sadly, these birds are nearly extinct, which is bad news for them, but good news for us.'

He tapped away at his computer. 'I can narrow this down further,' he said. A few moments later he stabbed at the screen with his finger.

'Bingo!'

'We have it?' asked Helen, eyes wide with excitement.

'We have it,' he whooped. 'Given what Kumari says about her kingdom, it's got to be one of these two spots.'

'I'm speechless,' said Helen.

'Me too,' said Theo, gazing into her eyes.

'So,' she said, after a moment. 'When can we take her there? I can ask Daddy to organise a plane. He's already offered to pay.'

'I guess so,' said Theo. 'It seems such a shame to lose her. These markers, they are unique. Not really human at all. Perhaps that's what she means by "goddess". It could be some genetic aberration specific to her family. A condition they attribute to have divine significance.'

'Even Kumari doesn't think she's a goddess. She told me she gave it up. She said she chose to become a mortal, otherwise she'd die after a year and a day.'

'You can't give up your genetic make-up. It's in your bones, your blood. It would be like changing every atom, rewriting your DNA. If Kumari was born a different being, then that is what she remains.'

Helen gazed at him for a moment then curled her lip and shook her head.

'You really think there is something in it, don't you? I'm surprised at you, Theo.'

'Shakespeare said it all. We know so little, you and I. All of us humans, we use a tiny bit of our brains. Who's to say that the legends are not true? Maybe god-like beings did once walk the earth. It's possible they still do. Come here, I want to show you something. Look at this, through the microscope.'

He could smell her perfume as they both bent to the eye-piece. It was fresh and yet there was a *note*, a lingering under-tone of musk and spice.

'You see that crescent shape? No human marker looks like that.'

'What crescent shape?' said Helen.

'It was there a moment ago. Now, wait a minute.' He was fiddling with the microscope, moving the slide around. When he looked up, his face was pale.

'It's gone. So have most of the others.'

'What do you mean, it's gone?'

'Maybe it's just this one slide.'

He raced to the fridge for the other samples. Exactly the same result. Helen stared at him, bewildered.

'Theo, what's going on?'

'My guess is that it's what she told you. About having a year and a day to live. Kumari might think she gave up being a goddess but her samples tell a different story.'

'Are you telling me she's dying?'

'That's what it looks like to me. It's already started at a cellular level. Seems her time here is nearly up.'

Helen's hand flew to her mouth. 'Then we can't waste another second.'

She was out the door before Theo could grab his jacket, taking the stairs two at a time.

* * *

'All right, all right!' yelled Ma. 'Hold your fire. I'm coming.'

Kumari opened her eyes. It was still dark outside, the street light filtering through the thin curtains. Someone was banging on the door, in the middle of the night. Throwing back her covers, she peeked into the hallway. There was Ma in her marabou-trimmed dressing gown, opening the door to Ms Martin. With Ms Martin that guy, Theo. What was going on?

'Kumari!' Ms Martin was at her side in a trice. 'Kumari, we need to take another blood sample right now. It's very important.'

'It's the middle of the night,' said Ma. 'Can't it wait until morning?'

'I'm afraid not,' said Theo. 'This is something we need to check out now.'

At his tone, Ma went quiet. Kumari saw the fear flicker in her eyes.

'What's going on?' asked Kumari. 'Why do you need more blood?'

Theo knelt down beside her and placed his hand on her arm. 'I'm not going to lie to you, Kumari. Something appears to be deteriorating in your cells. I just need to check your blood against the samples we took.'

'What do you mean deteriorating? Something is wrong with my blood?'

'I need to be certain. Hold still. That's it.'

Kumari was too busy looking at Ms Martin's face to notice the needle going in. She, too, looked worried and her smile was kind of tight.

'What's happening?' It was CeeCee and LeeLee, shuffling out of their bedroom.

'Nothing,' said Ma. 'Go on back to bed.'

It felt so surreal, standing around in the hallway at 2 a.m. Ma must have noticed too because she began ushering them into the living room.

'Sit down, sit down. Can I get you anything?' she was fussing round, fidgeting, which was unlike Ma.

And then Theo was murmuring something to Ma and Ms Martin, all three of them turning to stare at her. She could see the shock on their faces and, worse than that, the pity.

'Kumari.' Theo was kneeling once again, his kind face inches from hers. 'Kumari, we have to get you home. This is not looking good. Your cells, they're slowly dying off. Your year and a day must be nearly up. We need to get you back to your kingdom as fast as we can. Hel . . . Ms Martin's father is organising a plane.'

'But that's impossible,' said Kumari. 'I gave up being a goddess.'

'Apparently not,' said Theo. 'Whatever you did can't have worked.'

Then she remembered. That weird inkling with Chico. No, more than an inkling. It had been her Powers all the time. So much for Renunciation.

'I knew it!' said Kumari. 'My rituals are as lousy as ever. I can't even get that right. I can't even *resign*.'

'There, there,' said Ma. 'You did your best, honey.'

'My best isn't good enough!' wailed Kumari. 'Besides,

how can I get home? There's no point organising a plane if you don't know where it's going.'

'But we do,' chimed in Ms Martin. 'Or at least, we can get very close. Theo has narrowed it down to one of two possible places barely a hundred miles apart.'

'You're kidding?'

'I'm not. Kumari, you're going home.'

'I'm going home. Unbelievable! Back to the Kingdom. *Ohmigosh!*' The tears started to fall. 'I can see Papa and try to rescue Mamma and . . . '

Suddenly she stopped. A very big *but* filled her brain. There was something she had to do first. Really *had* to do, for all her friends here, for many more besides. She had promised to help spread the possibility of Happiness and she had to keep her word. She could feel the fear bubbling in the pit of her stomach. *But what if I don't get back home in time? Just go!* And then another voice in her head: *You have to, Kumari. You promised.*

Taking a deep breath, she blurted before she could change her mind. 'There's the concert. The benefit. It's . . . tonight.'

In precisely eighteen and a half hours to be totally exact.

'Forget the concert,' said Ma. 'We need to get you on that plane.'

'But it's for HUNK,' said Kumari. 'It's going to be on TV!'

'Ma's right,' said Ms Martin. 'There will be other concerts.'

'There won't,' said Kumari. 'Not where I'm going. You see, it's not just any old concert. I promised to talk about Happiness, to spread the HUNK message. It's so important I do that. It might be the only chance the World Beyond gets

250

to hear about it. I gave Mr Raider my word. I *have* to be there.'

The adults all looked at one another. Written across their faces, 'She's insane.'

'You said my cells had *started* dying off,' said Kumari. 'How long have I got?'

Theo looked uncomfortable. 'It's hard to say for sure. Look, Kumari, I really think you should listen to Helen and, ah, Ma. It's still only a concert after all.'

'It's not only a concert. It's also a fundraiser for HUNK. It will get the message across to millions. And my school gets twenty per cent if I turn up.'

'Twenty per cent? Pretty good,' said Ma.

'Of gross. I negotiated with Mr Raider. So you see it's important that I go. I mean, like, crucial.'

The grown-ups exchanged glances yet again.

'You'd risk your life for this?' said Ms Martin.

'I promised,' said Kumari. 'I need to be there for my friends. Rita Moreno needs the money. The World Beyond needs to hear HUNK's message. I'm still alive, aren't I? I think I can make it through another day.'

'There's no changing your mind, is there?' said Theo.

Kumari smiled. 'Not a chance.'

'Then promise me one thing – we leave straight after the concert?'

'It's a deal,' said Kumari.

She dropped a kiss on Badmash's head.

'Hey, boy, we're going home.'

Badmash rolled on to his back and waggled his belly for joy.

CHAPTER 24

The roar filled her ears like a thousand hungry lions. Ranked in front of the stage, a barrage of cameras. Madison Square Garden: home to some of the greatest gigs in history. And now a platform for HUNK. Things did not get any better than this. Above the stage, a massive banner setting out HUNK's manifesto:

Get Happy
Stay Happy
Spread the Happiness Around!

Beside her, Jack Raider, oozing charm and confidence. And then he was taking her by the hand, leading her back on to the stage.

'Give it up, everyone, for Kumari!'

Another roar, this time deafening. He handed her the microphone. 'Go HUNK!' she yelled.

'Go HUNK!' they chanted. Now this was fun. She tried another.

'Get Happy, Stay Happy!'

Dutifully, they echoed. Raider snatched back the microphone.

'And now, everyone . . . Deranged!'

He did a sort of swivel-hip thing – Tragic Dad Dancing. Jack was not as cool as he liked to think. Kumari smothered a grin. In the front row she could see them all: Ma, the girls, Theo, Ms Martin. Still no sign of Chico. Where on earth could he be?

A crescendo of guitar chords drowned out her thoughts. Deranged were running on stage behind her. She recognised the intro: 'Heaven Sent'. Her favourite song ever. All of a sudden Pete, the lead singer, was beckoning to her. *Oh my god, no. This was not happening.* He was holding her hand.

Pete shot her a sideways glance, then grinned and began to sing. Behind them, a massive screen on which she was projected. The cameras were zooming in, the crowd singing along too. She thought she must have died and gone to heaven. It was worth it, all of it. How could she leave here now? How could anything beat this?

She glimpsed the front row.

He was there. Chico.

Now things were absolutely perfect.

Just when it was time to go.

In his room at the YMCA, the RHM stretched out on his bed. Jetlag dulled his mind. He might as well flick through the TV channels. Tomorrow morning, he would try once more to pick up Kumari's trail. This was his last chance to find her, his final trip to Manhattan. The year and a day was all but up. If he failed, he would have to tell the king to give up hope. Worse, he would have to alter his own plans. In the pit of his stomach, a lurking dread. Kumari was not coming home.

He gazed at the TV blankly, barely taking in the images as he channel-surfed. He was flicking through them so fast he almost missed the show. Scrolling back, he took another look. Astonishingly, there she was. The hair and clothes were different but it was definitely Kumari, standing alongside some young man, her face filling the screen. A caption flashed up, *Live from Madison Square Garden*. It was all the information the RHM needed. He was out in the street in a trice.

'Madison Square Garden,' he told the cab driver who stopped. 'Please hurry.'

He was only a few streets from his quarry. The hunt was back on.

On the other side of Central Park, someone else was watching television. Simon Razzle had it on in the background with the volume down as he tried to fend his creditors off by phone.

'Mr Razzle? I'm afraid he's not in. No, this is not Mr Razzle. I will tell him you called.'

The hired heavy by the door yawned, never once taking his eyes from the state of the art TV.

'Cute chick,' he growled, shifting his considerable bulk.

Irritated, Simon glanced up. The man was not paid to talk. For once, though, he was glad he had done. It was *her*, up there on the plasma screen. The telephone rang again.

'Mr Razzle? He's not here.'

His creditors were closing in on him. Before his very eyes, the golden ticket out of this mess. The passport to millions in the slender shape of one girl. All these weeks trying to think up some way to snatch her back without getting arrested and she was there, right in front of him. The kid. Kumari. The answer to his prayers.

'We're leaving,' snapped Simon, throwing on his cashmere coat. 'Where's that other idiot?' The heavies came as a matching pair.

At that moment, the door burst open and Simon instinctively ducked.

'I got hot dogs for everyone,' said the other heavy. 'You OK, Mr Razzle?'

'No, I am not,' snarled Simon. 'How many times have I told you not to burst in like that? You give the secret knock and wait. In any case, we're leaving. Get me to Madison Square Garden. Quickly, you morons.'

He had no idea what he would do once he got there.

But there had to be some way to get the girl.

CHAPTER 25

The stage lights dimmed. Another intro twanged out. As one, the audience flicked open their lighters. 'Shoot Me Down in Flames'. Kumari's second favourite song ever. She could hear the crowd screaming over the sound of the guitar chords. Their yells punctuated the drum beats. This was what it must be like to be so popular.

'Kumari!'

Wow. They were calling out her name as well.

Smiling, Pete led her forward to take a bow, right to the front of the stage. Hands were reaching out towards them, the audience stamping and whistling.

'Kumari! Kumari!'

They were pumping their fists, waving their hands in homage.

Suddenly, one of those hands had a hold of her. She stared down into eyes she recognised. It was that lunatic, Simon Razzle. And he was trying to pull her off the stage.

Staring up into the spotlights, Simon felt the fury rise. She was there, within feet of him. Salvation was inches away. He could hear the blood pounding in his skull; see it rise in front of his eyes. A scream formed behind his teeth, trying to force its way out of his mouth.

The pressure. He had to relieve the pressure. His head felt fit to burst. He thought his heart might explode. The girl was almost within reach. All he had to do was grab her. Never mind that there were thousands of people present. This was it, his one chance. And then she was right there, standing alongside the singer. Her smile was the final straw. How dare she look so happy? He had meant to wait for a more opportune moment, but he could not ignore the blood rush.

'Give me your gun,' he snapped, snatching it from one of his heavies. Thank God the goon was thick with a security guard who owed him a favour. Tucking it in his belt, Simon lunged for the girl.

It was almost too easy, the way he reached out and grabbed her ankle, holding on fast as she looked down and, horrified, met his gaze. Simon bared his teeth in a grin.

'I got you now, baby,' he crowed.

* * *

257

No one else had yet realised what was happening. Another tug and she'd be his. Desperately, Kumari lashed out, kicking with all her strength. Finally spotting her predicament, Pete hauled her back from the edge. She saw Simon's face as she was ripped from his grasp. His eyes were crazed, his mouth twisted in a snarl. Like a dog refusing to let go of a bone, he leapt after her, on to the stage. Suddenly, everything was chaos. There were people running on from the wings. And then the light glinted off something in Razzle's hand. He was waving a gun.

He grabbed hold of her once again. 'Stay back or I'll shoot!'

Now this was all too real. Security were hanging back, not knowing what to do. The band dived for cover. Everyone was screaming. And then someone else strode on stage.

'Let her go at once!' he demanded.

Kumari's head whipped round at the familiar voice. Could it really be him? Yes, it was the RHM, his face like thunder. At last – they had found her at last.

'Let her go,' the RHM said again. 'I command you to do so in the name of the king.'

'Says who?' sneered Simon, waving his gun. 'This makes me king around here, buddy.'

At that exact moment, a furious flurry of feathers attacked, pecking at Simon's eyes.

'Be careful, Badmash,' yelled Kumari.

A loud report as the gun went off. A few feathers floated to the ground.

'No, no,' Kumari sobbed.

And then a familiar squawk as Badmash swooped from the lighting gantry. Lashing out with his sharp talons, he swiped at Simon's cheek.

'I'll get you for that!' shrieked Razzle, swivelling, trying to find Badmash in his sights. There was another, enormous bang. Far too loud for any gun. It sounded more like thunder, a gigantic roar of rage from the heavens. As it died away, Badmash dived once more, slicing open Simon's hand so he dropped the gun. It skittered across the stage, with Simon in hot pursuit. Another rumble drowned out the yells of outrage from Razzle. One final deafening crack and the stage was plunged into darkness.

A figure emerged from the shadows.

Raised above the figure's head, a sword, fashioned like a scimitar.

Kumari let out a gasp. She would recognise the sacred sword anywhere. The sacred sword of the kingdom: one of the few ways to kill a goddess. And now it was pointing at her heart, coming closer and closer. A sudden blast of light illuminated the centre of the stage. Someone must have hit the emergency spotlight. Its beam bounced off the sword, momentarily blinding Kumari. Blinking into the white glare she could only make out a silhouette. And then the figure spoke. It was a voice she had known all her life.

'I should have killed you then. That day on the mountain. But it was far too dangerous. There are eyes everywhere in that wretched kingdom. Instead, I chose this, the World Beyond. A slow death in some ways. A slow, complicated death as it turns out but with a profit margin that made it worth it. Or it would have done, if it hadn't been for all those bungling fools and your own efforts. You are too much trouble, Kumari. But then, you always were.'

From behind the figure, more emerged, fanning out to form an arc. One in particular bared his teeth in a semblance of a ghastly smile. She felt a wave of faintness crash over her. She was looking at her kidnappers. Suddenly, it all made sense. And it was that knowledge that broke her. Falling to her knees, she felt the fight drain away.

It had been her Ayah all along.

CHAPTER 26

The sword was at her throat now, pressing into her flesh. She could see the tooled and bejewelled hilt. Wrapped around it her Ayah's hand, knuckles white as she clutched it. She looked up then, into her Ayah's eyes. They shone with pure hatred. How could she have been so blind? The Ayah was her enemy. The woman who had helped bring her up now wanted her destroyed. Confused, disbelieving, Kumari could only stare. Her throat tightened at the touch of cold metal. She stifled a scream.

'One stroke of this,' the Ayah crooned. 'And you're dead, Kumari. As dead as that mother of yours. My saintly, beloved sister.'

Her sister? Surely not. Mamma had been the Ayah's cousin.
Despite her breaking heart and bewildered mind, Kumari struggled to work it out.

'Yes, that's right.' It was as if she'd read her thoughts. 'You're my niece, Kumari.'

'Then how could you do this?' said Kumari.

'Believe me, it makes it much easier.'

She swung back the sword and the entire stadium gasped. At that precise moment, Kumari dived. Rolling backwards, she flung herself to her feet, arms outstretched as she had been taught. Karali was a magnificent art but it was no match for a sword. Laughing, the Ayah lunged again and again, slashing with the deadly blade, trying to find Kumari's weak spot. Jumping, ducking, dodging, Kumari fought to evade her. She could see the kidnappers encircling, blocking off any exit.

Still the Ayah came at her, unstoppable, frenzied. For once in her life, Kumari was thankful a ritual had not worked. Not a single one of her Powers had been renounced. She was still a goddess. And it looked like the only way out of this was to summon up divine help. Faced with the sacred sword, Kumari knew that not even her Powers would be enough. Frantically, she rubbed at her amulet, trying to remember the ancient words.

'OM TARE TUTTARE TURE SOHA
MAMA SARVA RANDZA ... '

Duck, dodge. Slash, slash, slash. The Ayah was gaining ground. Any moment now she would thrust through her skin. And that would be the end of her.

I don't want to die, thought Kumari. *I'm not going to let her kill me.*

'DUSHEN DRODA SHINDHAM KURU SOHA . . .'

Chanting, howling to the gods. *Come on, come on, help me!*

And then she heard it, the roar again. The sound of a thousand lions. Except that there was only one and it was stalking across the stage. A gorgeous monster of a beast, its massive white head framed by a flowing silver mane. Its tail swished as it padded towards the Ayah, a flick, flick of fury. A collective gasp of disbelief, the crowd paralysed by the spectacle. On the lion's back, a woman clad in burnished gold and scarlet robes, her black hair rippling down her back. The woman's lovely face bore an expression that would turn fire to ice. Her eyes locked on to the Ayah's, inexorable in their hatred.

'Mamma!' cried Kumari.

The lion opened its jaws and roared again. Its massive teeth glinted. In one bound it was by the Ayah's side and then it snatched her up. Dangling, shrieking, from its mouth, the Ayah gibbered in terror. The sword fell from her outstretched hand and clattered to the floor.

Frozen to the spot, Kumari stared. *She had done it. She had summoned Mamma.*

'Mamma!' she called again and staggered towards her, reaching out for her hand.

Oh, to hold her, to touch her.

Her Mamma turned and looked into her eyes, her fierce expression suddenly gentle.

'I have to go now, little one. Be brave, Kumari.'

'No!' Kumari sobbed, almost at her side. 'Don't go. Don't leave me.'

There were so many questions still to ask, but this was not the time.

For one split second, her fingers met her Mamma's. The briefest touch and she was gone. Rising up, up above the crowd, a goddess riding on her lion. Still screeching, the Ayah in its jaws, legs kicking, arms flailing. The tears streamed down Kumari's face, blurring her last sight of her Mamma. All at once, the lion disappeared from view. They were gone, flying towards the heavens.

Brushing her tears away with her sleeve, Kumari turned to see her kidnappers running, throwing their weapons to the ground, begging the gods for forgiveness. An arm slipped around her shoulders. The RHM hugged her. Stern, crusty old RHM was actually holding her in his arms.

'Come, Kumari,' he said. 'Dry your tears. It's all over.'

Carefully, he bent and picked up the sacred sword.

'We will take this home with us.'

A soft cooing as a feathery missile hit her chest. It was Badmash, snuggling up, kissing her. And then they were all there, her friends, surrounding her with their love. The lights went up, the crowd began to cheer, feet stomping, hands clapping. Convinced it was all part of the show, they shouted their appreciation. Jack Raider ran out on stage.

'Give it up for Kumari!'

She could see Simon Razzle being lead away, Deranged dusting down their stage outfits. It was business as usual for

HUNK. Suddenly, she felt very tired.

'I want to go home,' she said.

'We're going to take you there,' said Ms Martin.

They left Raider standing on the stage, soaking up the glory.

CHAPTER 27

The plane sat on the tarmac, engines fired up and running. The steps stretched up ahead of her. At the top of them stood the RHM, beckoning her inside. Ms Martin and Theo were already aboard. She placed one foot on the bottom step and then stopped, unable to take another. Turning, she looked at each face in turn: Ma, CeeCee, LeeLee. Hannah. Charley. Chico.

'I don't want to leave you,' she cried.

'You have to go, Kumari,' said Ma.

Kumari gazed at that kindly face all crumpled up and felt her own heart splinter.

'We'll think of you all the time,' said Ma as she gave her one last squeeze. Each in turn held her tight.

'Friends forever?'

'You bet.'

At last it was Chico's turn. The lump in her throat threatened to choke her.

'I got you this,' he said. 'It's why I was late.'

In his outstretched hand, a box. Inside that, a necklace. Dangling from it an intertwined K&C.

'So you don't forget,' he said.

Forget? How could she forget? Come to that, how could she leave him?

She looked back and saw the RHM. She knew now what she had to do. The old Kumari would have tried to stay. The new one knew it was impossible. She had grown so much, learned to think not just of herself. Knew who and what she was. Understood what that entailed. She did not belong here, in the World Beyond. She had a job to do back home. One day, she would take her place as queen. In the meantime, she had to learn all she could. There was still room, however, for one last impulsive act.

'Come with me,' she said, taking Chico's hand. 'As far as the Kingdom.'

That irresistible smile spread across his face. 'Just try and stop me,' he said. Whipping out his cell phone, he punched in a number.

'Just got to clear it with grandpa, you know.'

'Of course. I know.'

She walked ahead up the airline steps, leaving him to his

conversation, praying he would follow, wondering if he would. And then she heard his footsteps behind her. Her heart flooded with relief.

'It's OK,' said Chico. 'He says he trusts I'm doing the right thing.'

'He's a wise man,' smiled Kumari.

At the door, Kumari turned once more. They looked so small, standing there on the concrete. She raised a hand and waved. Ma blew her a final kiss. The RHM placed his arm across her shoulders.

'I'm proud of you,' he said. 'One day you will make a worthy queen.'

'You mean it?'

Incredible!

And then the RHM was ushering them in and she was strapping on her seat belt. She gulped and Chico squeezed her hand. The engines roared beneath them. Then the plane was turning, gaining speed, racing for the skies. She could feel a gentle touch brush away her tears. A touch as light as a feather. She looked down at Badmash, nestled in her lap, his wing tip wiping her face.

'We're on our way,' she whispered.

As she stared out at the night sky, she could have sworn she saw a lion flying.

In its mouth, the Ayah, mouth agape, screeching.

On its back, her Mamma, forever beautiful.

But only vengeance would set her free.

CHAPTER 28

The snows were so deep that even the Sherpas struggled.

'How much further?' gasped Ms Martin.

'You see that ledge?' said the RHM. 'That's where we leave the Sherpas. From there, we go on alone.'

Thanks to the RHM, they had been able to plot an accurate course.

Above them, the peaks reached up into the clouds. The air was so clean it was dizzying. As Kumari drew it into her lungs she could scent home. The Kingdom must be very close now. Although she did not want to say, she was beginning to weaken. Her legs were like two sacks of wet sand. Dragging them along, her footsteps faltered.

Instantly, there was a hand at her elbow.

'Keep going,' said Chico. 'Come on, Kumari, you can do it.'

'You betcha,' said Kumari. *Could she really?* She was not so sure. They had trekked now for hours and the clock was still ticking. It would only stop once she crossed the border and entered the Kingdom. All at once her tired eyes focused on a peak that she recognised.

'The Holy Mountain,' she whispered. Was Mamma back there in its foothills? Stuck in limbo with her fearsome lion? At least now the mystery of her death was resolved. Or so it seemed.

At last they reached the ledge and the Sherpas unloaded. Chico slipped the bag containing her journal over his shoulder. She had nothing else to bring, apart from her presents from all her friends. And what a present from Ma – her precious, feathered hoodoo duster. It poked out the top of the bag confusing Badmash somewhat. Occasionally he threw it a jealous glance or tried to peck it, convinced he had a rival.

'It's not a bird, Badmash,' said Kumari. 'You're the only bird for me.'

Still, he sulked all the way up the mountain, only perking up when they neared the peak. At the plateau before the peak, something wondrous appeared. Ahead, the fringes of a lush forest rose like an oasis above the snow. The borderlands, at last. Above the forest, a golden light as if the sun were bathing just this spot. Suddenly, a creature darted from between the dense green leaves.

'A snow leopard!' cried Kumari.

The leopard paused and stood stock still. It was as if it stood there in greeting. Just as suddenly as it appeared it was gone, vanishing into the snows. She knew, though, that this was a signal. That she was nearly home. Just a few hundred yards and they would be at the edge of the forest. Beyond the trees, the seemingly impenetrable petrified waterfall that protected the boundaries of the kingdom.

Branches brushed against her face as they made their way through thick pine and rhododendron, her hair snagging on a twig that sneakily stuck out. It brought it all back, that night running through the forest, her Mamma's hand freeing her from the branches. This time, though, it was Chico who helped her on her way.

'Not long, Kumari, not long,' called the RHM.

Ms Martin looked concerned. 'Just keep putting one foot in front of the other.'

Come on. I can do it. We're so nearly there.

And then they were there, standing by the vast wall of quartz crystal.

Concealed within the plunging folds of the solidified waterfall, the eastern entrance to the kingdom. The quartz wall rose hundreds of feet, smooth as glass, insurmountable. It practically encircled the kingdom, stopping short of the western frontier. The RHM stood to one side and gave a discreet little cough. Kumari knew in her heart it was time to say goodbye. Still, she stared at them all, taking in their features. Ms Martin, sweet Theo. Chico. Her friends.

'Thank you for everything,' she said as Ms Martin held her close.

'You're welcome. And Kumari, thank you.'

A hug from Theo and then she was gazing at Chico's feet. She could not bear to raise her head and look him in the eyes. Was it really so great being a goddess? With all the stuff that went with it? She was going back to that big, old empty palace. No friends to hang out with. No school to attend. No HUNK. No Ma. No Chico. For a long, long moment the world stood still as the thoughts whirled round her head. Then they settled and she knew what to do.

'Goodbye,' she said, holding out her hands.

He took them and pulled her to him. The kiss he dropped on her lips tasted sweeter than any candy.

'I got you this. If you need me, just call,' said Chico. He was pressing a cell phone into her hands. Sadly, she shook her head.

'That won't work here.'

'Then call out for me. In your heart. Wherever you are, I will find you.'

She had to go now or she knew she never would. Turning, she walked to the waiting RHM. Badmash flew ahead, leading the way as they slipped between the rocks and disappeared. She could hear Ms Martin sob and then all was silence, as if a veil had been dropped between them.

Behind her, the friends she would never see again.

Ahead lay her home, Happiness and Papa.

KUMARI'S JOURNAL
(TOP SECRET. FOR MY EYES ONLY.
EVERYONE ELSE KEEP OUT!
THIS MEANS YOU!)

Home
Moon: Twelfth

Time to avenge Mamma.

THE EIGHT GREAT POWERS OF A GODDESS

1. The Power to be Invincible in Battle with the Sacred Sword

2. The Power of Extraordinary Sight

3. The Power to Run with Incredible Swiftness

4. The Power to Become Invisible

5. The Power of Rejuvenation

6. The Power to Levitate or to Fly Through the Sky

7. The Power to Move Freely Through the Earth, Mountains, and Solid Walls

8. The Power to have Command over the Elements

THE FIVE GREAT
GIFTS OF A GODDESS

1. The Gift of Eternal Life – and the power to grant the same

2. The Gift of Beauty – inner and outer

3. The Gift of Tongues – the ability to speak or understand any language

4. The Gift of Courage – often exhibited *in extremis*

5. The Gift of Wisdom – usually displayed by the more mature goddess

GLOSSARY

The spelling of these words can vary.

Ayah
South Asian word for nanny or nurse-maid – comes from the Portuguese *aia*, meaning 'woman tutor', which in turn is derived from the Latin *avia* meaning 'grandmother' (just in case you want to impress someone!).

Ay caramba
Flexible Spanish expression roughly meaning 'wow' – often used by Bart Simpson.

Badmash
Hinglish (a mixture of Hindi and English) for 'naughty'.

Bakwas
Rubbish/not very good.

Butter lamp
A metal container in which clarified yak butter or vegetable oil fuels a flame – often found in Himalayan temples.

Fatte	Awesome.
Gyps Vulture	Genus of Old World vulture now under threat of extinction in Asia.
Hoodoo	African-American folk magic.
Kumari	From the Sanskrit, meaning 'princess' or 'maiden'. Although there are living goddesses in Nepal known as Kumaris, there is no connection with our heroine.
Momo	Little dumpling filled with savoury mixture (yum!).

Loved this book?
Find out what Kumari does next!

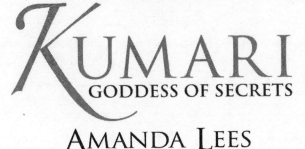

KUMARI
GODDESS OF SECRETS

AMANDA LEES

Kumari is back home, but everything has changed.
Papa has been struck down by a mysterious illness and
the Palace is full of danger. The fires of Happiness
are dying and the Hidden Kingdom is in crisis.

What's a girl goddess to do? Kumari's still struggling to
gain her Powers, while her quest to avenge her beloved
Mamma seems tougher than ever. And she's missing her
friends in the World Beyond – here, she has none,
apart from Badmash, her pet baby vulture.

Then unexpected visitors bring terrifying news.
With disaster looming, Kumari has to work in secret.
Can she outwit the thieves of Happiness and
save herself, Papa and the Kingdom itself?

ISBN: 978 1 85340 989 9
Coming soon to the World Beyond

Find out more about Kumari at:

www.amandalees.com

☆ Read the latest news about future *Kumari* books

☆ Enter competitions with fabulous prizes

☆ Download free *Kumari* wallpaper and banners

☆ Get to know author Amanda Lees

☆ Chat with other *Kumari* fans at the exclusive members' forum

☆

www.piccadillypress.co.uk

☆ The latest news on forthcoming books

☆ Chapter previews

☆ Author biographies

☆ Fun quizzes

☆ Reader reviews

☆ Competitions and fab prizes

☆ Book features and cool downloads

☆ And much, much more . . .

Log on and check it out!

Piccadilly Press

☆